BLOOD ON THE CARDS

By Chris O'Donoghue

A DI Sonny Russell mystery

First published in 2020 by Boghopper Books with PrintedWordPublishing

A catalogue record of this book is available from
The British Library
ISBN 978-1-91607-671-6

Typesetting in Minion Pro by Edward Sturgeon
Cover Illustration © Paul Harwood

Printed in Great Britain by Printed Word Publishing

PRINTED WORD PUBLISHING

Dedication

"Books are like Tarot decks. They provide answers and guidance but more importantly, they are doorways and portals to the otherworld and the imagination. They leave their imprint and keep whispering to us long after we close the pages or shuffle the deck."
– Sasha Graham, Tarot Fundamentals

My thanks go once again to my wife and soulmate, Greer, for her never-ending support and expert editing.
And also to Paul Harwood for yet another brilliant and germane cover.

Chapter 1

The Tarot began as *playing cards. In the late 18th century, some Tarot packs began to be used for divination and, later, specialist decks were developed for such occult purposes.*

DETECTIVE INSPECTOR Sonny Russell climbed the short flight of steps up to the gaily painted gypsy caravan. It was a bowtop wagon with intricately carved and decorated woodwork. Reaching the platform at the top he pushed the beaded curtain to one side, the glass spheres rattling against one another. After the bright sunshine outside, the interior was gloomy; just a single oil lamp burned, the smoky glass globe softening the darkness. As the policeman's eyes acclimatised he could make out a figure seated at a small cloth-covered table.

'Come in and sit down here, dearie,' she said. The sound of her gruff and nicotine tinged voice made him start. 'I've been expecting you.'

Russell walked forward, pulled the stool out and sat opposite her. 'Miss Lee?'

She cackled. 'You can call me Ivy Rose.' Then reaching forward she demanded: 'Show me your hands.' Without considering he held them out. The woman grasped them in her own gnarled hands which were tipped with sharp, talon-like nails. Deftly flipping them over, she stared hard at the palms. 'Mmm. You've a very long lifeline, but…' She bent forward, her face almost touching his palms, the fringes on her headscarf tickling his wrists. 'But, there are some significant events.' She looked up; her dark eyes seeming to burn as she stared at him. 'Something happened in your recent past – something unexpected and painful. Am I right?' The disturbing eyes bored into him.

'Maybe…' His answer was noncommittal but he felt an icy trickle of sweat rolled down between his shoulder blades.

'Thought so.' She gave a smug smile, as if she'd scored a point. 'This other line…' She traced it with the stained nail of her index finger. 'It suggests something momentous. Something that has just happened or is about to happen.' Russell shrugged. She pushed his hands away. 'Let's see what the cards have to say.' Reaching into the folds of her clothing she produced a small package wrapped in a velvet cloth. Reverently she unfolded the fabric to reveal a deck of Tarot cards. She pushed them towards him. 'Shuffle them, please.' He picked them up and did as she'd asked, then passed them back. Smoothing the cloth out flat she turned the first five cards over.

The five of Wands   The Hanged Man   The Knight of Swords

The Hermit   The Tower

The old woman stared intently at the cards for some minutes. Slowly she lifted her gaze and transferred it to Russell. 'Why did you come to see me?'

'I was curious.'

'Hmm.' She looked back down at the cards then adjusted them so they were perfectly in line.

'What do they say?'

'Ah, now there's a thing…'

'You came highly recommended.'

'Of course I did. That goes without saying.'

'So can you tell me?'

'I can. But I'm not sure how much help they will be, in your present situation.'

'Tell me anyway.'

She breathed in and exhaled noisily. 'Right. You hold a position of responsibility, yes?'

Russell nodded.

'This card,' she tapped the *Five of Wands*, 'shows me your determination. The next, *The Hanged Man…*' She paused and looked at him again for long moments. 'Interesting. Most people are alarmed. You've remained calm. Anyway, it doesn't necessarily mean anything bad, and taken with the other cards, it suggests that you're good at letting go, maybe turning everything upside down in search of the truth.' Russell gave a wry smile. 'It's confirmed by the next card.' She tapped the *Knight of Swords*. Again she paused and looked intently at him. 'You're a loner by nature, aren't you?' He gave a nod. She covered the next card, *The Hermit*, with the palm of her hand and grunted. 'This one confirms it. But the last card is curious. *The Tower* usually refers to accidents and losses. Have you had either of those lately?'

He nodded again. 'An accident, yes. But not serious.'

'I think you should be very careful,' she said slowly. Picking up the cards she returned them to the pack and folded it neatly in the velvet cloth. 'But you didn't come to see me about work, did you, Mr Policeman?'

Russell's eyes widened. 'How did you know I'm a policeman?'

She smiled, gold glinting in her mouth, and tapped the side

of her nose. 'Anyway, what did you come here for? It's about a woman, isn't it?'

Russell decided he wanted to hear no more. He cleared his throat and rose from his stool. 'I've taken enough of your time.'

She cackled again. 'You'll be lucky in love – eventually.' Her tone changed. 'Haven't you forgotten something?'

Russell turned and reached in his pocket. 'Sorry,' he said, and placed two half-crowns on the table. Quick as a flash she covered them with her hand and pulled them towards her.

After leaving he wandered round for a while – not going anywhere in particular, just turning over in his mind what she'd told him – trying to make sense of it. He'd experienced something unnerving. Her insight felt as if she knew more about him than he thought she decently should. It was as though his soul had been bared – well, perhaps not his soul but certainly his innermost thoughts. After half an hour of aimless meandering, and still uncertain about what she had meant, he found himself back at the foot of her steps. He hesitated briefly then made up his mind. He would ask her to explain – get his five bob's worth. As he was about to climb the steps again the beaded curtain was thrust aside with a loud clatter and the figure of a large man barrelled down the stairs, knocking him aside. Before Russell could react the man had disappeared out of sight between the vans. He shook his head – an unhappy customer presumably. He hesitated but before he had a change of heart he went ahead up to the caravan.

He was just about to push the curtain aside when a voice barked out: 'Go away! *I told you* – I don't want to see you again!'

'Pardon?' Russell said mildly.

'Oh it's you.' Her voice lost a little of its harshness. 'Sorry dearie. I'm closed for the day. Something's come up. You'll have to come back another time.'

'But...'

'I said come back another time.' There was a quake in her voice as she gave him a gentle push and pulled the door closed.

~O~

He had gone in to see the woman on a whim. He wasn't sure what he was going to ask but for the first time, for as long as he could remember, he felt he was entering into a romantic liaison – a relationship perhaps. It was completely out of character to seek advice from a fortune teller but he felt out of his depth. The object of his affections, Isobel Bailey, had been in hospital after being shot in the shoulder by a Frenchman who had been holding her hostage. He had been trying to fence a large quantity of valuable items stolen in Germany towards the end of WWII. Despite being injured in an accident involving a Post Office motorcycle in London, Russell had managed to get back to Compass Point in time to apprehend the Frenchman, recover the Nazi plunder and save Isobel from more serious injury. During his visits to the hospital they had become close and now they were seeing each other regularly. He shook his head. Reluctantly he pushed thoughts of Isobel to the back of his mind. Now, a week after his visit to the fortune teller he had a more pressing matter to deal with.

Russell was standing in the gathering twilight, with his DC, Johnny Weeks. They were on a damp river bank, next to a concrete pillbox just outside Appledore, waiting for the portly pathologist, John Crooks. He and his assistant were busy inside with the deceased.

'Do we know who it is, lad?' Russell asked Weeks.

'Not in detail, Sir. A woman in late middle age apparently.'

'Who found her?'

'A couple of schoolboys – out on a ramble. They thought she was a tramp. One of them gave her a shake and when she didn't move it spooked them. They ran into the village and told the local bobby, PC Gold. At first he didn't believe them but when he came here and looked he realised they were telling the truth. A phone call to the station at Collinghurst and the troops were galvanised into action.'

Russell stamped his feet and wrapped his arms round his chest. 'I just hope they don't take too long. It's getting chilly standing here.' His little terrier, Aggie, with her thick rough coat had no such problems. She was delighted to be somewhere different, somewhere with new sniffs. She scampered excitedly about but didn't stray too far.

Almost on cue the rotund form of the pathologist appeared. The entrance to the pillbox was narrow and he struggled to extricate himself. Russell disguised a smile with a hand held to his mouth. 'Ah, Sonny,' Crooks boomed. 'We've a right one here.'

'What do you mean, John?'

The pathologist chuckled. 'We haven't disturbed her. You take a look first and let me know what you think.'

'How long do you reckon she's been in there?'

'Difficult to say. About twenty-four hours, at a guess. I'll have a better idea when I've conducted a thorough examination.'

'So it's unlikely that whoever did it is still lurking around here?'

'Unless he's very stupid,' he snorted, his nostrils flaring like a bull's. 'Anyway, we'll go back in when you've had a gander. You'll need this, Sonny,' he said, handing him a heavy torch.

Taking it the officer clicked on the powerful beam. 'Thanks. Keep an eye on Aggie, will you? Best she doesn't come in.' He entered the pillbox followed by Weeks. As they rounded the internal wall the torch lit up a figure, fully clothed, in a seated position, leaning against the blockwork. It was a woman. Her eyes were wide open. 'Oh God!' Russell suddenly exclaimed and staggered backwards, nearly knocking his DC over. The beam of the torch shot up over the ceiling, down the wall and across the floor before he steadied it again on her face.

'Sir?'

'I know who it is. I saw her only a few days ago.' His voice was controlled – his tone hushed.

'Who is she?'

Russell took a deep breath. 'She goes by the name of Ivy Rose Lee. She's a fortune teller – a clairvoyant. She was at the funfair, on The Salts at Nottery Quay.'

'But how…?'

'Don't ask.' Russell bent down in front of the woman, careful not to disturb anything. Weeks was about to speak again. Russell held up his hand. 'I'll tell you about it later.' He leaned in closer. 'It's pretty obvious how she died.' There was a deep gash beneath her chin, running from one ear to the other. At first glance the blood that must have welled up wasn't obvious as she was wearing a dark red, velvet top. Russell peered intently at her. The top was a lighter colour at the sides, but the front was a deeper colour, stained by the blood.

'Why would anyone want to do that – and in such a bizarre place?'

'That's something we'll have to find out. It's too late to do much here tonight. We'll leave PC Gold guarding the site and send someone out to relieve him later. First thing tomorrow we need to round up as many uniforms as we can. They'll have to conduct a fingertip search as well as do a local door-to-door to see if anyone knows or heard anything. Then we'll need divers to search the canal. If we're lucky the murder weapon won't be far away. Come on. Let's get out; there won't be room for us as well as John Crooks. We might as well adjourn to the pub until they're done. I'm sure he'll join us when they've finished.'

~o~

They sat at the bar in the Red Lion. When they arrived Russell had shown the barmaid his warrant card and asked her if she had seen any strangers in the past couple of days.

She smiled sweetly. 'Sorry, Sir. I ain't been in for a while. I came in this evening to help out.'

Russell cocked his head to one side. 'Oh?'

'Yes, the landlord's been called away.'

'Where's he gone?'

'I don't know exactly. Said he had to go off urgent like. Think it might be somewhere on the coast. Sorry.' Her neck reddened and a blush spread to her cheeks.

Russell took pity on her. 'That's all right, dear. Do you know when he'll be back?'

'Oh, he said he'll be here tomorrow.'

'Let's hope he is. I need to speak to him.' Russell smiled warmly. 'What's your name?'

'Edna, Sir.'

'Right Edna, let's have two pints of your best bitter.'

~o~

They were on their second pint. Aggie was curled up at their feet. 'What do you think happened, Sir?' Weeks asked.

'I've no idea, lad.' Russell took a drink from his glass.

'It looks like she'd upset someone.'

'It certainly does – right royally, judging by the way she was killed.'

'Who would do a thing like that?'

'That's what we'll have to find out.'

Weeks rubbed his hands through his mop of dark curly hair. 'Blimey, where do we start?'

Russell shook his head. 'I don't know at the moment. Hopefully Crooks will be able to give us some clues.'

Weeks took a large gulp and set his glass down. 'Sir. You said you'd seen her recently.' He spoke hesitantly, aware that this might be a sensitive subject.

The DI sighed. 'I suppose it will have to come out at some time. I know I can trust you.' He looked pointedly at Weeks, who gave a slight nod. 'I'm sure you've noticed that I've grown fond of Isobel.' Another nod. 'It's a bit more than that. The bash on the head when I was clobbered by the motorbike in London made me think. It could have been a lot worse. I reckon I was lucky to get away with mild concussion.' He sipped some of his beer; a thoughtful expression on his face. 'Listen, I don't want this to go any further…'

Weeks wasn't sure what he was about to hear. 'Of course not, Sir.'

Russell stared straight forward, a distant look in his eyes. 'It was towards the end of the war. As you know, I finished up in Asia.'

'Yes, you told me. It's where you became interested in eastern philosophy. Isn't that why you became a vegetarian?'

'Yes, that's right. I also met someone out there – someone special.' The DC nodded but said nothing. 'She was called Lottie, a nurse. Look…' He reached into an inside pocket and brought out his wallet. From an inner compartment he produced a passport-sized photograph. Almost reverently he handed it to Weeks.

The picture was of an attractive, dark-haired girl, staring confidently at the photographer. Despite the small size of the photo Weeks could see a sparkle in her eyes and a mischievous smile playing on her full lips. 'She is a pretty girl, Sir.'

'*Was* a pretty girl, lad.' A shadow passed across Russell's normally cheerful face.

'Oh? What happened?'

'A stray bomb – one of ours, unfortunately. Hit the hospital she was working in.'

'She was killed.'

'No, not then, worse luck.' Weeks didn't understand but waited for his boss to explain. 'It would have been better if she had. What happened was that she received horrific injuries, but survived – for a while anyway. She was in hospital – intensive care – for several weeks. I visited as often as I could. She told me not to – to just forget her. We both knew that she would be seriously crippled and would need constant care for the rest of her life. She told me to go away and find someone else. I told her no – I would stand by her, look after her when she came out. We both knew this wouldn't be for many weeks – if at all. The last time I saw her she said I wouldn't have to worry about her any more. I asked her what she meant but she refused to say. I went in the next day and they said she'd passed away in the night.'

'I guess her body just gave up.'

'That's what they said.'

'It seems logical.'

'That's what I thought – at first. But she had such spirit. I couldn't believe she would have given up without a fight – it just wasn't like her. Then I though back to her last words to me:

"You won't have to worry any more". The more I thought about it the more it seemed wrong somehow. I decided to investigate – probably where my interest in becoming a policeman started.' He gave a grim smile. 'I tracked down a couple of her colleagues – nurses who'd worked the same wards. At first they were reluctant to talk. Then one took pity on me. I think I was in a bit of a state and she felt sorry for me. She wouldn't say exactly what happened but hinted that, because of the confusion, things were a bit lax.'

'Confusion?' Weeks had been reluctant to interrupt. Russell had never opened up to him before like this. During the time he had been talking his second pint had been drunk and the barmaid had replaced it with a third one which was already half-empty.

'Yes, as you know, although Germany surrendered in May '45 the war in the East went on for a few more months. It was grinding to its inevitable conclusion in August and things were all over the place.'

'How did that affect her death?' Weeks asked, gently.

'I never did find out for sure.' There was a pause while they both sipped their pints then Russell spoke, his voice just above a whisper. 'I could only conclude that she managed to get hold of a quantity of pills – enough to end her life. But I decided not to pursue it any further. Didn't want to get her friends into trouble.'

'It must have been hard for you.'

'Yes, it was – agonising. I was fortunate though.'

Weeks was puzzled. How could his boss possibly consider himself fortunate after what had happened? 'In what way?'

Russell smiled, a faraway look on his face. 'It was the monks. I'd been spending some time with them. There was a bit of a language barrier but their compassion cut through any difficulties we had and they were able to offer me great comfort. I'd never had any strong religious beliefs, but their simplicity appealed to me and helped me to find some sort of peace.' Another drink. 'I've never forgotten her though – she was special. Probably why I've never really been drawn to anyone else – until now.' He let out a sigh. 'Now you know.'

'Thank you, Sir. I appreciate it. Don't worry though, I won't breathe a word to anyone.'

Russell turned to him and smiled. 'I know you won't, lad.'

The two men sat, lost in their own thoughts for several minutes.

'Sir…'

'Yes, lad?'

'You were going to tell me why you went to see the fortune teller.'

'So I was.' He chuckled. 'After Lottie I'd been wary of getting involved with anyone – until Isobel. On a whim I decided to find out if the gypsy could give me any indication if this one might work out better.'

'And did she?'

Before Russell could answer the door swung open and the pathologist came in and strode across the bar, a galleon in full sail. 'I'll have whisky please – a large one.' This brought the conversation to a swift conclusion.

Russell signalled to the barmaid. 'A double whisky and two more pints, please.'

While the drinks were being poured, Crooks settled his bulk on the stool. It creaked ominously; the little terrier darted away. Crooks took his drink and toasted the detectives, 'Cheers,' he said, then took a large gulp.

'What do you make of it, John?'

'I can't really say. Once I get the poor soul back to the lab I might know more.'

'But why her, Mr Crooks?' Weeks asked.

'No idea, lad. Have you, Sonny?'

'Look, keep it under your hat – I don't want it spread about, but I visited her last week.'

Crooks's narrow eyebrows shot up towards his receding hairline. 'Really? What for?'

'I'd rather not go into details for now. Suffice to say, I found her to be uncannily accurate in her readings and yes, I warmed to her.'

'Fair enough. Where did you see her?'

'She was part of the travelling funfair camped out on the Salts.' He paused. 'Hang on, when do they move on?'

'I think they're around for another day or two,' Weeks said.

'Then we need to get there and talk to them before they go off to their next stop. I'm coming back here tomorrow. Can you organise that?'

'Yes, Sir.'

'Do you mind doing the *death knock*?'

Weeks tried not to look too crestfallen. 'No, that's okay.'

'Take WPC Nettie Sharpe with you. She'll be a great help. And you'll have to find someone who can officially identify the body – maybe there'll be a relative at the fair. Oh, and make sure her caravan is secured. Lewis will want to go over it when he's finished in the pillbox.'

Chapter 2

A pillbox is a type of *blockhouse, equipped with loopholes* through which to fire weapons. U*sually made of concrete or brickwork it is reinforced to protect against small-arms and grenades and elevated to improve the field of fire.*

THE NEXT morning, at first light, a dozen uniformed constables squeezed into a Bedford CA minibus. There was coughing; fags were ground underfoot; grumbles at the early start. The vehicle travelled along the Military Road, a low mist lying on the marsh; a suggestion of a warm day ahead. There was little conversation. It was too early for banter – that would spark up later. In half an hour the bus arrived at the bridge over the canal and came to a halt. The back doors opened and the men tumbled out. A police Wolseley was parked at the side of the road, Russell and Sergeant Wickstead already on the scene, Aggie sitting obediently between them.

'Beaumont. I you want you and PC Gold to go into the village. Knock on every door – ask if anyone saw or heard anything. Find out if there have been any strangers hanging around.'

'When were they likely to have been here, Sir?' PC Beaumont's voice was hoarse – it had been an early start.

'The day before yesterday. The pathologist reckons she'd been dead for over 24 hours. Right, off you go.' The two men peeled away from the group and set off along the road. 'The rest of you are going to conduct a detailed search of the area around the pillbox. I want this done methodically, no rushing. Hopefully we'll find some important evidence, maybe even the murder weapon. And use these.' He passed a handful of bamboo canes to PC Lee. 'Stick them in the ground to mark out a grid, so you know where you've been and you don't cover the same area twice. As I said, *take your time*. I don't want anything missed.'

It was a relatively narrow strip between the road and the Royal Military Canal, maybe 40 yards wide at most. A bridge, crossing the water, marked the boundary at one end, not far from the pillbox. In places the bank was steep and uneven leading down to the edge of the canal, fringed with tall Phragmites – common reeds, swaying gently in the breeze. Surrounding the WWII structure where the body had been found was scrubby grass liberally threaded with stinging nettles and vicious brambles.

The PCs walked slowly in a line abreast, staring intently at the rough grass surrounding the pillbox. The area had been marked out and each held a cane which they used to poke the ground. Wickstead watched the men with an eagle eye, prodding them if they strayed away from the strict line and offering words of encouragement when they stumbled. After a couple of hours, when all that had been found was a kettle, rusted through, and the skeleton of a discarded umbrella, the sergeant said: 'Right lads, time for a break.' There was a murmur of approval and the men started turning back. He held up his hand. 'Not so fast. Please stick your cane in the ground where you've reached, then we'll know where to carry on.' The policemen made their way back to the bus, grabbed haversacks and poured strong tea from Thermos flasks. As they sat around, eating corned beef and Spam sandwiches, the conversation was about everything but the task in hand.

Meanwhile, Russell had been examining the pillbox. Ivy Rose Lee's body had been taken to the mortuary the evening before but he was looking for clues to her murder – before the forensics team turned up. The interior of the room was barely 10 feet across. The concrete walls were dank and unwelcoming. Russell smiled wryly at the graffiti: A heart with ***Adolf loves Eva*** had faded almost to nothing. The legend: ***YANKS GO HOME*** had stood the test of time and was much clearer.

The floor was littered with empty bottles and broken glass, rusty tin cans and torn newspaper. He guessed that kids sometimes used the place as a camp and the occasional tramp dossed down there. But it certainly wasn't a very inviting space. Holding a slim torch he crouched and looked carefully around the spot where Ivy Rose Lee had been found. With his free hand he pulled a handkerchief out of his pocket, placed it on the ground so he could rest one knee on it and lean closer towards the floor. He took out his fountain pen and pushed some dead leaves aside. Something caught his eye. It was a ticket for the local narrow gauge railway.

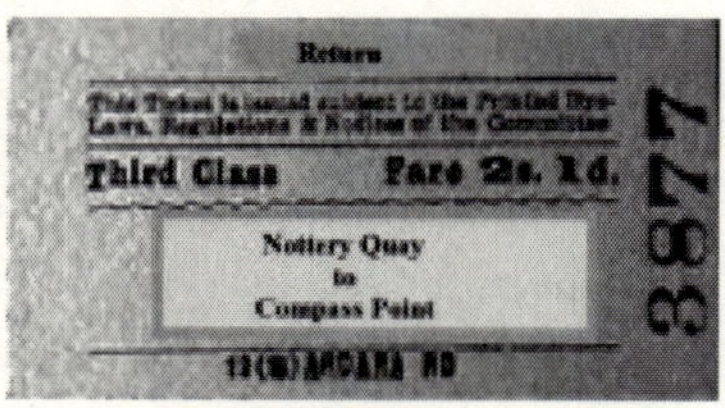

He was just about to rise when the torchlight reflected off something metallic that he'd disturbed. Moving another leaf with his pen he uncovered what appeared to be a gold ring. But not the ring for a finger, but an earring. The sort that a gypsy might wear. He would have to check if Ivy Rose had lost one. He heard a noise outside; the beam from a powerful torch cast a pool of light on the ground and Lewis, the forensics man, entered.

'Hello Sonny. Found anything interesting?'

Standing upright, with a gasp at the effort, Russell answered. 'I think so, look.' He pointed towards the floor.

Lewis shone the torch down, the light flickering on the ring. 'Well done,' he said. Then looking round: 'You haven't touched anything, have you?'

'*Touched* anything?' Russell's voice was filled with mock indignation. 'You should know me better than that.'

Lewis chuckled. 'Sorry. I knew you wouldn't have done, really.'

~O~

In Nottery Quay DC Weeks and WPC Sharpe had arrived at the funfair on the Salts. The rides were silent; the chairoplanes hung limp on their chains, swinging gently in the breeze; the sideshows shuttered. The grass between the attractions was flattened by the dozens of feet that had turned up to see all the fun of the fair. Smoke curled lazily from the chimneys of half a dozen caravans and living vans. A mean-looking dog barked at their approach, straining at the chain that tethered it. They gave the hound a wide berth.

'There's her caravan,' Nettie said. She pointed towards a bowtop which stood out among the others. The curved green canvas stretched over the roof looked new and the carved woodworked was freshly gilded and sparkled in the morning light. A piebald mare was tethered to one side, munching at a full hay net hanging from the side of the caravan. Someone was obviously looking after the horse. They approached and could see a board propped against the steps declaring:

THE ORIGINAL
GYPSY ROSE LEE
PALM READING
TAROT CARDS
CRYSTAL BALL

'Not likely to be anyone home. Better check to see if it's locked.' Weeks climbed the steps and tried the handle. 'Yes, it is. I suppose we'd better see who's in charge.' As they stood deciding which way to go a grubby urchin shot out from between the vans. When he saw the uniformed policewoman he stopped, eyes widening in surprise. He hesitated for a moment too long before turning, about to retreat. Nettie was quicker and grabbed him by the sleeve.

'Waddyer yer want?' He tried to shake her off but her grip was strong. 'I ain't done nuffink.'

'I'm not sure that's the whole truth,' she said, grinning at him. 'But we're not interested in you. Who's in charge round here?'

'What's it to you?'

Weeks let out a sharp breath and crouched down, his face a few inches from the boy. 'Look, lad. We're not here to cause trouble. We just want to know who runs the funfair.'

The boy scowled. 'It's me dad.'

'That's better. What's your name?'

'Duke,' was the sullen reply.

'Now, Duke. Please show us where he is.' Nettie kept a tight grip as the boy weaved his way between the stalls and rides, pulling like a dog on a lead. He stopped in front of an impressive living wagon standing on pneumatic tyres. It was painted a deep maroon, the panels expertly lined out in gold. At the foot of the short flight of steps stood a polished milk churn. Another dog lay beside it, quiet this time, head on paws, one watchful eye open.

'Dad!' the boy yelled. 'Da-ad!'

The door of the wagon opened and a man appeared. His frame was stocky, but muscular; his curly blond hair flopped over his forehead, startling blue eyes flashed beneath. He was wearing a collarless shirt open to reveal a thick matt of hair, with a red spotted scarf knotted round his throat. His legs were clad in a pair of corduroy trousers, cinched at the waist with a thick leather belt. 'What?' he growled. 'What do you want? D'you know what time it is?'

The boy shook himself free. 'Sorry Dad. These rozzers wanted to talk to you.' He dashed off again. They didn't see him disappear round the corner and run up the steps of the strongman's van.

Weeks took a step forward. 'Sorry, Sir. Could we have a word with you?'

The man scowled, a look of defiance spoiling his matinée looks. 'Go on. I'm listening.'

'Could we come inside? It's a rather delicate matter.'

'I suppose so.' He turned and went back into the van. The two constables looked at each other. Nettie mounted the steps followed by Weeks.

The interior of the wagon was a symphony in mahogany and brass. Everything was polished to a high gleam, reflected in numerous ornate mirrors. The two officers were invited to sit on a plush, fitted settee, opposite an immaculate cast iron range. A cheery blaze flickered behind the glass door.

'Right then. What can I do for you?' The man stood in front of the fireplace, his muscular arms folded across his chest.

'Could we have your name first, please?'

'It's Vado Boswell. Now what do you want?'

'I think it might be an idea if you sat down, Mr Boswell,' Weeks suggested.

The man's arms tightened; his face hardened. 'I'm all right standing,' he said.

'Fair enough. I'm afraid we have some bad news.'

'Oh yes?'

'You have a fortune teller here by the name of Ivy Rose Lee.'

'Yes, what of it?' Nettie, who had been watching Boswell carefully, saw him swallow. His neckerchief rose and fell as his Adam's apple bobbed briefly.

'She was found dead yesterday.'

'What? Where?'

'I'm afraid I can't give you that information at present.'

'What happened to her? Was it an accident?'

'No. We suspect foul play.'

'Really?' The man appeared genuinely shocked. 'How did she die?'

'Again, I can't say at this time.'

Nettie spoke. 'Didn't you notice that she wasn't around?'

The man shook his head, a blank look on his face. 'No. I don't keep tabs on all the showmen and women. It's up to them when they operate. If she hadn't opened up for a few days there would have been complaints, but nobody's said anything.'

'Did she have any family, do you know?'

Boswell shook his head slowly. 'Not that I'm aware of. She only turned up a few weeks ago.'

'Strange.' Nettie said. 'I would have thought a fortune teller is an important part of any fair.'

'It is.'

'What did you do before she came?'

There was a hesitation, then, 'Oh, we had another one – a man.'

'What happened to him, Sir?' Weeks asked.

'Oh, he went.'

'Why was that?'

Boswell appeared to consider. 'Um, I think he went off to join another fair.'

'You think?'

He seemed to make up his mind. 'He did. Yes.'

'Do you know why, Mr Boswell?'

He paused for a moment. 'Not really. Probably fancied a change.'

'How long had he been with you?'

'Six months or so.'

'Isn't that a bit strange, going off like that?'

He gave a shake of his head. 'Not really – people come and people go.'

'But after six months?'

Boswell exhaled. 'You know how it is.'

'Not really, Sir.' Weeks said, frowning.

'We *are* known as travellers. Or didn't you realise that?' Up until then the man's tone had remained even. Measured. Now it had an edge. He turned away from the officers and opened the door to the range. Crouching he took a small shovel and filled it with coal from the gleaming copper scuttle. He shot the fuel into the grate and shut the door. Then stood and faced them again, his eyes hard and his mouth set in a thin line.

Weeks decided to change tack. 'Did Ivy Rose have any friends here?'

'Doubt it. She hadn't been here long enough.'

Weeks rose from his seat. 'Do you mind if we ask around?'

'Feel free. I wouldn't think anyone can tell you anything about her.'

'Thank you. And would you be willing to identify the body?'

Boswell shrugged. 'I suppose so. When?'

'We'll let you know. Thank you for your time.' Nettie rose and made her way to the door with Weeks following. Just before they reached it he turned. 'I don't suppose you've got a key to Miss Lee's caravan?'

'Afraid not.'

'We'll need to search it so we'll need access.'

Boswell looked blankly at him. 'Not my problem. You'll probably have to break in then.'

Weeks nodded. 'Oh, by the way. What was the name of the other fortune teller, Sir?'

'He called himself Petulengro, Gypsy Petulengro.' His blank expression distorted into a grimace. 'Though I doubt that was his real name.'

'It sounds as if you didn't like him.'

Boswell shrugged. 'He was okay – did his job well enough – brought the punters in and told them what they wanted to hear…'

'But?' Nettie asked.

'If you must know, he was as queer as a coot.'

'Sir?'

'A homosexual,' he snarled.

'You don't approve?'

Boswell looked uncomfortable for the first time. 'I don't care either way. Long as they keep themselves to themselves.'

'And he didn't?' Weeks asked.

'I'm not saying that…'

'What are you saying, Sir?'

'I'm not saying anything. I was just glad when he upped sticks and left.'

~o~

Russell had left Lewis and his team to their work. There was little room in the pillbox and he didn't want to get in their way. So he'd set of for the Red Lion, hoping the landlord would have returned. As he left the site he looked round and was pleased to see that the Bobbies were back in line, walking slowly and prodding the ground. He was hoping that they would be lucky in finding something significant, but doubts were creeping in.

The Inspector walked the quarter of a mile to the village, passing elegant Georgian brick cottages and the medieval church – the little terrier happy to trot at his heel – before arriving at the pub. Pausing he looked up at the sign above the door.

JACK MILLS
LICENSED TO SELL WINES, SPIRITS, BEERS AND TOBACCO ON AND OFF THE PREMISES

He tried the door but it was locked. He rapped on the panelling. 'We're closed!' a gruff voice came from inside.

Russell put his face close to the door. 'I don't want a drink, I just want to talk.'

'Go away! Come back when we're open.'

Russell snorted. He could feel irritation bubbling to the surface. 'Mr Mills. It's the police. I suggest you let me in.' He only had to wait a few moments before he heard bolts being slid back and a key turning in the lock. When the door opened he did a double take. The man was the spitting image of his boss, Superintendent Vic Stout, the same overweight frame; the same florid complexion. The man even had a small cigar clamped in the corner of his mouth. His mode of dress was different – a singlet stretched over his ample belly and a pair of slim braces holding up a pair of grey flannel trousers – but everything else about him seemed the same. Until he opened his mouth. Then all similarities ceased. Stout's accent had a local ring to it. This man's voice was less Romney Marsh – more Hackney Marshes.

The landlord looked suspiciously at the dog who sat at Russell's heel, but didn't comment. 'Waddyer want?'

'Could I come in, please, Sir? I'd prefer to speak to you inside but if you insist on conducting the conversation on the doorstep...'

Mills just took the cigar out of his mouth, grunted and headed towards the bar. He picked up a steaming mug and took a swig. Turning, he regarded Russell with piggy eyes. 'Well?'

Russell decided that a direct approach was called for. 'We're conducting a murder enquiry.'

Mills's eyes widened and his jaw dropped, as if the muscles had failed. After a moment he regained enough to composure to utter: '*What? Murder? Who?*'

'The body of a woman was found in the pillbox by the canal. Can you tell me where you were yesterday?'

'I, er – 'ad to go away on business,' the man blustered.

'Can you tell me where, Sir?'

'I don't see 'ow my whereabouts is relevant.'

'It would help us to eliminate you from our enquiries.' Russell said, evenly.

Mills put the mug down. 'I'm not 'appy about it.'

'Perhaps not, Sir.' Russell paused. 'But if you'd prefer we could continue this conversation down at the station.' The DI set his mouth in a determined line.

Mills seemed to consider, then appeared to make a decision. 'Fair enough. I 'ad to go and see an old mate.'

'Where does this *old mate* live?'

'Where? Er, over Dungeness way.'

'According to Edna, you went off in a hurry. What was the reason for your visit?'

'Oh, er… my mate wasn't very well.'

Russell frowned. 'Strange. You said just now that you had to go away on business.'

'Did I? Oh yeah. I meant family business.'

'But I thought he was just a *mate*.'

'Yeah, well, I've known 'im a long time. We're more like brothers.'

Russell's puzzlement increased. 'So you dashed off to see this mate, who's more like a brother. And Dungeness is what, about 15 miles away. Journey that would take no more than half an hour, tops. Why couldn't you have come back last night?'

'He's sick. I didn't want to leave 'im.'

'I see. And does this *brother* have a name?'

'Name? Oh yeah… Albert.'

'And does Albert have a surname?'

'Albert Stern.'

'And would he be able to corroborate your story?'

'Corry – what?' It was Mills's turn to frown.

Russell sighed. The expression – *like pulling teeth* – came to mind. 'Would Mr Stern be in a position to confirm your story?'

Oh, right. Yeah, I'm sure 'e would.'

'Then perhaps you could furnish me with an address?' Russell reached into his overcoat pocket, produced a notebook and pen and peered expectantly at the landlord.

'Oh yeah, well. I'd 'ave to check.' He flailed his arms, ash flying from the cigar gripped between thumb and forefinger. Russell had rarely seen anyone so flustered.

'But I thought he was such a good mate?'

'Well 'e's moved recent like.'

Russell decided it was time to stop playing games. 'Look, Mr Mills. Either you know his address or you don't. I suggest you think of it quickly or I'll have you for obstruction.'

This had the desired effect. The man's memory seemed to improve, suddenly. 'I just remembered. It's Prospect Cottage on the Dungeness road.'

'Right. Thank you.' Russell took his time to write down the details.

The man picked up his mug and took a deep draught. Then immediately spat it back. 'Eugh! Cold!'

Russell tried hard not to smile. Instead he wrote down his telephone number on the notepad. He tore the sheet off and handed it to the landlord. 'That's it for now, Sir. If you think of anything else that might help, perhaps you'd be good enough to give me a ring.'

'Doubt if I can 'elp,' the man said, a sour look on his face.

'Just in case,' Russell replied, smiling politely. He put the notebook away and clicked his fingers. 'Come on Aggie.'

~O~

As soon as the door had closed behind the policeman, Mills lifted the counter flap and slid behind the bar. 'Bloody interfering rozzer and his mangy mutt,' he said, under his breath. He reached out and lifted the telephone handset. Holding it against his ear he dialled four digits with the other hand then waited.

The dialling tone continued for what seemed an age until finally, 'Hallo?' a gruff voice asked. 'Who is it?'

'Albert? It's Jack.'

'Ah. What are you ringing for? I only saw you a couple of hours ago.'

'Listen Albert. We might have a problem.'

Stern sensed the urgency in his friend's voice. 'What's up?' he asked suspiciously.

'I've had a copper round here. He's just gone.'

'What's he found out?' Stern spoke quickly.

'Nothing about us, don't worry. Some woman was found dead near here.'

'Oh God. Did you know her?'

Mills realised he hadn't asked who she was. 'Shouldn't think so. The copper didn't tell me.'

'What's it got to do with me?' he asked suspiciously.

'I told him I visited you last night, because you were poorly.'

'Why the hell did you tell him that?'

'I wasn't going to tell him the real reason, was I?' Mills sounded tetchy.

'I suppose not.'

Mills took a breath. 'Anyhow, be prepared for the boys in blue turning up on your doorstep before long.'

'What shall I say when they do?' His voice was pleading.

'Nothing!' Mills snapped. 'Tell them you've been ill and I came over to see that you were okay. Got it?'

~O~

After leaving Boswell the first vehicle Weeks and Nettie came to was a fairly plain looking cream-coloured, twin-wheeled caravan. To one side was what looked like an ex-army, Canadian built CMP truck with a canvas cover over the rear body. On the other was a large khaki tent. But what caught their notice was an elaborately decorated board leaning against it. In glowing colours it depicted a larger than life-size portrait of a man wearing a leopard-skin leotard. His raven hair was parted in the centre and greased down to a glossy shine. The ends of his equally dark luxuriant moustache were twisted into curlicues above gleaming white teeth set in a fixed grin. He held a bar across his chest with a large black ball on either end, his bulging biceps and forearms suggesting its great weight. Across the bottom of the board, in elaborate lettering was the legend,

CHARLES ATLAS – THE WORLD'S STRONGEST MAN

Weeks stepped up to the door of the caravan and rapped with his knuckles, then stood back and waited. After a few moments it opened and a cartoon version of the portrait on the board filled the doorway. To begin with, the man who stood there wasn't wearing a leotard, but a grubby string vest and baggy corduroy trousers. His hair had flecks of grey in it, the curls standing out like broken bedsprings and his moustache drooped, more Foo Manchu than Charles Atlas and curiously, he was wearing a pair of black silk gloves. But, he was impressive, nonetheless. He was tall but almost as broad as he was high; muscles bulged beneath the vest and his arms were more than equal to those on the painted image. He glanced down at Nettie then looked back at Weeks, his gaze flicking down to his feet, up to his tousled hair then locking his small, dark eyes on the detective's face.

'Yes, can I help you?' His voice was as light as his body was heavy, seasoned with a delicate lisp.

Initially taken aback, Weeks quickly regained his composure. 'Is that your real name, Sir?' he gestured towards the board.

'Yes, it is. I had it changed by deed poll,' he lisped.

'We'd like to talk to you about Ivy Rose Lee.'

The man stiffened. 'Oh yes?'

'I'm afraid she's been found dead.' The man's eyebrows rose a fraction but there was no other sign of emotion.

'You don't appear to be surprised, Sir,' Nettie said.

He shrugged. 'No. Can't say I am.'

'Why's that, Sir?'

'She was poison.'

'Sir?' Week's cocked his head to one side and stared at the man. 'That's rather strong.'

Atlas sniffed. 'You didn't know her. She drove my best friend away.'

'Your best friend?'

The man looked close to tears. 'Yes.' His voice was almost a whisper.

'And who might that be?'

'Pilgrim. Pilgrim Petulengro.'

'The fortune teller?'

Atlas's voice took on a harder tone, the lisp all but gone. 'He was more than that. He was a gifted genius!'

'You say he was driven away.'

'Yes, by that bitch!'

'Have you any idea where he is? Mr Boswell said he went off to join another fair.'

Atlas gave a dismissive shake of his head. 'He would say that. *He* was glad to see the back of him.'

'But you weren't,' Nettie said gently.

'No, I wasn't. Worst day of my life when I found he'd gone.'

'You don't know where?' Weeks asked.

Atlas shook his head, a single tear rolling down his cheek. 'No. But if you find him, can you let me know?'

The two constables spoke to several other members of the fair: the man on the dodgems, the lady who ran the hoopla stall, the two brothers in charge of the helter-skelter, but none could add anything to what they'd already heard.

As they walked back through the stalls and sideshows Weeks asked, 'What did you make of Mr Atlas?'

'I thought he was sweet?'

'Sweet!' Weeks exclaimed. 'He's built like a brick outhouse!'

'Ah, but inside that body of a he-man is the gentle soul of a poet.'

'Really?' He stopped walking and stared at his companion.

Nettie giggled. 'Well, perhaps not a poet, but he's certainly sensitive.'

'You can say that again.'

'Now, now.'

'He obviously had a thing for Petulengro.'

'I don't think it was returned though…'

'No?' Weeks had started walking again.

'No. I think it's what's known as *unrequited love*.'

'Is that what you call it?'

'Something like that. Must be difficult – if you're that way inclined.'

'Anyway, about this caravan,' Weeks said, quickly changing the subject.

'Which one?'

'Ivy Rose Lee's. We need to get inside. I suppose we'll have to force the door. Or get a locksmith.'

As they approached the van a cheeky grin lit up Nettie's face. 'We might not have to resort to either.' Climbing the steps she reached into her bag and brought out a fabric pouch. From it she produced a slim metal tool. She saw Weeks looking quizzically at her. 'It's a cuticle pusher,' she explained, 'but it does have other uses.' Crouching, she pushed the tool into the keyhole and started gently manipulating it, her tongue sticking out between her lips as she concentrated. After a few moments there was a click and she stood, smoothing down her skirt. 'There,' she said, a triumphant look on her face.

'Where on earth did you learn to do that?'

She tapped the side of her nose. 'Never you mind. I'll tell you someday. Now, let's see what's inside.'

~o~

When he left the Red Lion, Russell walked back to the canal, Aggie at his heel. He could see the line of uniforms, heads bent, moving slowly forward. Pushing through the gate by the bridge he started along the path between nettles and brambles. He guessed they obviously hadn't combed this part yet. When he reached the pillbox, Lewis came out through the doorway. As usual his dress was casual but smart: a blue woollen pullover and moleskin trousers, tucked into new looking wellingtons.

'Ah, Sonny,' he said, slipping off a glove and holding out a hand. Russell took it and received a firm handshake.

'What have you found? Anything interesting?'

'Apart from the earring and ticket you uncovered earlier?' There was a twinkle in his eye.

'Hope I didn't disturb anything.'

'I don't think there was anything to disturb.'

'Why do you say that?

I'm pretty sure she wasn't killed here.' Lewis pointed over his shoulder with his thumb.

'Really?' Russell's fears were beginning to come true.

'I can't be definite, we'll have to wait until Crooks has done his stuff, but I'm fairly certain.'

'What makes you think that?'

'For a start, there was very little blood on the floor. I would have expected her to be sitting in a pool of it.'

'True.'

'And if she had been killed in the pillbox there would have been blood spatters – but there's nothing.' He tapped the concrete wall.

'Curious.' Russell said.

'Quite. I can only think that whoever did the deed, slit her throat then brought her here. Probably hoping that the body wouldn't be found for some time.'

Russell nodded. 'Obviously not making allowances for a couple of curious schoolboys.'

'That's right. Anyway, I'm about done here so I'll head back to the station.' His assistant came out of the pillbox weighed down with a camera sporting a large flash gun and various other pieces of equipment. Lewis took some of it from him and the assistant nodded his thanks. 'By the way, do you know if Weeks has had a chance to look at our gypsy's caravan yet?'

'He's over there now.'

'Right, I'll head that way instead and see what he's found.'

Russell held up his hand. 'I've just had a thought. Do you mind if I tag along?'

'Not at all. But shouldn't you stay here – in case they find anything?'

'No, I'm sure Wickstead can cope for the time being. He'll let me know if anything turns up. Just give me a moment and I'll have a word with him.' He turned and walked toward the line of uniforms. When he reached them he spoke to the Sergeant.

'No problem, Sonny. I'm not hopeful we'll turn anything up – but you never know. If we do I'll radio from the car.'

Russell nodded and started making his way back. Just as he arrived a Morris Commercial PV van pulled up behind the forensics vehicle. As it rocked to a halt the doors slid open and two burly figures tumbled out. 'I'm looking for Russell,' the taller one said.

'I'm Inspector Russell. What can I do for you?'

'We're the divers you requested.'

'Oh – right.' The DI realised that the search would probably be fruitless. He had to make a decision and as they were there he thought he had better let them do their job – until it was confirmed that the death had taken place elsewhere.

'What are we looking for?' the diver asked.

'A knife. Afraid I can't tell you what sort.'

'That's okay. Where do you want us to search?'

Russell pointed towards the pillbox. 'If you start in the canal near there and work your way out.'

'How far do you want us to go?'

'About as far as someone could reasonably throw it.'

'Fair enough. Leave it to us.' While the diver spoke to Russell his colleague was unloading equipment from the back of the van – rubber suits, masks, flippers.

'I've got to go over to Nottery Quay so Sergeant Wickstead will be in charge.' Russell pointed towards the slow moving line of policemen.

'Okey doke. We'll let him know if we find anything.'

It was a bit of a squeeze in the van the flash and dab boys used. Lewis in the driving seat, Russell on the other side of the engine cover that protruded into the cab – Aggie happily sitting on his lap, watching the world go by. Lewis's poor assistant had drawn the short straw and was bundled up in the back with all the equipment. With the engine so close between the front seats and the limited range afforded by the three-speed gearbox, conversation was difficult so most of the journey to Nottery Quay took place with little being said. Russell took advantage of sitting in the passenger seat with nothing to do but look out at the scenery. On the left, trees dotted the raised bank separating the road from the canal. Every mile or so, a salient on the canal caused it to kink, creating an S bend in the road that made the occupants of the van sway one way and then the other.

Peering through the windscreen to the right he could see gently undulating fields full of lush grass, dotted with grazing Romney Marsh sheep. Some half a mile or so beyond the meadows the land rose to form what was once a cliff. This had been the barrier to the sea before the great storm of 1287 and the reclamation and draining of the marsh in the 14th century moved the coast some miles away. The squat tower of St Mary's church in Stone passed by in the distance – then steep Knock Hill, climbing up to the top of the landlocked cliff. Soon the sloping ground faded away, leaving a wide, flat swathe of arable land and the van jinked again as they crossed the bridge over the River Rother, the limit of the canal, at this point. As they approached the outskirts of Nottery Quay, Lewis slowed the vehicle, considerably reducing the engine noise.

'I understand you met the deceased a few days ago, Sonny,' he said, turning briefly towards his passenger.

'Crikey! News travels fast. How did you find out?' Lewis was about to reply but Russell stopped him with a raised hand. 'No, let me guess: Crooks.'

Lewis gave an affirmative nod.

'Thought so.'

'Sorry, Sonny.'

Russell snorted. 'It's all right. It was bound to come out sooner or later.'

'It's not like you – to visit a fortune teller.'

'She was a bit more than that…'

Lewis cocked his head to one side. 'Really?'

'Yes. It's difficult to explain.' Russell was quiet for a moment. 'She seemed to have, I don't know, presence, I suppose you'd call it.'

Lewis turned his head towards him again, a puzzled look on his face. 'What made you go to see her?'

'Ah, now, that's something I'm *not* prepared to discuss. Not at the moment anyway. It's not relevant to this investigation.' Russell's lips formed a thin line and he stared ahead, through the windscreen.

'Fair enough, Sonny.' Lewis knew his friend well enough and wasn't inclined to push him. He changed the subject: 'Anyway, we'll reach the Salts soon. Let's hope that Weeks has turned something up.'

~O~

Nettie pushed the door open and immediately gasped, putting her hand to her mouth.

'Jesus Christ!' Weeks exclaimed, following close behind. Then quickly: 'Sorry about my language.'

'That's okay. It is a bit of a shock.'

The interior of the caravan was a shambles. The table and stools were upturned, bedding was strewn across the floor; broken glass crunched underfoot. On the walls, on the curtains and on the woodwork were dark smears. Blood – everywhere. It looked like a massacre had taken place.

'This must have been where she was killed,' Weeks said, unnecessarily.

'What do you think we should do?' Nettie asked, her grey eyes clouded with worry; uncertainty in her voice. 'What would Inspector Russell want us to do?'

'I think he'd want us to leave well alone until forensics have been over the place.'

'I agree.' The two colleagues backed carefully out of the caravan.

As Weeks pulled the door closed he said: 'Do you think you can work your magic with that tool of yours – lock the door again?'

Nettie reached into her bag. 'I think so. I'll give it a go, anyway.' Crouching down she pushed the little metal gadget into the keyhole. She twisted it gently for a minute or two until there was a satisfying *click*. Standing again she gave a thin smile. 'There, that should keep it secure.'

Weeks frowned. 'Maybe, but I don't think we should take any chances. You stay here while I go back to the car and ring the station.'

Nettie stood at the bottom of the steps. The fairground people had started moving about, beginning the preparation of their stalls and sideshows for the entertainment later in the day. Although they glanced curiously in the direction of the policewoman they kept their distance. Perhaps they shared the strongman's dislike of the gypsy Lee – or the police uniform.

After a few minutes Weeks returned. 'Lewis is on his way. He's finished at the pillbox and is coming straight here.'

'Good. I could do with a strong cup of tea. It was really creepy in there.' Nettie shuddered.

'Not a pretty sight, I'll admit. Wonder what happened?'

'Judging by the state of the caravan I reckon there must have been a fight.'

A shadow passed across Weeks's face. 'Unless someone turned the place over and she came back and surprised them.'

'I suppose that's a possibility,' Nettie said slowly. 'But why move the body?'

'I don't know. Hopefully we'll find out more later.' They stood, talking quietly, while the fairground people went about their business, still pointedly ignoring them. Vado Boswell's son came tearing round the corner and skidded to a halt, a few feet from the constables.

'Oh. You're still 'ere, then?' he said, then slunk away without a backward glance.

~O~

It was something of a relief when Lewis's green Morris J-type van appeared between a showman's wagon and the shooting gallery. Even though the van was narrow it was a squeeze but by careful manoeuvring it arrived unscathed in front of the bowtop. Weeks was even more relieved when the door slid open and his boss, Sonny Russell, clambered out of the passenger seat, grinning.

'Good to see you, Sir, but I'm afraid it's not very pleasant in there.'

Russell's smile faded and his eyebrows flickered upwards. 'You've been inside?' he asked. 'Wasn't it locked?'

Nettie stepped forward, a bashful look on her face. 'I'm afraid I'm guilty, Sir. It was me who opened it.'

'And is it still open?'

'No, Sir, I locked it again.'

'Good girl. But perhaps you'd do the honours and unlock it again? I'd prefer that we didn't have to force it.'

'Sir.' Nettie took out her cuticle pusher again and within a couple of minutes, Russell and Lewis were making their cautious way up the steps.

'Johnny was right,' Lewis said quietly. 'It appears that there's been a bloodbath.'

'And you were right,' Russell agreed. 'Looks like this is where she was killed.'

'I take no pleasure in that. I find the whole thing particularly saddening. Why would anyone want to kill a fortune teller?'

'Hopefully we'll find out. My question is: why would they go to the trouble of taking the body from here, all the way over to Appledore, then dumping it in that pillbox?'

'I've no idea, Sonny. Perhaps John Crooks will turn up something.'

Russell stepped back from the doorway. 'There's so little room I'll let you get on with your work. Give me a shout when you've finished and I'll have a look round then.' He made his way back down the steps to the waiting constables. 'I want to know what you've found out. But first, I could do with a cuppa.' He smiled grimly. 'And looks like you could do with one too. I don't suppose there's anywhere around here we can get one?'

'There's Terry's teas. He's got a van parked in the lay-by.'

'That'll do. At least it'll be wet and warm.'

Chapter 3

A wild goose chase *is any senseless pursuit of something non-existent or unobtainable – a hopeless enterprise.*

THE SMELL of frying came from within the van as Terry prepared bacon butties for a couple of dustmen who'd parked their cart in the lay-by and stood waiting for their food. Next to the griddle where he was busy cooking, a shiny tea urn bubbled and belched steam and a stack of white sliced bread and a block of paper-wrapped marge waited to be made into sandwiches. The three police officers stood at the counter with steaming white china mugs of tea. Aggie sat at their feet, sniffing the air appreciatively. Russell and the others made small talk until Terry had finished and the two men collected their order and went back to the cart, one of them casting furtive glances at Nettie. He apparently wasn't used to seeing a policewoman in uniform drinking tea at a roadside caff. Terry busied himself in the back of the van.

'Right, now you can tell me about your findings,' Russell said, taking a slurp from his mug.

Weeks flipped open his notebook. 'We first spoke to Vado Boswell – he runs the fairground.'

'What's he like?'

'Handsome. If you like that sort of thing,' Nettie said. 'Not my type though.'

'I meant, what's his manner?'

Colour spread from the policewoman's collar and her cheeks turned pink. 'S-sorry, Sir,' she stammered.

Russell grinned. 'That's okay. He's obviously a charmer.'

'He *thinks* he is. But I reckon he has a cruel streak.'

'What makes you say that?'

'It wasn't so much what he said, more his attitude.'

'Can you be more specific?'

Nettie thought for a moment. 'When he was talking about Petulengro…'

'Petulengro?' Russell interrupted.

'Yes, Pilgrim Petulengro. He was the fortune teller in the fairground before Ivy Rose Lee.'

Russell gave a slight nod. 'I see.'

'When Boswell talked about him there was real venom in his voice. I got the feeling that he would be capable of killing someone if provoked.'

'Do you think *he* killed the gypsy, then?'

Nettie shook her head vigorously. 'I don't think so. His anger was aimed at Petulengro because *he* was *queer*.'

'I see. So he didn't feel strongly about Lee?'

'No,' Nettie said.

'He actually sounded genuinely shocked that she'd been killed,' Weeks added.

'Wasn't he concerned by her absence?'

'Apparently not. Said he'd only have noticed if she hadn't shown for a few days.'

'Hmm.' Russell's chin sank on to his chest. He appeared deep in thought. Weeks and Nettie waited. Finally he looked up and spoke. 'What happened to Petulengro?'

'He left.'

'Why?'

'Boswell said he didn't know. He thought he might have joined another fair.'

'We need to find out where he's gone.' Russell took a sip of his tea. 'I think he may be an important element in this investigation.' Weeks made a note on his pad. 'Did you speak to anyone else?' Russell asked.

'Ah, yes, Sir. We spoke to the strongman,' Weeks said, looking up from his notebook.

'And?'

'It was rather interesting, Sir,' Nettie continued.

'How so?'

'Despite looking like you'd expect a strongman to look he was, er, not what we expected.'

'Can you explain?'

'You'd expect the voice to match the physique.'

'And it didn't?' Russell suggested.

'N-no.' Nettie stammered. She seemed lost for words.

Weeks took over. 'Instead of a deep voice, it was light – almost feminine.'

'I can see that would be a surprise.'

Nettie seemed to regain her composure. 'It wasn't just that. He obviously had definite affection for Petulengro – seemed heartbroken that he'd upped sticks and gone, without saying where. Asked if we'd let him know if we find him.'

'But why did he go?' Russell's normally smooth brow was furrowed.

'Atlas said that Lee had driven him away,' Weeks said.

'Strange.'

'Why do you say that, Sir?'

'Well, it seems odd that a woman would have driven a man away – especially as he was obviously a fixture at the funfair. I think we need to look into this more carefully. Talk to the people here again.'

Weeks wrote in his notebook again.

'And we need to find Petulengro.' Russell drained his mug. 'Right, I think we'll see if Lewis has finished in the caravan. Then we can have a look around.'

~O~

But Russell didn't make it as far as the caravan. Weeks had dashed to the Wolseley to use the phone to report in. Just as the DI and Nettie were strolling into the fairground he rushed back.

'Sir! You're wanted at the station.'

Russell stopped suddenly. 'Why?'

Weeks was flustered. 'Superintendent Stout wants to see you – urgently.'

'Oh Lord. What have I done now?' His eyes rolled heavenwards. 'Can you drive me?'

'Certainly.'

'Nettie, you stay here. Keep any rubberneckers at bay. I'll send someone out to relieve you.'

~O~

'What is it you're not telling me, lad?' Russell was slumped in the passenger seat of the police car.

'I'm sorry, Sir. I *had* to tell him.'

'Tell *who what*?'

'Superintendent Stout. He answered the phone.'

'*He* answered the phone? Where was Wickstead?'

'He's out at Appledore,' Weeks said quietly.

Russell took a deep breath and let it out noisily. 'Oh yes.'

'I had to tell him about the state of the caravan.' Weeks paused while Russell considered. 'And he knew about the frogmen, too.'

'Ye gods and little fishes.'

'Sorry, Sir.'

'Not your fault lad. I should have run it past him first.' He sighed. 'Too late now – I'll just have to face the music.'

The rest of the journey passed in silence, Russell brooding and Weeks appearing to concentrate on the road – although he was actually giving his boss some thinking time. He felt bad about spilling the beans to Stout, but he knew her really had no option but to tell him what was happening. He was well aware of the Super's short fuse but knew that Russell was up to the challenge of defending himself – he hoped.

~O~

Russell walked into the station. As he passed the unattended front desk and went along the corridor his way was barred by a smirking DI Bonnie Parker. 'You're for the high jump, matey. You won't get away with it this time.' He took a drag on his Capstan Full Strength, let the smoke circulate fully around his lungs then blew out a long stream of blue smoke, into Russell's face. 'You've really done it now.'

Russell tried hard not to choke. 'Of course, you've never got it wrong.'

'Not on this scale, mate. If they gave awards for cock-ups you'd get first prize,' Parker added. He guffawed, then broke into a fit of coughing.

As he doubled over Russell gave a sly grin. 'I'm sure you'll manage it one day. Anyway, I've an appointment. Mustn't keep the Super waiting.' He pushed passed, still chuckling, and walked up to Stout's door. He knocked lightly.

'Come.' The growled summons was far from inviting – Russell couldn't have felt less welcome. His smile dissolved and his heart plummeted. He entered the room with its familiar aircraft-carrier sized desk and pleasant views across the park. Stout, as usual, was wreathed in a blue haze from the cheroot he was smoking. And, as usual, he made a point of ignoring the inspector, instead concentrating on his paperwork, until he was good and ready to begin the roasting. There was no invitation to sit down so Russell remained standing. After several long minutes Stout looked up, piggy eyes glittering above florid cheeks.

'Inspector Russell…' There was a resigned weariness in his voice.

The DI feigned innocence. 'Sir?'

Stout shook his head, slowly from side to side. 'This time you've gone *too* far.'

Russell frowned but didn't respond.

'I can't believe you would do this to me.' The Super's voice was low and venomous.

'I'm not sure what you mean, Sir.'

Stout brought his fist down so hard on the desk that the heavy glass ashtray jumped in the air, scattering cigar butts across the polished wood.

'You had the sheer, bared-faced cheek to organise a fingertip search – taking a large number of my uniformed constables – and the desk sergeant – away from more important work...'

'But...'

'*SILENCE!* Don't interrupt me when I'm speaking! Not only that but you requested a team of divers...'

'Only two...'

'*I haven't finished*! You decided to organise all this manpower to pursue a wild goose chase – without consulting me. What was the point of it when the victim was actually killed several miles away?' He violently stubbed out his cigar and waited for a reply. '*Well*?'

Russell kept his voice low and level although inside he was churning. 'I didn't know at the time that she hadn't been killed where she was found.'

'Well you should have bloody well found out, before wasting police resources on a pointless exercise!'

'Possibly, Sir.'

'*Possibly*?' Stour thundered. His colour had risen as his temper had exploded. He was now a livid red from his collar to his hairline. '*Definitely*! You should have consulted me before leaving an empty police station! I want those men back here now.'

'But what about the door-to-door in the village?'

With a supreme effort Stout reined his anger in. 'Look,' he said, slightly more reasonably. 'You might think that it's important but she was just a gypsy, after all. A traveller. Should we really be wasting police time on someone like that?' He spread his arms wide.

Russell clamped his teeth together. If he hadn't he would lost his temper and said something that he might have lived to regret.

Stout mistook his silence for agreement. His voice dropped several semitones and his colour returned to a lighter puce. 'I'm glad you see it my way.' He took a deep breath and let it out noisily. 'But, I can't trust you to investigate this case any more. I want DI Parker to take over.'

'But Sir!'

'No buts. You've made me look stupid. The Chief Constable has been giving me a hard time about this year's budget and you've just blown it for me.'

'I'm sorry, Sir.' Russell tried to look contrite.

Stout waved his hand dismissively. 'It's too late for sorry.'

He took his time to select a new cheroot from the tin on his desk. Then even longer to get his Zippo lighter fired up and the tip of the cigar glowing. He took a long drag, savoured the nicotine, tipped his head up and blew a plume of smoke towards the ceiling. Russell could only stand and wait, wondering what else was coming.

'You've some leave due, haven't you?'

'Yes, Sir.' Russell's heavy heart became leaden.

'I think it might be an idea if you take a few days off.'

'Really?'

'Really.' Stout pursed his lips, the gripped cheroot pointing outwards; his arms folded.

Russell tried one more time. 'Couldn't I work alongside Parker?'

'*No!* I'm away for the next couple of days and I don't want any trouble between you two. I know how you feel about him.'

'It wouldn't be a problem.'

'I said… *Take – Some – Leave.* Now go.'

'But…'

Just get out!'

Defeated, Russell turned to go.

'And send DI Parker in. I want a competent detective on this case.'

Russell left the room. Outside Parker was leaning against the wall, a fresh Capstan Full Strength clamped in the corner of his grinning face. He'd obviously overheard much of the conversation. 'That went well.' The grin widened, the cigarette dangling off his lower lip. Russell could only stand and stare. As Parker pushed past he said: 'I'm looking forward to taking over. I expect I'll wrap it up pretty quickly.' He entered the Super's office and the door closed behind him. Russell stood breathing heavily for several minutes, the stale smell of Parker and his foul cigarettes a bitter reminder of his blunder.

~o~

Back in his office, Russell sat slouched in his seat. He was bemused by Stout's apparent confidence in Parker. The man was a bumbling buffoon and had proved himself incompetent on numerous occasions. He knew his own failure to toe the line angered the Super but at least he got results. His normally positive disposition had deserted him; sunshine had disappeared behind heavy cloud cover. He realised now that he should have cleared it with Stout before taking so many men away from the station but… At the time he had felt it was necessary to get a fingertip search underway as soon as possible. Before any evidence was lost. If he'd known earlier that the gypsy had been killed in her van… Well, it was no good being wise after the event. He linked his fingers behind his head and pursed his lips. But he was too down to produce a cheerful ditty. Instead he exhaled noisily. There was a loud knock on the door.

'Come in,' he said wearily.

Weeks put his head round the door, his face like thunder. 'I don't believe it!' he exclaimed.

'I know, lad. I'm not very happy about it either.'

'What?'

'The Super taking me off the case…'

Weeks looked baffled for a moment. Then his blank expression turned to one of understanding. 'Oh. Sorry, Sir. Y-yes,' he stammered. 'Rotten luck. But it's not that.'

Russell sat up and put his hands flat on the desk. 'What is it then?'

'Bloody Bonnie Parker! The Super says I've got to go with him!'

'Really? What about Barrow?'

'He's off sick – again.'

'So you're going to be his DC.'

'Yes I bloody well am, apparently. Not my choice though.'

'Never mind, lad. At least you'll be able to keep me informed about what's going on.'

Weeks sighed. 'There is that I suppose.' He shook his head. 'Sorry, Sir. I shouldn't have flown off the handle like that – not when Stout has been so unpleasant to you.'

'Don't worry about that.' Russell smiled warmly. 'I've got a thick skin, and besides, I might do a little snooping on my own.'

'Really?'

'Yes. I've got some ideas that our Inspector Parker won't have thought of. Not a word to anyone, mind.'

'Of course not, Sir. You can rely on me.'

'I know I can, lad. Presumably you'll be going off with Parker in one of the pool cars?' Weeks nodded. 'Any chance I could borrow your car?'

'Of course, Sir.' Weeks fished in his pocket and brought out the keys. He grinned. 'I won't ask where you're going.'

Russell smiled back. 'Thanks, lad. Best I don't tell you – for now. But if you let me know what Bonnie's up to, I'd be grateful.'

~o~

Weeks was driving DI Parker over to Compass Point. The only consolation was that he'd got a Wolseley from the car pool and not the dreaded Ford Pilot – with the impossible column change that had always troubled him. But it was small comfort. Parker was dozing in the passenger seat, a Capstan Full Strength stuck to his sagging bottom lip. It had gone out before burning down completely, a column of ash threatening to cascade down his already grey-flecked jacket and tie. Weeks was tempted to swerve so it did fall but decided it would be preferable to have a few more minutes' peace and quiet. However, he had the satisfaction of seeing the DI's head flop forward as he stopped a little too sharply on arrival.

Parker shook his head and looked round, a puzzled frown on his face. 'What the bloody hell…?'

'We've arrived, Sir.'

'Oh really' He opened the door and, hanging on to the frame, levered himself out. Spitting out the spent fag end and pulling a pack from his pocket, he took a crumpled cigarette and lit up. 'Right,' he said. 'Where's this gyppo's caravan?'

Weeks led him to the bowtop, where Nettie was still keeping watch. Parker barely acknowledged her as he pushed past and puffed his way up the steps.

He opening the door and peered inside. 'Hell's teeth! What a mess.' He turned to the DC who had come up behind him. 'Why on earth did Russell send all those men over to Appledore when it was bloody obvious that the woman was done in here?'

'He didn't know at the time,' Weeks answered, adding: 'Sir', when the DI glared at him.

Parker harrumphed. 'Very likely, I don't think.'

Weeks decided not to reply. His lips formed a thin line.

Sucking hard on his cigarette Parker surveyed the interior of the caravan, taking in the shambles and the bloodstains. 'Why would anyone want to do this?' He shook his head, a look of incomprehension on his face. 'She may only have been a bloody fortune teller, but to do this…' He let the words hang in the air. He shook his head again, this time appearing to clear his thoughts. 'Right. Where do we go from here?' He looked expectantly at Weeks.

'Er…'

'Come on, boy. You need to be quicker than that if you want to be my wingman.'

Weeks swallowed then answered quickly. 'Lewis and his team have been and looked for fingerprints and any other evidence, so there's not much we can do here. I suggest we interview the other people at the fairground, again.'

'That's more like it.' Parker grinned, showing a row of nicotine-stained teeth. 'Where shall we start?'

Vado Boswell had been watching them from behind a net curtain. As soon as they had gone towards the fortune teller's caravan he had slipped out of his home. He jumped lightly down the steps to where his pride and joy, an imported Chevrolet pickup, was parked. Powerful enough to tow his showman's van he kept it in immaculate condition. The cream paintwork gleamed and the chrome hubcaps sparkled, especially as he'd recently scrubbed it out. He got in the car, started the V8 engine and set off, heading north.

Chapter 4

Advance-Design *was a truck series by* ***Chevrolet****. It was the company's first major redesign after WWII and from 1947 until 1955 they were the best-selling trucks in the United States. There were three main sizes: the half-, three-quarter-, and full ton capacities in short and long wheelbase.*

RUSSELL KEPT the Chevrolet in sight but stayed well back. He doubted that Boswell would suspect a humble Ford Popular was following him but he didn't want to take any chances.

~o~

After leaving the police station earlier he'd driven Weeks's car back to his railway-carriage home. He had quickly changed out of his suit and donned a pair of worn corduroy trousers and an ex-naval, white wool roll-neck sweater. He'd exchanged his polished brogues for well-worn walking boots and jammed a battered trilby on his head. Back in the car Russell had headed for Nottery Quay and the Salts. He'd parked a little way back from the funfair, the vehicle partly concealed behind some bushes. He turned off the engine and sat waiting, slumped low in his seat. After a few minutes the police Wolseley had driven past, and turned into the site. Not long after, as he'd hoped, the Chevrolet had nosed out from between a Scammell and Bedford lorry.

He followed the truck out of town and up the hill. When it reached the Peace and Plenty it forked right towards Iden. Russell had to wait while an Austin Atlantic turned on to the road in front of him. This suited him as now he could follow without appearing obvious. They drove through the village, round the double bends and were soon descending the steep hill towards the river bridge, the brake lights of both vehicles glowing red. As they reached it the driver of the pickup slowed, stuck his arm out the window and turned right. Once clear, the Austin roared off. Russell followed at a more sedate pace and pulled into a farm gateway. He climbed out of the car, his terrier scampering behind him.

'Aggie!' he called. 'Come to heel.' They crossed the road and walked down the track the pickup had taken. It was stony and rutted; the river on one side and open fields on the other, initially bordered by mature trees. A little farther on it opened up to what could only be described as a motor graveyard. There were vehicles in various states of decrepitude. Russell didn't know a lot about cars – they were only useful for getting him to where he wanted to go – but he could recognise at least a couple of Model T Fords, three or four Austin 7s, the odd Standard and even what looked like a Bentley – all of pre-war vintage. Partly dismantled engines, gearboxes and differentials lay around along with tyres, wheels and pieces of metal he couldn't identify. All very interesting but his destination was further on. The pickup was out of sight. He presumed it was beyond a distant clump of elders. Rather than observing discretion he threw caution to the wind, pulled the brim of his hat lower and strolled on confidently – a country gentleman out for a ramble with his dog.

When he reached the trees he could see the Chevrolet tucked into a clearing. Drawing closer he was surprised to see beyond it, a gypsy caravan. He carried on walking past, whistling nonchalantly, Aggie rootling excitedly around in the undergrowth. He went on another 20 yards or so before he risked looking round. All was still. He obviously hadn't been seen, or been paid any attention. Quietly calling the dog, he slipped her lead out of his pocket and clipped it on to her collar. Moving more cautiously he retraced his steps. When he reached the elders he stopped and peered through the emerging greenery. The door to the caravan was open and he could hear raised voices.

'You said she wouldn't be found for days!'

'She shouldn't have been.' Russell thought he recognised Boswell's voice.

'What do we do now?'

'I don't know.'

There was a pause, then, 'What's happened to your ear?'

'Oh that. I've lost an earring. Must have got torn out when we were moving her. Solid gold it was. Bloody annoying.' Russell started. There was an earring found where Ivy Lee's body had been found.

'Where do you think you lost it?'

'How the hell should I know?' The voice was agitated.

'All right, keep your hair on.'

'Must have been when we were carrying her along the river bank or somewhere.'

'I hope the rozzers don't find it!'

'Doubt it. Could be anywhere.' Another pause. 'Anyway, it's best if you lie low for the time being. Nobody knows you're here. I'll come out again with some grub. Okay?'

Nothing more was said and Boswell appeared in the van's

doorway and descended the steps. Clutching the terrier's lead tightly Russell held his breath and watched the man get into the truck, start the engine and reverse out on to the track. The vehicle turned and set off back to the road. The DI waited, watching the open doorway of the caravan. A man appeared. He was thickset and stocky. A russet-coloured scarf was tied round his head; dark curls escaping from underneath, the colour matching the moustache on his upper lip. He wore a loose shirt, the same shade as his headscarf. His trousers were black and Russell noticed his feet were pushed into a pair of curious looking slippers. They had an eastern appearance, but what stood out most was the bright pompom atop each of them. The man stood for some moments, hands on hips, looking out at nothing in particular before turning and going back inside and closing the door. Russell waited for a few minutes before retracing his steps, making his way to the car.

What should he do? Judging by what he'd just heard, Boswell and the other man – Petulengro? – may well have killed the gypsy, Ivy Rose Lee, or at least been involved in her death, somehow. Stout had taken him off the case but this was too important to keep to himself. He made a decision. He would go back to the funfair and tell Parker what he had heard. Then the man would have to do something about it, wouldn't he? He started the engine, turned the car in the gateway and set off back towards Nottery Quay.

~o~

When he arrived at the Salts he was alarmed to see Charles Atlas being led away in handcuffs by a uniformed officer and bundled into the back of a police car. His shoulders were so broad it took some effort to get him in. The shambling figure of DI Parker followed behind, a self-satisfied grin on his face, a customary fag clamped between his lips. Weeks brought up the rear, his bewildered expression the counterpoint to the DI's. Russell got out of the Ford and made his way across to his opposite number.

'Russell,' Parker said, a gleeful look on his face. 'I've done your job for you.' He folded his arms across his chest, the grin spreading, Cheshire-cat like.

'What do you mean?' Russell asked.

'We've got the murderer.'

Russell couldn't believe his ears. 'Atlas? The strong man?'

'That's right. Got him banged to rights.'

'But how do you know he did it?'

'More or less confessed. Said he hated the woman – wanted her dead.'

'What about evidence?'

'Evidence?' Parker gave a shrug. 'I'm sure we'll find it.'

'I think you're wrong.'

Parker snorted, a shower of ash cascading down his front. 'Listen,' he said, walking up to Russell and prodding his chest with a finger. '*You* are off the case. *I'm* in charge now. So get used to it.'

Russell tried once more. 'I think Boswell and Petulengro, the other fortune teller, did it.'

'Oh yes? On what do you base this *unlikely* idea?'

'I heard them talking.'

'You heard them talking.' He shook his head sadly. 'And you ask about me having evidence. Sorry mate, I can't see how I could have got the wrong man. You'll just have to lump it, I'm afraid. Now, if you'll excuse me.' He turned to the DC. 'Weeks – come on. I want to get back to the station. I've got a guilty man to question.'

With that he got into the Wolseley and settled himself in the passenger seat. Weeks looked towards Russell and shrugged. His expression was far from happy.

~o~

In Appledore Jack Mills was getting ready to open up the Red Lion for the lunchtime trade. With a sense of relief he'd seen the police pack up and go. Not that it had been bad for trade. A number of people had come in from outlying villages to see what was going on and had popped in to the pub for drinks and food. But the close proximity of the boys in blue had made him nervous.

As he went about his preparations Mills was worrying about his friend Albert Stern over in Dungeness. Well, he called him a friend but he was more of an acquaintance. He only remained in touch with him because he had a boat, capable of easily crossing the channel to France. And that was very useful to Mills. He was worried because he didn't trust Stern to keep his mouth shut if the police did call on him. He was unreliable at the best of times and if the police started probing, Mills was concerned he would cave in. He decided he would better go over and see him in person – sooner rather than later.

Edna had gone down to the cellar to stock up on bottles of bitter lemon and tonic water. The hatch opened, her tousled head appeared and she came up the steps.

'Jack,' she said. 'What's that stack of crates in the corner of the cellar?' Her face was a picture of innocence.

Mills's scowl was the complete opposite. 'What?' he growled.

'Big stack of crates – covered with a tarpaulin?'

'You keep your nose out of it,' Mills said. 'Nothing to do with you,' he said, and slammed the cellar hatch shut.

~o~

Russell was in a quandary. His intuition told him that Parker had got the wrong man. He knew from the conversation he'd had earlier with Johnny and Nettie there was no love lost between the strongman and Ivy Rose. He just didn't think he would actually kill her. But, judging by the conversation he'd heard out by the river, Petulengro and Boswell were much more likely candidates. The trouble was, Stout had made it patently clear that he was to have nothing to do with the case. And Parker obviously wasn't going to take him seriously. So what could he do? He sat in the Ford, his hands on the steering wheel, a frown on his forehead. Aggie seemed to sense her master's frustration. She lay quietly on the back seat, chin on paws, one eyebrow raised. Russell turned and ruffled her head.

'What should I do?' he asked, knowing he wouldn't get an answer. 'I suppose I could talk to Johnny – he might be able to persuade Bonnie Parker.' The terrier yawned. Russell smiled. 'Yes, I know how you feel. It all seems a bit of a trial. But I've got to do something – I hate the thought of an innocent man being convicted.' He sat for a while then made up his mind. 'Yes, that's what I'll do.'

When he arrived at the police station Wickstead was leaning on the counter, reading the racing section of the evening paper. 'Hello Sonny. I thought you were on leave?'

Russell chuckled. 'I am.' His expression turned serious. 'But I need to talk to Johnny. I fear our friend, Parker, is about to carry out a dreadful miscarriage of justice.'

'That sounds serious.'

'It is. Do you know where I can find them?'

'They've got that chap from the fairground, Atlas, in the interview room.'

'That's who I'm worried about.'

'But I thought he'd confessed.'

'Huh! That's what Bonnie said, but I don't think so.'

'Why didn't you tell him?'

'I tried, but he wouldn't listen.'

'No surprise there.'

'I'm hoping I can get Johnny to exert some influence.'

Wickstead gave a snort. 'Good luck with that. I can't see Bonnie Parker letting you anywhere near him.'

'Oh?'

'I think he's decided to hang on to him while his normal sidekick, Clyde Barrow, is off sick.'

'Charming. He *is* my DC.'

'Yes but Stout has suspended you, hasn't he?'

Russell nodded grimly.

'I'm afraid you'll just have to put up with it, until you're back at work.'

The DI let out a long sigh. 'I suppose you're right.' He turned and was about to leave.

'Oh, Sonny. Crooks, the pathologist just rang.'

Russell stopped. 'What did he say?'

'We-ell. I'm supposed to pass it on to the officer in charge. But as you're here…'

'Go on…'

'He's got the body of that gypsy on the slab. Apparently he's discovered something interesting.'

'I'm intrigued. Can you delaying telling Parker for a little while?'

Wickstead tapped the side of his nose. 'Leave it to me Sonny.'

DI Parker sat slouched in the interview room. His jacket hung untidily over the back of his chair; his braces strained over his ample stomach; his ash-flecked tie was loosened and askew. By contrast, DC Weeks sat neatly upright, his pen poised over a pristine page in his notebook. Even his normally unruly mop of dark curly hair seemed tamed – for now. The look on his face was one of quiet resignation.

'Right. Let me get this straight. The blood on your shirt is from when you cut yourself shaving,' Parker stated.

Not for the first time Charles Atlas shifted nervously in his seat. If he fidgeted much more the slender wooden structure was likely to give way under his weight. A rough, grey woollen blanket was wrapped round his muscular frame. 'Yes, I've already told you several times,' he answered. A bead of sweat rolled down the side of his face, dampening the extremity of his already moist moustache.

'Huh!' Parker exclaimed. 'A likely tale.' He reached for his cigarettes, withdrew one from the pack and jammed it into the corner of his mouth. Striking a Swan Vesta he applied the flame to it and sucked greedily. He held the smoke in his lungs for several seconds until, with a barking cough, he blew it out, not caring that it went straight into the face of the strongman. 'Now let's have the truth.'

'It *is* the truth!' Atlas protested.

Parker took another drag on his cigarette. 'We'll see. At this very moment our flash and dabs boys are examining your shirt.' He leaned forward, put his elbows on the desk and rested his chin on his knuckles. 'And let me tell you – *I* think we'll find it's the blood of that gypsy.'

'But I didn't kill her.'

'So you say. I think the evidence will tell a different story.'

'But why would I want her dead?'

Parker turned his head towards Weeks. 'Constable, read what he said when you interviewed him.'

Weeks flipped back a couple of pages in his notebook. He cleared his throat. 'He said, "I wasn't surprised that she was dead. She was poison".'

Parker smiled triumphantly. 'Now if that ain't a confession of guilt, I don't know what is.'

~o~

Russell stopped outside the austere façade of the one-time asylum. The Victorian red-brick building was now an annexe of the town's hospital, with the mortuary off to one side. He reached below the dashboard, pulled up the handbrake and switched off the engine. Exiting the car he climbed the steps to the front door, crossed the foyer and turned down the pea green and beige corridor that led to John Crook's domain. At the end was a door marked:

PATH LAB – ONLY AUTHORISED PERSONNEL TO ENTER.

Pushing the door open he crossed the small, plain anteroom containing just a row of filing cabinets and a pair of straight-backed chairs. On the other side was another door marked PRIVATE. Russell knocked then pushed the door open. The pathologist was bending over a body lying on a stone slab.

'Ah, Sonny,' he said, straightening up, the green gown straining over his ample stomach. 'I hoped I'd be seeing you instead of that appalling Bonnie Parker. He really is an unpleasant character – bumbling and incompetent, a real scruff of a man. Always puffing on one of those foul cigarettes and scattering ash over everything – mainly his own greasy suit. Eugh. Can't stand him.'

Russell was taken aback at the force of the outburst.

'You agree with me, don't you?' Crooks lowered his eyebrows and stared at the DI.

'I couldn't possibly comment, John.'

The pathologist let out a sharp breath and tutted. 'Anyway I'm glad it's you.' He turned back to the slab. 'Come over here. I think I might have found something rather interesting.'

Russell walked across to where the body of Ivy Rose Lee lay, modestly covered with a green rubber cloth. He was glad it was pulled right up to her chin, covering her throat which he knew wouldn't be a pretty sight. Her eyes were closed in her nut-brown face – she looked at peace, an image at odds to her violent end. 'What is it John?'

'I thought I'd wait until you – or that awful man – turned up, before revealing what I've found.' The gypsy's lips were parted, her mouth slightly open. Taking a large pair of tweezers from the metal tray on the end of the slab he carefully pushed them into the opening. Squeezing the blades closed he pulled out a piece of folded card. There was an elaborate pattern on the back. He put it on the woman's chest and returned the tweezers to the tray.

Russell leaned forward as the pathologist unfolded the card. 'Well I'll be…' It was a tarot card, featuring a lurid drawing of a skeleton, astride a white horse. His hand gripped a vicious-looking scythe; his mouth was set in a sickly rictus. **MORT** was written across the bottom in large letters.

'Oh, Death,' Crooks said. 'Any idea what it means? Apart

from the obvious, of course.'

'Not really. I suppose it might be some sort of message from the killer.'

'My thoughts, too.'

'I know the cards have different meanings. I'll have to look it up. Can I take this?'

'You'd better not. I ought to show it to Parker.'

'I suppose so. Shame, as it's rather intriguing.'

'But aren't you off the case?'

Russell grinned sheepishly. 'Doesn't stop me doing a bit of private investigating, does it?'

Crooks chuckled, his belly shaking. 'Nothing ever does.'

Russell paused for a moment, considering. Then spoke hesitantly. 'John,' he began. 'I've got a bit of a dilemma.'

'What's that, Sonny? Crooks replied going over to the sink and washing his hands.

'I suppose you've heard that Parker has made an arrest.'

'Yes, the news had reached me.'

'What do you make of it?'

Crooks shrugged. 'Not really given it much thought.' He looked directly at Russell, his bushy eyebrows low over his eyes. 'I suppose you're going to tell me he's got the wrong man…'

'As a matter of fact…'

'I knew it! Go on then. Spill the beans.'

Russell explained about the conversation he heard between Boswell and Petulengro.

Crooks, who had listened in silence, nodded. 'That's does put a different complexion on it, doesn't it? What are you going to do about it?'

'The Super is away so I tried to tell Bonnie but he wasn't having any of it.'

'No change there, then.'

'He's convinced he's got the right man. I wouldn't be surprised if he tried to fit him up – you know how he feels about homosexuals.'

'Yes, he is rather biased.'

'That's being polite.'

'But you're convinced the man is innocent?'

'Well, not convinced, but it does seem rather convenient.'

Crooks rubbed his chin. 'Listen. I've got an idea.'

'Oh yes?'

'Why don't you ring the station? No doubt you'll speak to Wickstead. Tell him you're a member of the public and you've seen a caravan that fits the description of the one that belongs to Pilgrim Petulengro. Get him to pass it on to Parker as an anonymous tip-off.'

'Do you think that'll work?'

Crooks spread his arms expansively. 'Of course, trust me. He's such a lazy sod he'll accept if without question and get someone else to follow it up.'

'Hmm. That's a good idea. Thanks, John. I'll give it a try. Meanwhile, I'll see if I can find out what this card means.'

Chapter 5

***The Reading** or kite wagon has straight sides that slope outwards towards the eaves, high arched wheels, and is relative light in weight.*

PILGRIM PETULENGRO lay back on the plush velvet sofa in his van, his hands clasped behind his head. His was a Reading wagon, elaborately decorated in red, with details picked out in yellow and green. The interior was equally decorative with ornate bevelled mirrors; painted cupboards and seat lockers where goods were stored when the van was on the move. But none of this finery gave him any comfort. Boswell's visit had rattled him. He'd been so casual about the gypsy Rose Lee. The man had been certain that the body wouldn't be found for weeks. By then Petulengro would have been miles away, working in another funfair. Instead he was stuck, far too close to where they'd dumped her body. His van was in good condition and his horse, young and fit. But he could still only travel at a few miles a day and would be easy to spot. Much as he disliked it he was just have to stay put for the time being. Boswell had assured him that he would be safe where he was. He said he knew the bloke who owned the land – and the cars dumped there – and nobody came down this track. He let out a long sigh, closed his eyes and drifted off to sleep. He couldn't know it was a sleep he would never wake from.

Chapter 6

Aleister Crowley was an English *occultist, ceremonial magician, poet, painter, novelist and mountaineer. A prolific writer, he founded the religion of Thelema and published widely over the course of his life.*

'RIGHT, LET'S get this straight.' DI Parker had levered himself out of the chair and was walking round the room. 'You still claim that you had nothing to do with the death of this gyppo, Ivy Rose Lee.'

'I've already told you that – several times. I might not have liked her, even hated her, but I *didn't* kill her. Why would I? She was nothing to me. She *may* have driven Pilgrim away, maybe not, but I had nothing to gain from her death.'

Parker shook his head sadly. Coming up behind the strongman, he placed his hands on the back of the chair. He leaned forward until his lips were almost touching the other man's ear. 'But the evidence will tell a different story,' he said, in a throaty whisper. He stood upright and was returning to his chair when there was a knock at the door. 'Come in,' he growled, lowering his bulk on to the seat.

The door opened and Lewis appeared. In contrast to Parker he was the height of elegance, a neat side parting in his well-cut hair. 'Can I have a word?'

'I suppose so.' Parker groaned as he heaved himself out of the chair again. When they were in the corridor he said: 'I hope you've come to tell me the blood on the nancyboy's shirt is a match.'

Lewis shook his head. 'I'm afraid not.'

'*What?*'

'I'm sorry to let you know that he was telling the truth. It looks like he really did cut himself shaving.'

'I don't believe it.'

'I'm afraid you'll have to. The evidence is conclusive.'

'Hmm.' Parker paused, his brow furrowed. 'What about fingerprints in the gyppo's caravan?'

'Oh there were lots.' Parker's face brightened. 'But none matched Atlas's,' Lewis said.

'Bugger. So we've got nothing to hold him on then.'

Sorry. Wish I had better news.'

'Double bugger! I suppose I'll just have to let him go – for now.' A sickly smile crept across Parker's face – like an oily tide coming in over a muddy riverbed. He leaned towards Lewis 'Listen. We're both men of the world, aren't we?' Lewis's affirmative nod was almost imperceptible. 'We both know he's guilty as hell, don't we.' It was a statement not a question so Lewis remained silent. 'I need some evidence, so I suggest you go back and find me some. Okay?'

'If you say so. But I don't hold out much hope. We've been very thorough.'

Parker put his hand on the door knob. 'I don't doubt it, old chum. But another look ain't going to hurt, is it? I want him convicted.'

The door hadn't been closed properly while they talked. The strongman couldn't help but hear every word.

~O~

"Death, or Mort, signifies change. The figure of death is a living skeleton surrounded by the dead and dying – kings and paupers – signifying that no one can cheat death". On a shelf of the bookcase in his railway-carriage home Russell had found a well-thumbed book called *The Meaning of the Tarot.* He recalled buying it some years before from an antique shop housed in one of the warehouses in Nottery Quay. He remembered paying for the book and the man snatching the ten shilling note with bony fingers that ended in talon-like nails emerging from grubby fingerless gloves. Then almost throwing a few coppers change back to him.

Squeezed between a shop dealing in good quality oak and another selling slightly battered utilitarian furniture was a dingy weatherboarded warehouse, the timber rotting and the floor uneven. It was filled with a kaleidoscopic selection of antiques. The interior was so gloomy it was difficult to tell if there was anything of value or if it was just all just junk. The owner's name was Septimus Pike, a wizened man, of indeterminate age, straight out of a Dickens novel. Russell had known him for some time.

When he had asked if Pike had a copy of a book on Tarot cards he said: 'What do you want it for?' his voice a cross between and rasp and a croak.

'Just idle curiosity,' Russell answered

'You ought to be careful. Dabbling with the occult can be dangerous.'

'And you would know about that?'

'Maybe I would and maybe I wouldn't,' Pike said, stroking his wispy beard with dirt-ingrained fingers.

'I'd be interested to hear your thoughts, Septimus.'

'I'm sure you would, my friend.' He made an elaborate flourish with his arm and gestured towards a leather armchair. 'Take a seat and I'll tell you what I know.' Russell gingerly lowered himself into the chair. The leather was torn and stained and as he sat he could feel a broken spring pressing into his thigh. He shifted to make himself more comfortable.

'Right. What do you know?'

'Have I ever told you that I met Aleister Crowley?'

Russell's eyebrows shot up in amazement. He knew of the man but was surprised that Pike would have known him. 'Really? Wasn't he called "*The most evil man in Britain*"?'

'Well, "*The wickedest man in the world*", actually.' The antique dealer rose from his chair. 'Just a minute.' He walked across to a shelf and ran his finger along the spines of the books on it. After a few moments he stopped at one and pulled it out. He placed it on the low table between them and settled back in his chair. Russell picked up the volume. It had a rich blue cover with a beautifully painted illustration of a Tarot card in the centre. Above the picture were the words **THE BOOK OF THOTH** *(Egyptian Tarot)* and below, by **THE MASTER THERION** *(Aleister Crowley).* He opened the cover and inside the flyleaf the author had signed his name. The signature was most distinctive, the capital 'A' forming a crude representation of a man's genitalia. Russell looked up to see Pike staring at him grinning, his hand caressing his beard.

'That shocked you, didn't it?'

'It is something of a surprise, I must admit.'

'Not as surprising as the man himself.'

'Is that right?'

'Yes. I didn't actually see him until he was near his end. But he still had something about him – some strange power.'

'Tell me about it. How did you come to meet him?'

Pike put his elbows on the arms of his chair and steepled his fingers, carefully resting his whiskery chin on the upturned talons. 'Well, I do a bit of house clearance, from time to time. This is how I got a lot of this stuff.' He nodded to the room in general. 'It was towards the end of '47. A lady came into the shop – I don't know why she chose me – must have been my magnetic personality.' He chuckled, a deep phlegmy sound. 'And she really was a lady. Have a look inside the cover.'

Russell opened the book again. On the frontispiece he read, "Illustrated by Lady Frieda Harris". 'Golly' was that her? A *real* lady.'

'She certainly was. We got chatting and she confided in me. She'd been friends with Crowley for years, apparently. As far as I could make out she was some sort of disciple and had followed his teachings on something called, I think, *Thelema*. Some mumbo jumbo, anyway. He had come to live in Hastings – she'd heard he was ill and had travelled down from London to check on him. Apparently he was dirty and neglected so she arranged for a nurse to look after him. Anyway, she asked if I was interested in old books. I wasn't going to turn down a chance to meet him so I said yes. He was in lodgings at Netherwood House on The Ridge in Hastings and I visited him there.'

'What was he like?'

'He was an old man by then. Early seventies, I think. He wasn't well, coughed a lot and looked pale and drawn. I understood he was addicted to heroin. But there was something in his eyes. I don't know, a darkness or something. His room was number 13…'

'Of course.'

Pike nodded. 'Despite being near the end he still had a huge presence.'

'What did you talk about?'

'Nothing of consequence, as I recall. Chess – he was member of the local club; hadn't ever been beaten, apparently. The weather – he found the climate in the South good for his bronchitis. Lady Frieda showed me some books that he wanted to sell. They were old but there was nothing particularly special so I offered a few shillings, which she seemed happy to accept.'

'Is that how you came by this?' Russell tapped the book.

'Oh no.' Pike leaned forward, his eyes sparkling. 'He *gave* it to me.'

'How come?'

'Before I left, I went over to say goodbye – he was sitting in a large wing chair. He grabbed hold of my hand – almost pulled me on top of him. I was amazed at his strength – he looked so feeble. He stared into my eyes. I can't tell you how it felt. Creepy I suppose. Strangely compelling. Then he relaxed his grip and said: "You must have this," and gave me the book. I heard that he died not long after.'

'Is he buried somewhere nearby?'

'No, no. The people of Hastings thought he was evil so he was cremated in Brighton.'

'I see.' Russell sat up in his chair. 'Are you going to sell me this book then?'

Pike let out a gasp which sounded like the cry of a mythical bird. 'Not likely, my friend!' He scooped up the volume and clutched it to his chest. 'This is precious to me.'

'Fair enough,' Russell said, feigning indifference although he rather fancied owning it. He started to rise from the chair.

Pike shot out a hand and gripped the DI's wrist. 'Not so fast. You can't have this one but I have another you can buy.' That is how Russell came to be in possession of a less valuable and more battered book on the Tarot that he was now perusing.

~O~

The landlord of the Red Lion, Jack Mills, was in a foul mood, even though the journey had only taken 20 minutes, as that bloody policeman had relished in pointing out it would. Why the hell someone had to dump a woman's body in the pillbox up the road from the pub he just couldn't imagine. He could well do without nosey coppers making their bloody enquiries around Appledore. Thank God they'd found out that she hadn't been done in there but over at Nottery Quay and buggered off. He gripped the steering wheel of his Standard Vanguard pickup tightly and stared angrily out through the dusty windscreen as he travelled along the straight road approaching Dungeness. He forked right, crossed over the little Romney Hythe and Dymchurch Railway level crossing and was soon pulling up outside Stern's house. He switched off the ignition, the engine tinkling as the metal cooled.

Mills could see Albert's van parked in the drive, so presumably the man was home. He walked up the path and knocked on the door. He waited a few minutes but no one came. Cursing, he rapped again. Still nothing. Making his way along the side of the house he walked into the back yard. At the far end, on a patch of hardstanding, Stern was kneeling down, bent over a BSA motorcycle. It had seen better days, showing the ravages inflicted by the salt-laden, seaside air. The tank and metalwork were pocked with rust and there was a dribble of black oil on the concrete beneath it. Stern was so intent on some intricate operation that he didn't hear Mills come up behind him.

'What are you up to then?' the landlord asked.

Stern shot in the air as if fired from a canon and turned as he did to face Mills. 'What the bloody 'ell did you do that for?'

'Jumpy, ain't we?' said Mills, grinning.'

'You could've given me an 'eart attack, comin' up behind me like that.' Stern was breathing heavily, his heart beating fast in his beanpole-thin frame.

'You got a guilty conscience then?' Mills's grin had turned into a deep-throated laugh. He was enjoying the other man's discomfort.

'You can put a sock in it. It's your fault I'm jumpy.'

'Why's that then?'

'Bloody coppers 'ave been nosin' round.'

Mills grew serious. 'They didn't find nothing, did they?'

'Course they bloody didn't. Ain't nothin' 'ere for them to find. Last lot went over to your place, remember?'

'Don't remind me. I been sweating buckets since they discovered that woman's body. Swarmin' all over the village they were. Luckily they didn't stay long.'

'They found out who she was yet?'

'Some gyppo fortune teller, apparently.'

'Where was she done in then?'

'Funfair on the Salts at Nottery. Mate of mine's been 'elpin' out on the dodgems. Said her caravan was drippin' with blood.'

'Charmin'.'

'Right mess it was.'

'Do they know who done it?'

'Got some bloke banged up in the local cop shop. My mate said 'e was the strongman – Charles Atlas.'

Stern snorted.

'Funny thing is, apparently 'e's built like a brick shit'ouse but 'e's a pooftah – a fairy – bats for the other side.'

'Takes all sorts.' Stern paused and wiped his hands on a greasy rag. 'Is 'e guilty then?'

'Who knows? Suppose 'e must be. Anyway, what did the coppers 'ave to say?' Mills asked.

'Oh, it was only one of them – the local bobby. I know 'im a bit. Well, when I say I know 'im, we nod to each other in passing.'

'All right, I don't need the ins an' outs of your relationship.' Mills gave an exasperated sigh. 'For Christ's sake, What did 'e *say*?'

'What? Oh yeah. 'E just wanted to confirm that you'd spent the evenin' over 'ere.'

'An' did you tell 'im?'

'Course I bloody did. What d'you take me for?' Stern asked tetchily.

'Keep yer 'air on. I was only askin'.'

'You should know me well enough, by now.'

'Suppose I should.' They stood in silence looking down at the motorbike for a while – each lost in thought.

Stern looked up. He cleared his throat. 'I'm glad you came over. I've got somethin' I've been meanin' to say for a while.'

Mills tipped his head to one side and frowned. 'Oh, yes?'

'There's no easy way to say this – I want out.'

Mills's eyebrows shot up. '*What*?'

'I don't wanna do no more trips.'

'You're jokin', ain't yer?'

'No. I'm deadly serious. I've 'ad enough. It's too risky.'

'Bloody 'ell man! How am I supposed to get my cheap booze and fags?'

'That's up to you. I just know I don't want nothin' more to do with it.'

'Thanks a bunch. What do I do now?' Mills scratched his head, a miserable look on his face.

Stern took pity on him. He sighed. 'All right, just one more trip.'

'Thanks, mate,' Mills said, his smile returning. 'When can we go?'

'Let me think. The moon's nearly full and there's not gonna be much cloud – plus the tide's right.'

'So tonight?'

Stern sighed again. 'I suppose so.'

'Thanks mate. I'll make sure it's worth your while.'

'You'd better. An' don't forget – this is the last time.'

~o~

'Sonny, I'd recognise your voice anywhere,' Wickstead chuckled.

'But will you do it?'

'Of course I will. You can rely on me.'

'Thanks. I appreciate that.'

'You can show your appreciation in the pub when you're back.'

Russell put the phone down and smiled to himself. Hopefully Crooks's idea would work out.

True to his word, Wickstead sought out DI Parker, He found him in his office, his feet up on the desk. The room was wreathed in smoke and a customary cigarette smouldered in the overflowing ashtray.

'Sergeant. What can I do for you?'

Wickstead held his hand up to his mouth and coughed. 'I've just had a phone call from a member of the public, Sir.'

'That's interesting,' Parker said indifferently.

'Apparently they spotted the caravan belonging to the other fortune teller, – the one that disappeared from the funfair.' Parker looked blankly at him. 'The gypsy, Petulengro, Sir.'

'I *do* know who he is. What of it?'

'Er, I thought you might like to talk to him, see if he can help with the enquiry.'

A sickly smile crossed Parker's face. 'Well that's very nice of you, but I think I've got the case wrapped up.'

Wickstead was afraid the deception had backfired. 'Oh, right,' he said and turned to leave. He was just going out the door when Parker spoke.

'Just a minute, sergeant. Weeks has been moping around with a face like a wet weekend. It would be good to get him out from under my feet.' He scowled. 'I'll be glad when DC Barrow is back at work.'

Wickstead sneaked a crafty smile. 'Right, Sir.'

'Tell him to take a look – although I doubt it will turn anything up.'

'Yes Sir. Thank you.'

~O~

Russell was in the little kitchen in his railway-carriage home. Though small in proportions it had everything he needed. One compartment housed his living room, with an efficient coal stove, another, his bedroom. The kitchen was equipped sufficiently so he could produce meat-free meals. Towards the end of the war when he'd been stationed out in the East he'd spent time with Buddhist monks. He had been so impressed by them and their philosophies that he became a vegetarian on his return to England, quite unusual for the time. It caused a few raised eyebrows and made eating out tricky but he'd stuck to it and felt better for the change.

He filled the kettle and put it on the stove. Striking a match he turned the switch and lit the gas underneath it. He took a tin off the shelf, removed the lid and took out a slab of fruit cake. Aggie stood in the doorway, wagging her tail and looking up expectantly. Russell grinned. 'Not for doggies!' He reached for another tin and took out a Bonio. He crouched and held it out. The terrier sat and lifted a paw, which Russell shook, then she gently took the treat in her jaws. Standing, Russell smiled and continued with the preparation of his tea. When it was done, he went through to the living room and sat in his armchair. He put the tray on a little side table and waited for the tea to brew. His mind wandered to his new situation.

A woman had come unexpectedly into his life. It was a surprise as he thought he was settled into the life of a bachelor, wedded to the job. But Isobel Bailey had turned his head. He'd met her earlier in the year during a case involving stolen Nazi plunder that a shady Frenchman was trying to sell. She was an antique dealer and craftswoman, specialising in jewellery and small items, and had become embroiled in the case. At the denouement she had been injured and Russell had ended up with suspected concussion.

There had been a possibility that she would have been convicted of handling stolen goods or obstructing the course of justice but Russell managed to keep her out of it. Since then they had grown close and had spent time together. She had visited his unconventional home and had seemed to approve of it but he wondered if she would rather that he lived somewhere more conventional. He sighed. He loved his railway carriage but he was starting to wonder if it was time to move on. He was just about to pour himself a cup of tea when there was a knock on the door. Aggie started rushing round excitedly then began bouncing up and down like a ball by the door.

'Afternoon, Sir,' Weeks said, standing in the doorway, grinning.

'What are you doing here, lad? Good to see you. Come in, I've just made tea.'

There was a twinkle in Weeks's eyes as he sat down. 'We received an *anonymous* tip-off about a caravan. I thought you might know something about it.'

Russell laughed. 'The ruse worked then. Crooks said it would.'

'Yes, it did. Bonnie Parker was only too keen to get rid of me. That man…'

'Has he made any progress with the case?' Russell asked, passing the DC a cup.

'I don't think so. He's convinced that Atlas did it.'

'But where's the evidence?'

'He hasn't got any. Lewis told him the blood test and so on came back negative but Parker told him to look again.'

'I doubt he'll find anything.'

'That's what I thought but he's made his mind up.'

Russell nodded. 'Well it's down to us – I mean *you* – to prove him wrong. Come on, drink up and I'll show you where the caravan is.'

Weeks glanced at his boss's slice of cake.

'Oh all right then, Russell laughed. 'But you'd better bring it with you.'

Russell led the way in Weeks's Ford and the DC followed in a police Wolseley. They bumped down the track, passed the car dump and pulled up in the clearing by the caravan. All was quiet, just a tethered piebald grazing on the scrubby grass. Even the birds were silent. Russell had a bad feeling as he approached the steps to the van. He recalled the last time he had seen Petulengro when Boswell had been to visit him. He tried to remember his impressions of the man – whether he had appeared disturbed by the visit. It had been hard to tell – the gypsy fortune teller had seemed unaffected. But something told him, some sixth sense, that now all was not well. Climbing up he went to tap on the door but it swung open. As his eyes adjusted to gloom within he felt a creeping sense of *déjà vu*.

'Oh no,' said Weeks, following close behind.

'I'm afraid so. Don't touch anything.' The interior of the van wasn't as much of a shambles as Rose Lee's had been; there weren't any obvious signs of a struggle, but blood had soaked into the fabric of the sofa and the rag rug on the floor. There was no sign of Petulengro. 'Better radio for Lewis and his team.' They returned to the Wolseley and sat, waiting for the forensics man to arrive.

'What do you make of it, Sir?'

'I don't know, lad. I had Petulengro down for Ivy Rose's murder but now I'm not so sure.'

'Could it have been Vado Boswell who did for both of them?' Weeks asked.

'Possibly. Although I'm not so sure about that either.'

'Why's that, Sir?'

Well, I can understand that he *may* have killed Lee, but I'm struggling to accept that he killed Petulengro as well. Despite what he'd said earlier, from the conversation I overheard between them, it sounded like they were on friendly terms. Boswell left saying he was going to return with some food. He'd hardly say that if he was going to come back and do him in.'

'I suppose not. Then who did it?'

Russell heaved a huge sigh. 'That I don't know. Someone who doesn't like fortune tellers, perhaps?'

'But why?'

'That's a puzzle we'll have to try to unravel – sorry – *you'll* have to try to unravel. I'm off the case, don't forget.' He smiled wryly.

'Then why are you here, Sir?'

'I had to show you the way, didn't I?' Russell's eyes twinkled.

'But you're still here...'

'I just thought I'd wait around to see Lewis – if that's okay with you?'

It was the DC's turn to smile. 'I doubt I could stop you if I wanted to.'

It wasn't long before they heard the rumble of an engine and the forensic department's Morris J-type van appeared. The driver's door slid open and Lewis got out, smiling, as dapper as always. Russell and Weeks stepped out of the Wolseley, ready to greet him. The passenger seemed to be struggling with his door. Lewis walked round to assist. When the door finally opened, the detectives expected to see a forensic assistant. They were more than surprised to see the crumpled form of DI Bonnie Parker emerge, start coughing and immediately begin complaining.

'Christ, Lewis. I wish I'd not bothered to come. I'm beginning to wonder if there is any point in me being here.' He'd been bent over coughing for the first few seconds and as he slowly stood upright his eyes lighted on Russell. 'You! What on earth are you doing here?'

'Me?' Russell said, feigning innocence. 'I'm merely a member of the public. Just a bystander.'

At first Parker looked puzzled, then a sickly smile began spreading across Parker's face. 'Just a bystander? It was you – the anonymous tip-off.'

Russell held his hands out. 'Don't know what you're talking about.'

'A likely tale. I suppose you've had a look?'

'Don't worry, I haven't touched anything.'

'I should bloody well hope not.' He turned to Weeks. 'Right then. Let's see what you've found. I just hope it's worth my while coming out here in that rattletrap.' The DC nodded and led the way up the caravan steps.

Russell stood by the cars with Lewis. 'Did you find any evidence to incriminate the strong man?' he asked.

'Of course not. I knew I wouldn't.' He looked towards the caravan to make sure he couldn't be overheard. 'To be honest, I only had a cursory look. I agree with you that Atlas is innocent.'

'What happens to him now?'

'They've nothing to hold him for. They had to let him go.'

'So, back to square one for Parker.' While the men were talking, the terrier had been excitedly sniffing around in the undergrowth – on the hunt for rabbits or rodents. Suddenly, she stopped, head erect, nose twitching, then shot off. She rocketed across the stony track, up over the raised bank and disappeared towards the river. '*Aggie*!' Russell shouted. '*Come here!*'

Lewis laughed. 'She might not be a bloodhound but she's got the scent of something. Let's go and see.' Following the path the dog had taken the two men climbed over the bank and down on to the flat grass along the riverside. They could just see the terrier, tail wagging madly, nosing around the plants growing at the side of the river. Lewis, the more nimble of the two, reached her first.

'What have you found, little dog?' He crouched and parted the reeds. 'Well I'll be…' he exclaimed. 'Aggie! Leave it!' She backed away and danced about. 'Sonny, take a look at this.'

With a sharp exhalation Russell knelt down. 'A slipper! It's what Petulengro was wearing when I saw him.'

'So it belonged to the gypsy? It doesn't look like it's been here for long.'

'Do we get the frogmen in?'

'*We*? *You* don't do anything,' Lewis stated.

Russell stood up and sighed. 'I keep forgetting. Will you?'

'I'd better not act before consulting Parker. But I won't suggest divers – just yet. The body will most likely float downstream so I'll suggest he scours the riverbank for a mile or so.'

While they had been talking, Parker had finished his cursory examination of the caravan and had come looking for Lewis. He came puffing over the ridge, almost losing his balance as he slithered down towards the river bank. He cursed loudly then said: 'Ah. This is where you're hiding.'

'I think you'll want to see this,' Lewis said.

With an effort Parker bent down and looked where the forensics man was pointing. 'It's a bloody woman's slipper,' he said, straightening up again.'

'Not a woman's,' Russell corrected.

'Who asked you?' Parker demanded, facing up to the DI.

Lewis stepped between them. 'Steady on. He saw Petulengro wearing them. It's a *man's* slipper.'

'Bloody pooftah's, more like. What's it doing here then?'

'Looks like our man was dumped in the river.'

'Oh Christ. Does this mean I'm going to have to get the divers in?'

'Not necessarily,' Lewis said. His tone was measured and mild, matching his appearance. 'Why don't you get some men to walk down the river for a mile or so. It's flowing quite slowly so the body can't have gone far. May even have snagged on a branch or got caught up in some reeds.'

Parker nodded. 'Good plan.' He looked back the way he'd come. '*Weeks*!' he yelled.

The DC came over the rise. 'Sir?'

'Radio through to the station. Get Wickstead to round up as

many bodies as he can. We want this river searched.'

Lewis spoke. 'Right, now you've organised that, I'll see if I can find any clues in the caravan.'

Parker nodded. 'Good man. Just what I was going to suggest.' He turned to Russell. 'I suppose I owe you an apology,' he said, struggling to get the words out.

The DI was surprised. 'You do?'

'Yes. You were right about the strongman. It wasn't him.'

'Right.'

'No. It was obviously Boswell. Killed them both.'

Russell just stared.

'I'd better get back to the Salts before he does a bunk.'

'But...'

Parker smiled. 'No, I don't need any help, thanks. You can enjoy your time off.' With that he turned and clambered back up the bank, yelling for Weeks to get the car ready.

Chapter 7

***Smith's Potato Crisps Ltd** was founded by Frank Smith and Jim Viney in the United Kingdom in 1920. The crisps were sold in greaseproof paper bags, with a blue paper twist of salt. The firm started in Cricklewood, London, reputedly in Smith's garage.*

RUSSELL STOOD on the riverbank, staring at the slow-moving water. He felt at a loss. Lewis had said goodbye and gone to examine the caravan. Bonnie Parker had made Weeks drive off in such a hurry he hadn't had a chance to exchange a word with him. He wasn't used to this – not being in the thick of it. He was certain that Parker was on the wrong track – pursuing Vado Boswell – something he'd find out in time. He hoped it wouldn't go too far before he realised his mistake and had to let the gypsy go. But there was nothing he could do to prevent the man following his fools' errand. Aggie was quite happy, dashing around, following scents only she could detect. But Russell was unable to share her contentment. He felt frustrated and kicked at a clump of grass with his polished brogue. He could go and see Isobel – that was tempting, but he knew that she was busy working on a prestigious jewellery commission and he would rather not disturb her. He walked disconsolately along the river bank and his thoughts turned back to the beginning of the case.

If he hadn't been so hasty in sending the entire staff of the police station off on a fingertip search, but had consulted Stout first, he would still be on the case. But he had, and there was no going back. It would be a while before the Super allowed him to deal with anything more demanding than minor crimes. As his mind roved he recalled his visit to the Red Lion in Appledore, and the shifty landlord, Jack Mills. What was that all about? The man obviously hadn't been involved in the murder of the gypsy but… he wasn't telling the whole truth.

The germ of an idea started forming in Russell's mind. There was something going on – something Mills hadn't wanted to share. He was sure that whatever it was, it was connected with his mate over in Dungeness. What was his name? Russell felt in his pocket and produced his notebook. Flipping through the pages he found it. *Albert Stern, Prospect Cottage, Dungeness.* The idea started as a vague framework, but the more he thought about it, the more it began to take on a discernible form. He realised that he was moving outside the bounds of accepted behaviour but he just couldn't help himself. He needed a challenge – a puzzle to unravel. And the more he thought about it, the more he was convinced this was the one. He knew that Stern had received a visit from the local bobby, but only to confirm that Mills had visited that evening, which he had. But in the PC's report he'd mentioned that he didn't think that Stern looked unwell. So why had the landlord said he was? Russell decided he would like to know more. For the first time in ages he started whistling. Inspired by his location it was *Down by the Riverside*. Feeling more cheerful than he done for a while his step was light as he climbed up the bank and made his way to the car he'd borrowed from Weeks. First he set off for his home.

~o~

Back in his little kitchen he made himself a flask of tea and a round of cheese and tomato sandwiches. He wrapped them in greaseproof paper and put them in an ex-army knapsack, added an apple and a bag of Smith's crisps. Then he changed out of his work suit. He replaced it with a pair of worn corduroy trousers and a white submariner's rollneck sweater. His brogues were exchanged for a pair of sturdy walking boots. He took a camel-coloured duffle coat and a Breton cap off the peg. To this he added a pair of naval binoculars. They were bulkier than he liked, but would have to do. Thus prepared, he returned to the car, whistled for Aggie to join him and headed off for Dungeness.

The journey was uneventful, the landscape becoming increasingly flat and barren as he approached his destination. In just over half an hour he was nearing the level crossing at the approach to the estate. He slowed the car and was able to stop easily as one of the Romney, Hythe and Dymchurch railway 15-inch gauge trains rattled across the road. The one-third full-size locomotive was at the head of the rake of chocolate and cream carriages, with smoke streaming from the chimney, its whistle shrieking a warning. Russell smiled. He was used to the three-foot gauge railway that ran near his home and on to Compass Point but this was quite different. By comparison *his* railway was almost staid and the carriages almost full size. This outfit had the feel of a mainline railway, just on a much smaller scale. If you half closed your eyes it could be an express, thundering up the east coast main line. Almost as soon as it appeared it had gone, snaking its way through the shingle to the station near the distant lighthouse.

As Russell passed Prospect Cottage he could see a van parked out front, presumably belonging to Stern. He drove further on up the road until it turned to the right where he pulled on to the side, so the car would be out of sight. He turned off the engine and got out. Reaching into the back he took out the duffel coat and cap, put them on, grabbed the knapsack and walked back the way he had come, Aggie happily sniffing out new scents. He was just an ordinary man taking his dog for a walk. Approaching the cottage he could see what looked like a derelict shed about a hundred yards away on the other side of the road. He set off diagonally, crunching across the shingle. When he reached the building he pulled at the door, which opened with difficulty, the hinges complaining and the bottom scraping noisily on the ground. The terrier scampered in after him and he hauled the door shut.

As Russell's eyes grew accustomed to the dark interior he took in his surroundings. Inside was a jumble of broken fish boxes and unidentifiable lumps of rusty metal. There were three windows, missing most of their glass. One faced towards the distant beach and a handful of fishing boats pulled up on the shingle; a second gave a good view of Prospect Cottage; the third looked out sideways. A few feet away were the rusty tracks of one of the hand-worked fishermen's railways. This traversed the shingle, elevated in places, raised up on piles of planks where it crossed dips in the terrain. At the inland end a flat wagon sat on the narrow track, a large, crude wooden box balanced on top.

Looking round the interior of the shed he found the remains of a chair, its back missing but the legs intact. Gingerly he lowered himself on to the seat. Despite an alarming creak, it held his weight. He opened the knapsack and took out the binoculars. Focussing on the cottage he could pick out the details of the door and windows but was unable to see inside. He swivelled to look the other way and had a clear view of the half a dozen boats pulled up on the shingle. He wasn't sure what to expect or what he was going to do but he had a gut feeling that he was in the right place at the right time. Russell settled down for a long wait.

~O~

The immaculate Chevrolet pickup was parked alongside the immaculate living van so it was reasonable to assume the man was at home. Leaving DC Weeks standing next to the Wolseley, Bonnie Parker stomped up the steps and hammered on the front door. It was only a few seconds before the door suddenly swung open and the stocky figure of Boswell stood staring at the policeman, a belligerent scowl spoiling his handsome face.

'What the bloody hell do you want?'

Parker was unaffected by his glowering presence. He puffed out his chest. 'Vado Boswell, you are under arrest. You are not obliged say anything unless you wish to do so but whatever you say will be taken down in writing and may be given in evidence.'

'*What*? You must be joking. What I am I supposed to have done?'

'The murder of Pilgrim Petulengro, for starters, and probably of the gyppo Rose Lee.'

Boswell held his hands out. 'I don't believe it… Where's the evidence?'

'Don't worry, sunshine. We'll find it.' He turned to PC Beaumont who had come up the steps behind him. 'Cuff him constable. We'll continue this down at the station.'

As the junior officer reached out with the handcuffs Boswell looked quickly from one side then to the other. In a flash he pushed Beaumont hard on the chest, knocking him backwards into Parker who overbalanced, his arms windmilling. Both policemen stumbled backwards down the steps and fell in a heap. Boswell vaulted athletically over them, landing on the ground on all fours. Pushing himself upright, he ran towards the pickup and wrenched the door open. But, before he could get inside, Weeks was on him. The gypsy tried to shake him off but, although wiry, the DC hung on as tenaciously as a terrier. They fell to the ground, rolling in the dust. Parker had stayed down, groaning, but Beaumont was quickly on his feet and dashed over to the grappling figures. This time he did manage to get the handcuffs on Boswell's wrists and suddenly, the fight seemed to go out of him. Panting, Parker rose to his feet and tried to brush the dust off his suit jacket. It made little difference.

'*You!*' he said, his face red with rage. 'You're for the bloody high jump.' He leaned forward and gripped the spotted scarf round the suspect's neck. '*And* I'm going to do you for assaulting a police officer!' He let go of the scarf and pushed him away, a look of disgust on his face. 'Take him to the station and chuck him in the cells.'

Boswell said nothing as he was led to the police car.

'Where's Lewis?' Parker demanded.

Weeks looked blankly at him. 'Sir?'

'The bloody flash and dab bloke – the forensics man, whatever you want to call him.'

'He's over in Iden, Sir. At the other caravan.'

'Hell's teeth! We need him here. I want the case against this gyppo sewn up so bloody tight you won't be able to crack it open with a crowbar.'

'I'll go over and let him know, Sir.'

'Not before you've taken me back to the station. I'm not travelling in the car with that low-life. Don't know what I might catch.'

~o~

During Russell's time out in the East the monks had taught him how to meditate. When he'd tried to sit cross-legged they had laughed, good-humouredly. One, who spoke passable English, explained that westerners weren't flexible enough to take up the lotus position easily. If they tried, it would become uncomfortable after a while and they'd concentrate more on the pain and not the meditation. Once that was accepted, he'd learned the practice sitting in a chair and had become quite adept at it. So, sitting in the tumbledown shed he'd found no difficulty in maintaining his posture for quite a while. He tried emptying his mind, as he had been taught, but there were so many things spinning round in his head, demanding his attention, that he wasn't totally successful. But, the time passed easily enough. Aggie too, seemed content to curl up on an old sack and snoozed happily. After an hour or so Russell got up and stretched, poured a cup of tea from the flask and unwrapped the sandwiches. After an impromptu meal, which he shared with the terrier, he settled down again to wait.

It wasn't long before he heard the sound of an engine. Keeping well back in the shadows he saw a Standard Vanguard pickup pull up outside Prospect Cottage. The light was slowly ebbing from the sky but, with the aid of the binoculars, he was able to make out the distinctive form of Jack Mills. The landlord got out of the car and walked up to the front door of the cottage. The door was opened and he disappeared inside. 'Bingo!' Russell thought. So he was right to stake out the property. It wasn't long before the door opened again. Mills reappeared followed by another man. Where the pub landlord was broad and stocky, his companion was stick thin. Through the glasses Russell could see he had a long face with a sour expression that looked permanent. Albert

Stern, he presumed. The men came walking straight towards his hideout. He held up an admonishing finger to the terrier and melted further into the shadows, praying they wouldn't see him. When the two men reached the little railway track, they dumped the bags they were carrying into the box on the wagon. Mills took out a packet of Senior Service and offered it to Stern. Stern shook his head. The pub landlord shrugged, put a cigarette in his mouth, lit the end and sucked greedily.

'I'm not happy about this,' Stern complained.

Mills put his arm round the other man's shoulder. 'Don't be like that mate. Just one more time, one more consignment of booze and fags, then I'll leave you in peace.'

'You said that last time,' Stern mumbled, twisting away.

'I mean it, this time – honest.' Mills beamed at him.

'You'd better. Anyway, where's the meeting this time?'

'Wissant.'

Stern looked alarmed. '*Wissant?* I'm not landing on that bloody beach again. Last time we only just managed to get off before those French rozzers turned up.'

'Don't worry. This time Jacques is gonna meet us in his boat.'

'Hmm.' Stern paused – Mills drew on his cigarette, the tip glowing in the gathering gloom. 'What time are we supposed to be meeting him?'

'Midnight.' Mills slid his sleeve back. He peered at his watch. 'That gives us a good five hours before the *rendezvous*.'

'I suppose.'

'Come on, mate. Cheer up. You know you enjoy it really.' Stern gave him a look that said the opposite then bent and started pushing the wagon. The rusty wheels squealed in protest and it rocked alarmingly on the uneven trackwork. Mills took one more drag, dropped the cigarette end on the shingle and followed.

Russell sat in stunned silence. Even Aggie stayed quiet. The DI was astonished at what he had heard. He'd half-expected something of the sort, but to hear exactly what they were planning, exactly where and at what time, was more than he could have hoped for. He knew Wissant – had been taken there by his friend, Inspecteur Guillaume Bruissement, in the Citroën DS the French police officer had on loan. They had eaten an excellent meal in a restaurant – Le Vivier – in the centre of the pretty little coastal village and taken a walk to the flat, sandy beach. That was where Stern had mentioned. Now what to do? Cautiously Russell lifted the binoculars and followed the progress of the men as they made their way to the distant beach. Russell saw them throw the bags into one of the boats then put their shoulders to the bow. Slowly, the hull of the boat started sliding down the shingle ridge towards the sea.

But, *what to do*? There was little point in Russell making his way to the beach. The duo would have put out to sea before he reached it. And what could he do if he got there before they left? Nothing. All he'd heard was a conversation that they could deny if pressed. It would be his word against theirs. They'd say he'd misheard and all they were doing was going out night fishing. So there was no mileage in following that course of action. The words spun round in his head again – *what to do*? How could he stop them? He sat back on the rickety chair, his forehead creased in thought. Then he had a brainwave. *He* might not be able to do anything but he knew someone who probably could. Leaving the shed he set off quickly back towards the car.

Russell remembered he'd passed a red telephone box and reached it in a few minutes. Pulling the heavy door open, he whistled to the terrier who joined him inside. He took his notebook out of his pocket and flicked through the pages until he found the one he was looking for. He picked up the receiver and dialled 100.

'Operator,' a disembodied female voice said. 'What number do you require?'

'I'd like to make a reverse charge international call.'

'To what number?'

Russell read the number off the page. Holding the receiver to his ear he could hear a series of clicks, then the long series of purring notes he knew to be the French dialling tone. After what seemed an age, there was a final click, then,

'Allo?'

'I have a call from England,' the operator enunciated slowly. 'Will you accept the reverse charges?'

'*Mais ouis* – but of course.'

'Putting you through.'

'Guillaume?'

'Ah Sonny!' Russell could imagine his French opposite number's cheery grin beneath the luxuriant moustache. ''Ow wonderful to be 'earing from you. It 'as been too long.'

'Yes it has.' Russell was grinning too.

'What 'as caused you to call me on the telephone?'

'I need your help.'

Bruissement chuckled. 'But of course. That is why you are telephoning me at my home. Do not worry. I am very 'appy to be of service. What can I do for you?'

Russell explained what he had heard and how he felt powerless to act from his position.

'Look, my friend,' the Inspecteur said. 'I am understanding your concern, but do you not still 'ave shortages in *Angleterre*?'

'Yes, we do…' Russell said slowly. 'I'm sure you do too.'

'*Mais bien sûr.* But the authorities turn, 'ow you say, an eye that is blind.'

'But it's still smuggling, Guillaume.' Bruissement let out a laugh that was a cross between a roar and a bark. Russell smiled. 'So you don't think it's very important?'

'That is not what I meant.' His voice was serious now. 'If it is something that causes you distress then I will 'elp in any way I can.'

'I wondered if you'd be able to just take a look at what was happening on your side – in Wissant. I don't want you to do anything heroic, just observe.'

'Of course, I will do what I can for you, *mon ami*.'

'And no risks?'

'You know me, Sonny. I am not one to stick out my neck. I will just observe.'

'Right. I will ring you tomorrow, to find out if you have seen anything.'

'You do that. I will let you know if I 'ave any information that might be of 'elp to you.'

Russell finished the call, happy that his friend would take an interest. There was little point in going back to the shed; nothing would happen until the early hours when, presumably the smugglers would return. He decided to continue on to the Britannia pub and see if he could get something to eat.

As he approached the building his heart sank when he saw the sign, emblazoned with the word COURAGE, swinging in its frame. It was a long way from being his favourite beer, not something that Alf would dream of serving in the Shipwrights Arms at Compass Point. With a heavier heart he pressed on and pushed the door open, Aggie trotting behind him. The handful of locals turned to stare briefly at the stranger. Holding his head up, Russell approached the bar.

'I don't suppose there's any chance of some food?' he asked.

The landlord took his time drying the glass he was holding. After an unnecessarily long pause he spoke. 'We've got fish – fresh today.' His voice was gravelly, matching the shingle outside.

'Er, I'm afraid I don't eat fish,' Russell said apologetically.

The man's eyebrows rose slightly, but there was no other reaction. 'Might be some steak and kidney pie left.'

'Sorry, I don't eat meat either.'

This news was received with a sigh.

'I don't suppose you've got anything else?'

By now, the three men sitting at the bar had turned to listen and the old boys sitting nearby had paused in the middle of their game of dominos.

'I'll have a look to see if we've got any cheese.'

'Thank you. That would be good.' Russell was regretting his decision to come to the pub and could feel colour rising from his collar.

'I'll go out back in a moment. Do you want a drink while you're waiting?'

'Er yes. I'll have a pint please.' The words were out before Russell realised he should have ordered a bottled beer. When the landlord had pulled his drink, Russell took it over to table near the fireplace. A coal fire burned smokily in the hearth, giving out little heat. He sipped at the beer and grimaced at the soapy taste. This had nothing to do with cleanliness of the glass – there were definite fingerprints on the surface – just the poor quality of the brew. He sat for a few minutes, turning over the events of the evening. Then the landlord crossed the room and put a plate down in front of him, none too gently.

'That do?'

Russell looked at the uninspiring ploughman's lunch. 'Thanks,' he managed. The man grunted and stomped off. Russell looked down at the contents of the plate. The chunk of bread was obviously yesterday's; the cheese looked hard and was cracked with a gleam of sweat coating the surface. When he bit into an onion the taste was bitter – the onion insufficiently pickled. With a feeling of resignation he spread some of the dubious butter on the bread and chewed it unenthusiastically. Being a vegetarian was hard. He almost wished that he still ate fish – as they were so close to the sea it was bound to be fresh. He sighed. No, he'd made a choice and would stick to his principles. With that thought he ate as much of the unappealing food as he could manage.

While he chewed he thought about what had happened. It was pretty obvious that Mills and Stern were actively involved in smuggling duty-free goods into the country – and probably had been for some time. However, judging by the conversation, and Stern's reluctance to carry on, this could be the last time. Russell wasn't so sure though. It sounded like Mills could be very persuasive. Despite the end of rationing, there were still shortages, and people were often hard up. But the trade was still illegal. With his sense of duty he felt he ought to pursue it. He wondered what Guillaume might do. On the phone he seemed less than enthusiastic about following it up, but Russell knew his friend would help him out of a sense of loyalty. After working his way through half of the food, he gave up – even Aggie turned up her nose at the piece of cheese he offered her under the table. He just wasn't hungry anymore. And the pint remained half-drunk as he made his way to the bar. The landlord took his money with barely a word. With a sense of relief, Russell left the pub. Rather than drive home he decide to settle down in the car and wait for a few hours until the boat returned, in case he could spot anything.

Chapter 8

***A Flobart** is a traditional clinker-built fishing boat, unique to the northern French coast. It can float in a foot of water, making it ideal for launching off a trailer in the shallows.*

INSPECTOR GUILLAUME Bruissement *was* reluctant to drive the 20 or so kilometres to Wissant. He knew that goods were frequently smuggled across the Channel, but, like many of his colleagues, he preferred to turn a blind eye. People had suffered enough during the war and he felt they were entitled to a little leeway when it came to paying for luxuries. But… Sonny was his friend. They'd met while working on an unusual case.

The case had involved ex-Nazis being hunted down and killed by a strange pair of Germans who'd been seeking revenge for the death of their brother. Bruissement had a natural loathing for Hitler's elite. However, despite his feelings of leniency towards smuggling, murder was a much more serious crime, and in that instance he was happy to see the brothers finally captured and behind bars.

Despite the distance and the language barrier the friendship between the two policemen had grown. The Inspecteur might not feel so strongly about the illicit trade but he would follow it up for his friend's sake. So, just before 11pm, he left his *appartement* and lowered himself into the seat of his Citroën Traction Avant. Heading north from Boulogne he wound his way through the sleeping villages and hamlets. Wimereux, Audresselles, Audinghen and Tardinghen were passed. A few houses still had their lights burning and the occasional dog let out a warning bark as the car went by. When Bruissement reached Wissant he turned off the D940, drove down the main street and parked in the square between Église *Saint-Nicholas* and the *Hôtel Normandy*. He got out of the car and stood for a moment in the quiet square. Automatically he reached into his pocket for the pack of *Gauloises*. He was about to shake a cigarette out of the flimsy carton when he hesitated. 'No,' he thought. 'I will do without.' He thrust it back in his pocket and set off for the beach.

Walking past the *Hotel de la Plage* he turned down the unmade road that led to the sea. The track was rutted from the wheels of the tractors that hauled the fishing boats, on their crude trailers, down to the beach. Luckily the moon was almost full and gave enough light to enable him to make his way without stumbling. After a few minutes he reached the boundary where the scrubby grass ended and the sand began. There was a gap in the concrete barrier – the remains of the Atlantic Wall that the Germans had built – that led to the beach. Close by, on his right, was the solid shape of a German WWII blockhouse. Over the 15 or so years since it had been built, the shifting sands had gradually undermined the hurriedly constructed foundations and it now leaned at a jaunty angle. Bruissement made his way across the soft sand and entered, wrinkling his nose at the scent of damp and decay. Just enough light filtered in for him to see a low, concrete platform – presumably the mounting for a gun. He lowered himself on to it and sat, waiting.

Through the embrasure in the wall the French policeman had a good view of the beach. Like Russell he had developed an ability to wait patiently and, after half an hour, he heard the sound of an engine. In a few minutes the shape of a tractor hove into view, towing a traditional wooden *flobart* on a simple trailer. As it passed within a few metres, Bruissement could see there were just two figures – one driving the tractor, the other standing in the boat. He watched as the vehicle was driven to the water's edge. It then turned in a tight arc and started reversing into the sea. There was enough moonlight reflecting off the surface for him to see the moment when the boat floated off the trailer. Bruissement decided it was time to make a move and emerged from the blockhouse. Though short and round, he could produce a decent turn of speed. In a few dozen paces he had reached the tractor, as it dragged the empty trailer out of the shallows and rumbled up the beach. The driver, who had been looking over his shoulder, turned and saw the detective and brought the tractor to a halt.

'What the…?' he exclaimed.

'Doing a spot of night fishing?'

'Maybe. What's it to you?' he asked as he climbed down from his seat.

'I didn't think you boys went out after dark.'

The man squared up to Bruissement. 'I don't see that's any of your business.' Although a whole head shorter than the other man the detective stood his ground. After a few moments the man flicked his head upward in dismissal and made to turn away. Bruissement gripped his arm.

'I asked what you were doing.'

'None of your damn business,' was the terse reply. He tried to shake the hand off but Bruissement had a tight grip. The man growled and, with his other hand, pushed the policeman hard in the chest. This made him let go, stumbling to regain his balance as he staggered backwards. His heel caught the trailer drawbar and he toppled over, falling heavily on his arm. Bruissement let out a gasp. The man ignored him and stomped off down the beach towards the boat, riding in the shallows. As he clambered over the gunwale the other man, Jacques, spoke.

'What was that all about?'

'Just some nosey parker – wanted to know what we were doing,' the first fisherman, Jean answered.

'Who is he?'

'I dunno. Never seen him before.'

'I saw you shove him. He went down and didn't get up. Is he all right?'

'Why should I care?' Jean grunted.

'We should check.'

Jean let out an exasperated sign. 'We'll be late for the meeting.'

'It'll only take a moment.' With that Jacques started getting out of the boat.

'What the hell do you think you're doing?'

'I'll just check he's all right. It won't take long.' Jacques splashed through the shallows and walked hurriedly up the beach. In a couple of minutes he was back.

'Jesus!' he panted, scrambling back into the boat. 'I don't know what you did but he's out cold.'

'Must have banged his head or something. Is he breathing?'

'Yes.'

'Well he'll be okay then. He'll come round soon – with a headache. Serve him right for poking his nose in where it's not wanted. Come on. We've got to get going.'

Pushing against the sea bed with long oars they moved the

boat into deeper water, then turned it to face out. Jean swung the starting handle several times and the engine coughed into life.

~O~

The two men had gone out on the rising tide. On the barely sloping beach the incoming flood came in swiftly. Bruissement lay unconscious on the cold sand as the water came towards him. It lapped at his feet then dampened his trousers. It crept past his waist and darkened his jacket and shirt. The water lapped and rose up to his ear and moistened his moustache. It rolled between his lips, into his open mouth. When it started trickling down his throat he coughed then retched, bringing up bile and seawater. His body convulsed and he cried out.

'Mon Dieu! My arm!'

He managed to raise himself to a sitting position, cradling the injured limb. With an effort he got on to his knees, then struggled slowly to his feet. He gritted his teeth against the pain. Stumbling through the shallow water he made his way up the beach. It seemed to take forever, as he staggered up the track, finally reaching the *Hotel de la Plage*. Driving himself was out of the question, so he pushed the door open and walked slowly up to the bar.

'Sir?' the barman said. Then paused, looking more closely at the newcomer. 'Are you all right? You're wet. You look very pale.'

Bruissement took a breath, and then replied, almost in a whisper: 'It's my arm. I think it's broken.' He took a step towards the counter and leant against it, swivelled and slowly slid to the floor, his head slumped on his chest.

The barman came round from his side of the bar and took one look at the crumpled figure. 'My God! He needs an ambulance.'

Dashing back again he grabbed the telephone and dialled the emergency number.

~O~

At the funfair the rides and sideshows had shut down for the night. Once the garish, coloured lights were off there was little illumination. Out of the shadows a large, shadowy figure emerged from between the vehicles and furtively crept up the steps to Boswell's van. Carefully opening the door, he eased his bulk inside and closed it quietly behind him. He struck a match, cupped the flame with his hand and looked round. Once he had his bearings he blew the match out and crouched by the fireplace. Reaching forward his hand found the handle at the front of the range. It was lukewarm. He opened the door, took a small package out of his pocket and pushed it into the ashes. He closed the door, stood upright and left the way he had come.

Although the fire had been out for some time there was one gently glowing ember. The corner of the package touched it and the cardboard began to smoulder.

~O~

Russell spent an uncomfortable few hours curled up on the back seat of the Ford Popular. Sleep seemed to evade him. Finally, in the early hours, he gave up. Reaching for his knapsack he took out the flask and gave it a shake. Yes, there was still some tea left. He took the cup off the top and balanced it on his knee. Then, after removing the stopper, he poured the contents out. He took a tentative sip. He grimaced – it was barely lukewarm, but just about palatable. When he'd drained the cup, he pushed the car door open and stepped out into the night. He was stiff and cold. He shuddered and wrapped his arms round his body and bounced on the spot a few times. Aggie thought it was a game and bounced too.

Russell smiled, yawned and looked up. The moon had long since disappeared over the horizon; the sky was dark with pinpricks of stars. Looking east he could see the beginning of sunrise. He guessed it must be getting on for five. Shutting the car door he set off for his lookout. When he reached it, he once again settled down on the broken chair. It wasn't long before he was aware of movement on the beach. After a while he heard the *squeak-squeak-squeak* of metal wheels on rusty track. As the noise grew louder, he could make out two shadowy figures in the growing light. He couldn't believe his luck when they stopped in the same place they had been the night before. A match was struck, lighting both faces; grotesque masks.

'What was that all about?' Mills asked, drawing hard on a cigarette, making the end glow fiercely orange.

'Waddyer mean?' Stern's voice was low and ragged.

'Jacques. He was as jumpy as a frog.' Mills suddenly chuckled. 'Frog – geddit?'

'Very funny, I don't think.' He shuffled his feet. 'Come on. I want to get this stuff loaded in your truck. The sooner you're out of here the better.'

As the daylight increased, Russell could see the men more clearly. Mills put his arm round the other man's shoulders. 'Don't be like that. You know you like it, really.'

Stern shook the arm off. 'No I don't,' he said, anger rising in his voice. 'And, I repeat, this is the last time I do this.' With that, he heaved a box off the pile on the wagon and lifted it on to his shoulder. 'C'mon. It's getting light. I don't want no one spotting us. Plus, I need my bed.'

Russell sat quietly, the terrier at his feet, maintaining the silence. Bruissement obviously either hadn't bothered to try to stop the transfer of the goods or something else had happened. Either way Mills and Stern had taken delivery of the contraband. The two men made several journeys. By the time they made the last one, it was light enough for Russell to see distinctly the words on the side of the final box Mills was carrying:

COURVOISIER
VSOP

As Mills crunched away across the shingle Russell wondered what he should do. Weighing up the alternatives he realised there was very little he *could* do. His first thought – to burst out of his hidey-hole and confront the men *in flagrante*, as it were, now seemed foolhardy. Maybe he had got cold feet, but there were two of them and he didn't relish a possible beating. On the other hand, he knew he would be cross with himself if he didn't do something. He watched as the landlord put the box in the back of his pickup with the others and pulled the canvas tilt over the load and secured it. Stern had already gone into the cottage; Mills followed and disappeared inside. Without waiting to consider, Russell pushed the shed door open and crossed the road. Reaching the truck, he unclipped a couple of the loops of rope and rolled back the corner of the tilt. There was now enough light to see the containers, neatly stowed. As well as more boxes of brandy, there were packs of cigarettes. Russell let out a silent whistle. There must be several hundred pounds worth of goods – presumably all free of tax. He leant over further, the better to see the lettering on one of the packages. He was so intent that he didn't hear the man creep up behind him. All he knew was something hard hit him across the back of the head. He saw bright stars – then darkness descended.

Chapter 9

***Sea Kale** – Crambe maritima – is a member of the brassica family that grows wild on shingle beaches. It became popular in the early 19th century and was served to diners at the Brighton Pavilion.*

RUSSELL SLOWLY gained consciousness. His face was wet. His eyelids flickered open and he looked up into a pair of brown eyes. Aggie was licking his face and if a dog could look worried, the terrier projected concern. He smiled then winced at the pain. He looked around and took in his surroundings. He was lying on the shingle, a blue sky above. Gingerly, he turned his head to the left. A few feet away he could see an emerging clump of sea kale, the new growth a soft purple. Looking to the right he could make out the dark hull of a wooden fishing boat. Cautiously he raised himself on one elbow. The small dog wagged her tail, pleased by the movement. Russell wondered how long she had been standing guard over him. He screwed his eyes up and looked at the sun. It was well over the horizon. Painfully he pushed himself up until he was in a sitting position and felt the back of his head. There was a lump and his hand came away, sticky with blood. He looked round.

He could see farther now: Prospect Cottage was about 200 yards away. How had he got here? He doubted he could have crawled so he guessed the men must have picked him up and dumped him. Gingerly he eased himself up until he was standing, swaying unsteadily, a jackhammer threatening to break out of his skull. He walked slowly, following the rusty railway track as it dipped and snaked across the undulating shingle. When he reached the shed where he had been hiding he looked inside. He was surprised to see that his knapsack and binoculars were still there. Picking them up he continued towards the cottage. His brain was fuzzy from the blow on the back of the head and he wasn't sure what he was planning to do. As he neared the dwelling he could clearly see that there were no vehicles parked outside. Obviously no one at home. He shrugged, which sent a sharp wave of pain through his head. He stood, breathing heavily for a while, before trudging on up the road. When he reached Weeks's Ford Popular he opened the door and sank gratefully into the seat. The terrier jumped up on to his lap then hopped across to the back and burrowed into the blanket on the seat. Russell closed his eyes against the thumping in his skull and in a few moments had fallen asleep.

~o~

'Let me get this straight. You claim to have had nothing to do with the death of either Petulengro *or* Gypsy Lee?' DI Parker paced irritably, circling the dingy interview room liked a caged animal. Vado Boswell sat on one side of the battered table, his shoulders slumped and his head bent forward, close to its scored and battered surface. Weeks sat upright across from him, his chair pushed away from the table, his notebook in his lap. He wasn't enjoying the experience. In the hour or so they'd been there, Parker had chain-smoked his filthy Capstan Full Strength cigarettes and a pall of grey smoke hung a couple of feet below the stained ceiling.

'I told you…' Boswell said, his voice lacklustre, reflecting the constant repetition of denial. '…She was dead when we went into her van.'

'Why on earth did you bother to cart her body all the way over to Appledore and dump it in the pillbox then?' Parker rested his knuckles on the edge of the table and leaned close to the gypsy. 'Why didn't you come straight to us?'

'I thought it would be bad for business if she was found at the fair.'

'Then locking up and leaving her caravan splattered with blood for a load of bobbies to coming tramping round wasn't?'

'I hadn't thought that far ahead – I didn't think she'd be found so quickly,' Boswell said wearily.

Parker lit up again. 'Obviously not.' He blew out a cloud of smoke and circled the table again, hands behind his back, cigarette dangling from his lower lip. 'Right then. Suppose we believe what you say about that gyppo, what about the other one – Petulengro?'

Boswell looked up. 'I told you, I was a surprised as you were. He was my friend.'

'And a pooftah…'

'That didn't matter.'

Weeks spoke for the first time in a while. 'That's not what you said when we first talked to you.'

'What do you mean?' Boswell said sharply.

Flipping through his notebook Weeks came to the relevant page. 'You said, "He was as queer as a coot, a homosexual. I was just glad when he upped sticks and left."'

'Did I?'

'If he says you did…' Parker pointed at the DC, '…then you did. He's got one of them memories. What's it called?'

'Eidetic, Sir.'

'Yeah, well, whatever you say. Anyway, being a pansy is not enough reason to get yourself killed, so why did you do it?' Parker was back, leaning on the table, his face inches from Boswell's.

The man sat up straight, his brow lowered and his eyes flashing. 'I told you, I didn't bloody kill him. I liked him, even though he was a queer.'

Any further conversation was curtailed by a knock. 'Come in,' Parker snapped.

Lewis's head appeared round the door. 'Could I have a word please, Inspector?'

Parker tutted. 'I suppose so. We're not getting anywhere here.' He pushed himself away from the table and followed the other man out of the room.

'I think Boswell may well be telling the truth.'

'*What*?' Parker, stopped in the middle of lighting yet another cigarette.

'Well, certainly about Petulengro.'

'What do you mean?'

'We've examined his clothes and only found traces of Ivy Lee's blood, not the other fortune teller's. And if he had killed Petulengro, the caravan was such a mess he would be bound to have his blood on him, and we found none.'

Parker grimaced, the cigarette gripped between his thin lips. 'That's as maybe, but I was right about one thing.'

'What's that?'

'He did kill the gyppo woman.'

'I'm not so sure.' Lewis frowned.

'Oh?'

'He certainly handled the body. We went over his immaculate Chevrolet. The pickup body wasn't quite so pristine. It had obviously been thoroughly cleaned but we found definite traces of the gypsy's blood that had been missed. I'm guessing that he – and probably an accomplice – did as he said: took the body from the funfair and dumped it in the pillbox.'

Parker drew on his cigarette a thoughtful expression on his face. 'You say you're *guessing*?'

For the first time in the conversation the forensics man looked unsure. 'I can't be certain…'

'In fact, you don't have any proof that he didn't kill her, do you?'

'No.'

'Well. *I* still think he's as guilty as hell. I'll grant you that you were right about the strongman, but I think chummy in there did it. And I want you to find the proof. Go back over his van with a fine tooth-comb if necessary. Okay?' He prodded Lewis in the chest with his finger. 'Now I'm going to do my job. I suggest you do yours.' With that he dropped the cigarette end, ground it under his heel and re-entered the interview room.

Lewis stood for a few moments, stunned. Then muttered: 'Bloody man,' and stormed off.

~o~

Half a dozen uniformed policemen had been walking slowly along the riverbank for more than an hour when a shout rang out. '*Sir!*'

'Yes? Who's that?' Sergeant Wickstead asked.

'It's Beaumont, Sir. I think I've found him,' came the excited reply.

Wickstead made his way towards where the voice had come from. As he neared the river he could just make out the constable, crouching down in the reeds. 'Let me look, lad.' He made his way cautiously down the slippery bank until he could see what the PC had found. Face down in the water was a body. The water had darkened the shirt and headscarf making them almost as black as the trousers. One foot was bare but a slipper, matching the one found earlier, still clung to the other. The shirt had snagged on a branch, just below the water's surface, stopping the body from floating farther down the stream. Wickstead shuddered. He'd seen enough dead bodies in the force and during the war, but he still found it disturbing. 'Well done. Let's get some help to pull him out of the water.' With an effort, he scrambled back up the bank. 'Lee,' he said to the nearest constable. 'Go back to the car and radio in. Let DI Parker know we've found Petulengro.'

~o~

Parker arrived forty minutes later, accompanied by Weeks. Lewis and John Crooks, the pathologist, hung back behind them. Lewis was still smarting from the DI's comments. The spot where the body had been found couldn't have been more idyllic. A weeping willow hung over the river, the tips of the newly emerged leaves just touching the surface. A gentle breeze ruffled the water, sunlight glinting off the ripples. The reeds swayed rhythmically; a hidden warbler chattered his song and a pair of swans glided serenely by. The only thing that marred the sylvan setting was the body of the gypsy, laid out on a piece of tarpaulin – oozing water. The PCs stood about, smoking and quietly talking. Parker had knelt on a dry corner of the canvas and was peering at the body.

'Bloody hell. Same MO as the other gyppo – Ivy Lee, or whatever her name was. Throat cut from ear to ear.'

Lewis had crouched down on the other side. 'What's this?' he said, almost to himself. Rigor mortis had yet to set in and it wasn't difficult for him to prise the man's jaws apart. He inserted a rubber gloved thumb and forefinger and withdrew a piece of sodden card. A decorative pattern in blue and white covered the surface but, as Lewis unfolded it, a graphic illustration was revealed.

'What the hell is that?' Parker asked.

'It's a Tarot card. *The Lovers*. Like the one in Ivy Rose Lee's mouth.'

'What, the same?'

'No, hers was *Death*.'

'Why ain't his *Death*?'

'That would mean having two packs of cards,' Lewis explained patiently.

'Mmm. I suppose so. But what does it mean?'

'There I can't help you. You need an expert on the Tarot for that.'

Parker let out a heartfelt groan. 'Don't suppose you know one, do you?'

'Afraid not. Looks like the main two contenders are no longer available.'

'Eh?' The DI's face began as a picture of puzzlement, slowly changing as understanding dawned on him. 'Very funny, I don't think.'

'All very interesting, but perhaps you could allow me to confirm the cause of death.' The two men kneeling down looked up. Crooks was standing, his fingers linked across his ample stomach, his eyebrows raised.

'Pretty obvious, ain't it?' Parker said as he got creakily to his feet.

'That's as maybe. But best check, to be on the safe side, don't you think?'

~O~

It was the light that woke him. He had slumped in the seat, his head thrown back and now the sun was streaming in through the windscreen. He half-opened his eyes and winced. The brightness seemed to penetrate right to the back of his skull. Quickly he closed his eyes and took a few deep breaths, as waves of nausea swept over him. He tried again. This time it wasn't as painful. Slowly he sat up and took in his surroundings. To the left, across the shingle, he could see the huddle of huts, surrounded by a chain-link fence that housed the old radar station. Craning his neck round to the right he could just make out the Victorian lighthouse beyond the Britannia Inn, its black finger pointing skywards. Russell pulled back his cuff and looked at his wristwatch. The glass face was cracked, the hands motionless. He held his wrist up to his ear. No sound came from the watch. Must have stopped – maybe damaged when he was struck. He looked down at his clothes. Streaked with dust. He realised his body ached too. He had obviously been dragged across the shingle. Perhaps that was when the watch glass was broken. Looking again out of the windscreen, he reckoned it was probably something like 10am. He tried to think, but the blinding headache made recollection slow. What time was it that Mills had said they were making the rendezvous? The word midnight slowly formed in his brain. He tried to concentrate. If that was the case it would have taken Mills and Stern between four and five hours to get back. That would seem about right as it was just getting light when he saw them return.

Russell paused while muddled thoughts crowded into his brain. Then his mind cleared. So, assuming he'd been knocked out and dumped sometime between five and six o'clock, it had been around four or more hours since he'd woken on the beach. The effort had drained him and he breathed out a long sigh. He was still unsure what to do. Should he have confronted the men when he had a chance? Probably not. He might have ended up in a worse predicament than the one he was in now. Should he report what he had seen? Probably. But it would still be his word against theirs. They would be unlikely to have left any of the illegal goods in Stern's cottage. And he doubted whether Mills would be foolish enough to leave any evidence in the Red Lion. But you never knew. He had to do something so he started the car, turned it round and set off for Appledore.

~o~

In France, Inspecteur Guillaume Bruissement was sitting up in bed. When he had passed out the barman had called the emergency services. Not wanting to move the man before they came he had draped a blanket over him and waited. When the ambulance had arrived at the *Hotel de la Plage* the attendants had taken one look at the officer, and whisked him off to the hospital in Boulogne. He'd been diagnosed with a fractured radius bone which was now secured in a plaster cast from wrist to elbow, and held in a sling across his chest. His immediate superior had been to visit him earlier.

'Looks like you've been in the wars, Inspecteur. What were you doing in Wissant at that time of night? Care to tell me about it?'

Bruissement looked glum. His luxuriant moustache drooped and his cheeks were dark with stubble. 'I was following a tip-off.'

'Oh yes?' the boss's eyebrows formed two perfect, raised arcs.

'About smuggling.'

'I see. Presumably guns or other weapons.'

'No. Duty-free.'

'I don't understand…' The eyebrows stayed up, the brow furrowed.

'Alcohol and tobacco.'

'I'm puzzled. Why would a senior police officer involve himself in something like that – at night, on his own? I thought you usually turned a blind eye to such things?'

'It was a favour for an English friend.'

'Ah, I see.' The boss smiled. 'And might this English *friend* be the esteemed Inspector Russell?'

Bruissement looked thoroughly miserable. 'Yes,' he answered quietly.

'And this friendship has caused you to end up here…' He swept his arm out in a gesture encompassing the hospital ward. '…with your arm in a sling and on an enforced leave.'

'I suppose so.'

'And all for the sake of a few bottles of booze and a few packs of cigarettes?' The boss's face darkened. Bruissement recognised the signs and remained silent. 'You're an idiot! There's real crime going on here. You know we're short staffed and you go and put yourself out of action as a favour for a friend.'

'I'm sorry, Sir.'

'Sorry's not good enough. How long will that be on?' he gestured towards the plaster.

'Maybe a week or two.'

'And that's the hand you write with?'

'I'm afraid so.'

'*Mon Dieu*!' The boss stood up and rammed his hat on his head. 'You'd better learn how to use your left arm – and quick. You've got two weeks to sort yourself out.' After one final angry glance he turned on his heel and stormed out.

~o~

Russell pulled up outside the Red Lion just as the bolts were being drawn on the front door. He sat in the car for a few minutes, the thumping in his head slowly diminishing. He didn't think he'd been hurt badly. He hadn't felt quite right ever since he'd received a blow that had caused concussion some months before. He was prone to the occasional painful headache; he didn't always sleep well at night and occasionally felt himself nodding off during the day. He knew he should visit the doctor to get it checked but hadn't got round to it. He sighed and climbed out of the car, Aggie following happily in his wake. On entering the pub he was unsurprised to see not the landlord but Edna at the bar. She smiled shyly in recognition.

'What can I get you, Sir?'

'I don't suppose there's any chance of a cuppa?'

'You're in luck,' she beamed. 'I've just made a pot.' She disappeared through a door behind the bar and reappeared a few moments later with a steaming mug. Russell took it gratefully and cupped it in his hands as he settled on the bar stool.

After taking a sip, he spoke. 'How come you're here this morning? I thought Jack would open up.'

She blushed prettily, something, he realised to she was prone to do. ‘Oh, er, he had to go away, sudden like. I got a message asking me to do the morning shift.’

‘Any idea where he went?’ Russell asked innocently.

The blush deepened. ‘Something about moving some stuff to a safe place.’ She looked down, busying herself with wiping the bar top. Russell thought that was all he was going to get out of her. Then she looked up and spoke again. ‘This is difficult.’

Russell smiled gently. ‘Go on.’

‘I shouldn’t really say anything – it doesn’t seem right.’ She looked miserable and her hands twisted the cloth she was holding into a knot.

‘It can be between you and me,’ Russell said encouragingly.

‘Well as long as it doesn’t go any farther…’

‘You can trust me.’

‘Okay, then.’ She seemed to make up her mind. When she spoke this time it was with more confidence. ‘I was down in the cellar, getting some bottles, and I saw a big pile of boxes in the corner, covered over with a cloth. I had a quick look. It was crates of spirit and cartons of cigarettes. When I asked Jack about them he got quite angry – told me to mind my own business.’ She took a deep breath. ‘I’m worried that he might be doing something that’s not right – not legal.’

‘Are they still there?’

‘No. I had a look and they’re gone.’

‘Do you think that’s the stuff he talked about moving?’

Her face fell. ‘I suppose so. I feel bad about snitching on him now.’

Russell reached forward and patted her hand. ‘Don’t worry. It’ll be our little secret.’

‘Thanks.’ She smiled, reminding Russell how pretty she was.

He took a drink of tea then carefully put his mug down on a beer mat. 'Do you think you could show me where you saw the boxes?'

Confusion clouded her face. 'I-I don't know. Jack might not like it.'

'He doesn't have to know though, does he?'

'I suppose not.'

'Let's have a quick look then.' Before she could object, Russell had lifted the wooden flap and joined Edna behind the bar. 'Is this it?' he asked, pointing to the trap set in the floor. Edna nodded. Russell reached down, grasped the brass ring and lifted the door, revealing a set of stone steps leading into darkness.

'Let me go first,' she said. 'I know where the light is.' She descended the steps, flicked a switch and the cellar was illuminated with a pale glow. Russell followed her down, the terrier close behind. The room was bigger than he had expected. Along one wall were barrels on racks, with pipes leading back up to the bar. Next to them were wooden crates containing an assortment of bottles and on a shelf stood various cardboard boxes. Beneath the shelf was a space with just a tarpaulin, lying in an untidy heap.

'That's where they were,' Edna said, pointing.

Russell hitched up the knees of his trousers and crouched down. Aggie stood beside him, tail wagging, sure there was a game afoot. Russell gently elbowed her out of the way. He carefully unfolded the green fabric but, as he'd been told, the boxes had gone. He let out a long exasperated breath and started straightening up. He was just about to turn and head back up the stairs when the small dog let out an excited yelp. She pushed her muzzle into a fold in the canvas and wagged her tail even more furiously.

'What is it, girl?' Russell crouched again and bent back the tarpaulin to reveal a piece of card stuck to the material. Carefully, he peeled it off. Some of the surface came away but there was enough left to see the legend **LUCKY STRIKE** lettered in white on a circular red target.

'*American* cigarettes?' Edna sounded puzzled. 'But we don't sell those.'

'I don't think they were meant for sale here,' Russell answered quietly. 'Let's go back up.'

They ascended the steps, the trap door was closed and they took up their respected places either side of the bar.

'What does it mean?' Edna asked.

'I'm not entirely sure, but I think your boss may not be quite all he seems.'

Edna was thoughtful while Russell sipped at his tea. Suddenly she burst out: 'I shouldn't really be saying this but I've been suspicious about him for a while.'

Russell tipped his head to one side. 'Oh?'

'Yes. Calling me in at short notice – going off and coming back without warning. That sort of thing. I only put up with it because I need the money.'

Russell drained his mug. 'You said he was moving stuff to a safe place…'

The girl's blush returned. 'Yes.'

'I don't suppose you've any idea where he meant?'

'I'm really not happy about this…'

He reached out and patted her hand again. 'I said it would be our little secret.'

She was quiet for a while, then seemed to come to a decision. 'He mustn't know that this came from me.' Russell nodded his assent. 'He sometimes goes over to Snargate. There's an old church there – St Dunstan's, I think it's called. Legend has it that smugglers used to hide their contraband there, but that could be an old wives' tale. Anyway. So few people live there that they only have services in the church a couple of times a year. I don't know for sure, but he may store things there, from time to time. There, I've said more than I meant. He'll kill me if he finds out.'

'Don't worry – he won't. I shan't say a thing. Thank you, Edna, you've been very helpful. He stood up. What do I owe you for the tea?'

Her beaming smile returned. 'Nothing. It's on the house.'

~O~

When Russell got back into the Ford he suddenly felt weary. It had been a long night and he could do with a rest. Investigating the church at Snargate could wait. Deciding he needed a wash and a change of clothes he set off for home. There was little traffic on the road and less than half an hour later he was bumping along his stony track. He was just walking down the garden path, stepping over clumps of self-seeded *Centranthus ruber* when he heard the telephone ringing inside the house. He fumbled for his key and got the door open just in time to snatch up the receiver.

'Hello?'

The line crackled then a voice he recognised boomed out of the earpiece. '*Sonny*! I've been trying to make contact with you all morning. They said at the station that you were *en vacances*.'

'Guillaume. How good to hear your voice. Yes, I am *on holiday* but not of my choosing.'

Bruissement chuckled. 'That is what I thought, when I looked between the lines.'

'Anyway, my friend. How can I help you?'

'I wanted to ask a favour. I am *en vacance* but for a different reason. I want to come over to *Angleterre* and I would like to ask if you can suggest a nice place where I could stay for a few days.'

'Better than that. You would be welcome to stay in my little home.'

The chuckle became a belly laugh. 'I was 'oping you would say that.'

'When are you thinking of coming?'

'Ah, well. I 'ave already bought my ticket and booked the ferry. I will be arriving early *ce soir*.'

'Are you bringing your car?'

Again the familiar laugh. '*Mais non*. I am – 'ow do you say – *hors de combat*?'

'Sorry?'

'I am unable to drive at present. I can explain when I see you. I will catch a train at Dover. Perhaps you would like to *recontre moi* at the station in Collinghurst?'

'It would be my pleasure. Just let me know what time your train gets in.'

With thoughts of his friend's imminent arrival Russell's fatigue fell away. He washed, shaved and put on fresh clothes then set about tidying the carriage and getting the guest room ready. His spare bedroom was in another carriage, set behind his main home. It also contained a compact bathroom and a store room. Beyond that was a lean-to extension he used as a conservatory. Although the rooms were small, each man would have his own space. Russell worked steadily, happy to have the Frenchman's company for a while. He would introduce him to Isobel – he was sure they would get on.

It was growing dark when Bruissement's train pulled into Collinghurst. He had eaten on the ferry so was happy for Russell to drive him straight to Shinglesea. On the way he explained about the plaster on his arm.

Russell was concerned. 'I shouldn't have asked you to go to Wissant.'

'Nonsense, *mon ami*. It was my own fault. I should have taken more care. Anyway it is, 'ow you say, a disguised blessing, because 'ere I am!'

Chapter 10

*A **coffee percolator** is a type of pot used for the brewing of coffee by continually cycling boiling, or nearly boiling, water through the grounds using gravity until the required strength is reached.*

'LET ME get this straight. You claim you didn't kill the gyppo Lee – just dumped her body in the pillbox.'

Vado Boswell again sat at the battered table in the interview room. He'd spent a restless night in a cell, he had dark rings under his eyes and his shoulders drooped. 'I've told you a dozen times already that I didn't kill her.'

Parker continued walking slowly round the room. 'Right, for the sake of argument, let's say that I believe you.' He stopped circling and sat down heavily in the chair next to Weeks. He folded his arms and rested them on the table. 'I can see that a big lad like you could manage to get the woman's body out of her caravan and into that smart pickup of yours.' He took a breath then exhaled noisily. 'But I'm puzzled at how you managed to carry her from the road, across the rough ground by the canal, and into the pillbox.' When Boswell didn't respond he leaned forward and gripped his arm. 'You had help, didn't you?'

Boswell slowly lifted his head and made eye contact with the DI. 'I might as well tell you. I did… It was Petulengro.'

Parker's eyebrows shot up and his jaw dropped. 'But you didn't like him…'

'That's what I said at the time – to put you off the scent. He was a good mate.'

The DI sat back, temporarily stunned into silence. Automatically he reached into a pocket, pulled out a crumpled packet and shook a cigarette into his mouth. He sat for long moments, with it dangling from his lower lip while staring at Boswell. Finally he said: 'Say that again.'

'We were friends. And now he's dead.' The fairground owner looked thoroughly miserable. If his sadness wasn't genuine he was a very good actor.

Parker struck a match and lit the cigarette. He inhaled deeply then coughed as he breathed out. 'Right. So now you're saying you and Petulengro loaded the gyppo's body into your pickup and drove her over to Appledore?'

Boswell nodded.

'And you hoped she wouldn't be found…'

'For some time, anyway.'

'Why the hell didn't you come to us when you found she'd been done in?'

'I wish I had.' Boswell's voice was hardly above a whisper.

'So do I. It would have saved us all a load of trouble.'

~O~

Russell and Bruissement sat on the little bench in front of the railway carriage. They had gone outside on the Frenchman's insistence so he could smoke a *Gauloises*. Russell had received a phone call early that morning from Weeks, bringing him up to date with what had gone on and he had told

Bruissement how things stood.

The day was warm, with a slight haze over the rough meadow that separated them from the beach. Inside the chestnut fence that surrounded the dwelling the garden was coming to life. Sea kale, that had self-seeded, was starting to flower; the distinct scent of honey rising from the blooms. A *Cistus purpureus 'Alan Fradd'*, that Russell had planted, was showing the first of a succession of delicate papery blossoms – white with a yellow centre surrounded by five magenta dots. The architectural glaucous leaves of a *Cardoon*, each over three feet long, filled a corner of a garden. Soon the thistle-like artichoke flowers would emerge. *Alchemilla mollis* and scented thyme grew in clumps around the wooden stepping-stone path.

After discussing the murders the two men sat in companionable silence, each wrapped up in his own thoughts, the terrier dozing on Russell's lap. They had breakfasted on boiled eggs and toast. Afterwards, Russell had made coffee in a percolator. More accustomed to drinking tea he'd dug it out from the back of a cupboard and used ground coffee he'd bought some time before, hoping it would still be drinkable. Bruissement had been delighted at the gesture.

'So, my friend,' he said. 'What plans do you 'ave for us today?'

'We-ell,' Russell said slowly. 'We could go over to Snargate – have a look at that church. Or, I could take you into Collinghurst – introduce you to Isobel…'

Bruissement chuckled. 'Pleasure in front of business I think, *mon ami*. I know you are wanting for me to meet 'er.'

As they were not in a hurry they decided to take the train so walked the short distance to Shinglesea Halt. It was a simple affair: a rough, sleeper-built platform and a rustic, wooden waiting shelter. Bruissement smoked another *Gauloises* while they waited. A skylark was above them, valiantly piping its twittering song as it rose on fast-moving wings. The sound of the surf, gently falling on the shingle, could be heard on the distant beach. A rabbit popped its head out of a burrow 20 yards away but, although Aggie stiffened and pricked up her ears, she stayed at their feet. After a few minutes a thin column of smoke appeared in the distance and a reedy whistle sounded. The rumble of wheels on the metal track grew louder and soon a small steam locomotive came into sight, resplendent in gleaming scarlet livery.

'Ah, I see Captain Salt has brought *Cardinal* into service early.' As the train grew closer Russell explained the workings of the little three-foot gauge railway. 'The Captain tends to use the railbus set in the off-season as it's cheaper to run. This splendid engine generally only comes out when the tourist season gets underway.' The train came to a halt and the men climbed into one of the two chocolate and cream-coloured carriages. It was the first train up from Compass Point and they were the only passengers. They settled on the wooden seats, there was a toot from the whistle, the carriage jerked as the couplings took up the slack and they were off. The train rattled along, never exceeding 15 miles an hour.

Bruissement was happy to look out of the window so little was said on the journey. The scenery appeared unspectacular, but was deceptively subtle. Apparently flat, the patchwork of fields and meadows had gentle undulations, sewn together with reedy, water-filled dykes. Fat Romney Marsh sheep grazed on the lush grass, their new lambs dancing and gambolling. Every now and again they dipped their heads under their mother's thick woollen coats and sucked greedily. A green woodpecker flew by, overtaking the train, its flight swooping and dipping like the needle of a seamstress. A grey and white heron stood sentinel, with the stance of old warrior, at the edge of a dyke, patiently watching for suitable prey; a kestrel hovered low over a clump of reeds.

In less than 20 minutes the train was slowing to a halt at the terminus. It would have been easy to leave without paying but, before exiting the station, Russell went up to the little ticket window and handed over the money for their fares. Bruissement admired the Englishman's honesty.

'You are a man most honourable, Sonny,' he smiled. 'But then I am expecting nothing less.' He stood for a few moments, his free hand on his hip, looking round. 'So this is the famous metropolis, Collinghurst?'

Russell chuckled. 'Hardly a metropolis although it does have a certain something.'

'And does that *something* go by the name of Isobel?'

'Among other things.' There was a mischievous twinkle in his eye. 'Let's make our way to her shop. It's not far.'

They walked to the top of Station Road then turned left, past an inn and along the high street. Soon they reached the shop. Russell pushed the door open, making the bell tinkle. At first Isobel didn't react, keeping her back to them, intent on something on her workbench. When she did turn and saw who it was her face broke into a delighted grin and in one graceful movement she stood, turned and quickly covered the few feet between them.

'Sonny,' she said, pecking him on the cheek. 'How lovely to see you. And this must be the famous Inspecteur Bruissement.' She held out her hand.

Instead of grasping it he gently took her fingers and held them up to his lips. He beamed at her. 'You are even more beautiful than he has told me you are.'

Isobel almost blushed. *Almost*. 'And you are just as charming as I thought you would be.' She bent to pat Aggie who was keen not to miss out. Straightening she asked: 'What brings you here? Not that I'm not pleased to see you. I thought you'd be tied up with that dreadful case involving the murdered fortune teller,' she added.

'Ah well, you see,' Russell said seriously. 'I haven't been able to let you know. I'm off the case.'

Isobel's face registered real concern. 'Oh Sonny, Why? What have you done?' Before he could answer she said: 'I know, it's that awful boss of yours, Stout.'

'Well partly. Although it's my own fault really. Listen I know you're busy.' He nodded towards her bench, where a piece of jewellery sparkled beneath the Anglepoise lamp. 'But have you got time for a cuppa?'

'For you and this handsome gentleman? Of course.' She turned back to the bench and switched the light off. Picking up a card reading:

BACK IN 20 MINUTES

she tucked it in the window frame.

Conveniently located next door was *Miss Smollett's Teashop*. The three made their way inside and settled round a table near the window. Miss Alex Smollett herself served them. She was dressed in her customary grey – grey woollen skirt, neatly belted and reaching just below her knees, Lisle stockings and suede shoes with a little strap across the ankle. On an older woman it would have looked severe but the proprietress carried it off with style. She recognised Russell from previous visits. 'Inspector. How are you?'

'Very well thank you. May I introduce you to Guillaume? A friend of mine from Boulogne.'

Before she could react Bruissement took her hand and kissed it as he had done with Isobel. '*Enchanté*.'

This time the lady did blush. 'You're too kind,' she mumbled. After a moment she sniffed and regained her composure. 'I heard about that terrible case on the Salts. That poor woman who was murdered. Have you found out who did it?'

Russell looked up. 'As I'm sure you realise, I can't discuss the case, but if you have any information…?'

Miss Smollett shook her head. 'I'm afraid not, Inspector, but if I do hear anything, of course I'll let you know. Now, what can I get you?'

Isobel turned to the Frenchman. 'Tea for you, Guillaume? Or would you prefer coffee?'

'Tea would be *parfait*. I am *très friands* of your English beverage. I am often 'aving a tisane myself in my 'ome.'

'Tea for three, then Alex,' Isobel said. 'I'd prefer Earl Grey, please.' This was something Russell didn't know and he filed it away for future reference. When Miss Smollett had gone off with their order, Isobel lowered her voice and spoke again. 'So if you're off the case, do you know what's happening?'

Russell smiled. 'Luckily Johnny Weeks is keeping me informed. As I'm sure this won't go any further I'll bring you up to date with what we know. There's been another murder.'

Isobel looked shocked and put her hand to her mouth. '*No*! Who was it?'

'It was the fortune teller who'd been at the fair before Ivy Lee – Pilgrim Petulengro. They found his body in the river. Initially it was thought that he was involved with the first death but it seems that he and Vado Boswell, the fairground owner, just moved the body. Naturally, Bonnie Parker is not convinced, but Lewis has been unable to find any evidence to link them to the actual murder.'

'Who do *you* think did it?'

'I've really no idea. I thought at first that Petulengro had killed Ivy but again Lewis can find no evidence.' A waitress arrived with the tea so he said no more until she had gone. 'There is something curious about the case though.'

'Oh yes, what's that?' Isobel asked as she poured their drinks.

'What do you know about Tarot cards?'

Isobel watched as Bruissement spooned sugar into his cup. She smiled, her eyes twinkling. 'Probably more that I should,' she said.

Russell looked at her quizzically. 'Oh yes?'

She nodded. 'First, tell me why you ask.'

He looked around to make sure they weren't being overheard and leaned in towards her. 'Both the victims were found with a Tarot card stuffed in their mouths.'

'Curious,' was all she said. Then: 'I don't suppose you know what cards they were?'

'If I tell you, do you think you'd be able to interpret their meanings?'

She nodded slowly. 'Possibly.' Then, after taking a sip from her cup she said: 'Listen. Why don't you come round for supper later? You can tell me more and I will see if I can help. I'm sure you can find plenty to occupy yourselves until then.'

~O~

Boswell had been sent back to the cells and Parker had returned to his own office. He had his feet up on the desk, trouser cuffs hitched up over scuffed brogues. A customary Capstan Full

Strength dangled from his lip, the blue smoke curling upwards. The DC sat opposite, his notebook open in front of him. 'Right, Constable Weeks. What do we know?'

'Sir?'

'About the bloody murders, *obviously*'

'We-ell,' Weeks began hesitantly. 'It appears that neither Boswell nor Petulengro had anything to do with the murder of Gypsy Rose Lee.'

Parker grunted. 'Go on…'

'And it's unlikely that Boswell had anything to do with Petulengro's death.'

Parker sucked hard on his cigarette then took it out of his mouth. After exhaling noisily he said: 'I'm not so sure…'

'But Lewis hasn't found any evidence.'

'Yet… I'm still to be convinced. However, we seem to have hit a brick wall. What do we do to get this bloody investigation moving?'

Weeks flipped through his notebook, his dark curly hair flopping over his face as he bent forward. 'Um. I think we should talk to the fairground people again.'

Parker leaned back in his chair. 'Good idea. Anyone in particular?'

'We didn't really talk to Boswell's son, Duke. He seemed a bright boy. I expect he sees most of what's going on.'

'A kid? You reckon he might know something?'

'We can but ask.'

'We? I think you should go. And take that Wopsie with you. The boy might respond to the feminine touch.'

'Wopsie?'

'Yeah, you know, WPC Sharpe, whatever her name is. I've got plenty to be getting on with here.' He sat up and started shuffling papers on his desk. When Weeks didn't move immediately he looked up. 'You still here?'

~O~

'Do you think he'll be able to tell us anything?' Nettie asked.

Weeks wrestled with the column change on the Ford Pilot, crunching the gears – yet again. 'I hope so. It's bad enough having to work with Bonnie Parker. This investigation has stalled and won't be going anywhere unless we get some more information.' Finally he got the car into gear and they set off.

When they reached the Salts they were rather alarmed to see that many of the stalls had been packed up, the rides were being dismantled and some of the fairground people had already left. However, Boswell was still awaiting release, pending bail, so his immaculate caravan and pickup were still there.

'We'd better see if we can find his lad.'

As they walked towards Boswell's wagon they spotted Duke, chatting to a very large man dismantling the Waltzer. When the boy saw the two constables he stopped talking to the man who looked up quickly and disappeared behind the machinery. Duke ran towards them and skidded to a halt, a couple of feet away. '*You!*' he said accusingly, 'what you doin' arrestin' my dad? 'E ain't done nuffink!' He stood, hands on hips, glaring at them. He was trying to look menacing but at five-foot-nothing he wasn't quite pulling it off.

'That's not strictly true,' Nettie said gently.

''E ain't killed no one anyhow.'

'That's true, but he did move the body.'

'So?' The boy stuck his chin out and tried for belligerence.

Nettie suppressed a smile. 'Listen. How do you fancy a hot dog and a bottle of pop?'

The jutting chin was joined by a frown. 'You what?'

'Terry's tea van is over in the lay-by. Bet you're hungry.'

'Might be.' The chin softened and the boy affected a look of *laissez faire*.

'Well I could do with a cuppa, anyway.'

'Is 'e comin'?' Duke pointed at Weeks.

'If that's all right.'

'S'pose so.' He stuck his hands in his pockets. 'C'mon then. What are we waiting for?'

They walked the few hundred yards to the lay-by and Weeks placed the order. When the food and drinks arrived they took them over to a table and chairs at the side of the tea van. The boy bit into the ketchup-smothered hotdog and chewed hungrily. Nettie waited until his mouth was almost empty and he'd sucked greedily on the straw sticking out of the bottle of Vimto. He wiped his greasy fingers on his shorts, the oily marks blending with the streaks of grime already present. He belched noisily.

'Now, waddyer want? I know you ain't bought me some grub for nuffink.'

Nettie did smile this time and took a sip from her mug. 'You really are a bright boy, aren't you?'

He shrugged. 'I *can* read an' write, if that's what you mean.'

'I'm sure you can. And I bet you don't miss much.'

'I keep me eyes open.'

'Would you like another bottle of pop?'

'Don't mind if I do.' He was enjoying the attention.

Nettie looked towards Weeks. 'Johnny?' Happy to leave his colleague to do the talking the DC got up and went back to the counter. She turned her attention to the boy. 'Did you see who visited the fortune teller, Ivy Rose Lee?' she asked.

'Yeah, I did. Spent quite a lot of me time spyin' on 'er visitors.'

'I thought you probably did. Anyone in particular catch your eye?'

'That policeman, 'e went to see 'er.'

'Which policeman was that? Nettie asked gently.

'Short bloke. Got a big chin and small dog.'

'DI Russell?'

'Yeah, that's 'im. Came over later with that fingerprint bloke.'

'Right. Anyone else unusual?'

'Maybe.'

Nettie smiled. 'Do tell.'

Duke looked down, staring at his hands, clasped on the table. He paused for so long Nettie thought he was going to clam up. Then: 'I *know* it weren't my dad what killed the fortune teller.'

'You do?' Nettie said, keeping her voice level, not wanting to put the boy off.

He frowned. 'Yes, for sure.'

Weeks returned with another bottle of Vimto. Nettie looked up. 'Do you think it might be an idea if you went and talked to some of the other folk – before they all leave?' Taking the hint he nodded and set off back to the fairground. Turning to Duke she said: 'What makes you think that?'

'Cos it was someone else.'

'Oh yes? Who?'

The boy shifted uneasily in his seat, concentrating on sucking on the straw. Nettie waited patiently. After a long pause, Duke looked up, his face serious. 'I can't say.'

'Why not?' She said gently.

'It wouldn't be fair.'

'But if you know who killed her…'

'No, I can't.' Nettie realised the boy was near to tears.

'Surely…' But she got no further. Leaping up and knocking his chair to the ground Duke rushed off before she could stop him.

'Damn!'

~o~

After Isobel had made her excuses and returned to work, Russell and Bruissement made their way to the station, arriving in time to catch the train back to Shinglesea. The Frenchman was keen to take a look at the church in Snargate so they set off in Weeks's car. As they were travelling he said: 'What is it you are more interested in – the murders of the two fortune tellers or the smuggling of spirits and cigarettes, without the taxes being paid?'

Russell chuckled as he changed up into third gear. 'Obviously the murders, but I'm off the case.'

'But that would not stop you *normalement*. It would be, 'ow you say, like showing a bull a rag red.'

'You know me too well, Guillaume. But I've decided to stay away – for the time being – to see if Bonnie Parker digs a big enough hole to bury himself in.'

Bruissement let out a deep guffaw. 'That would indeed be a sight to be seen!'

They travelled along the Military Road and on reaching Appledore, Russell slowed the car and pulled over to the side. 'There,' he said pointing towards the pillbox. 'That's where the body of Ivy Rose Lee was found. Where my troubles began.'

'Very interesting, but do not forget, the case no longer belongs to you.'

'Fair enough.' Russell put the car in gear and drove off, turning right over the bridge, then sharp left to travel along the other side of the canal. They followed the winding lane for a couple of miles and bumped over the level crossing at Appledore station. The road wound between newly green hedges of hawthorn and field maple with an occasional willow already standing taller. In a while they had reached Snargate. Russell turned into the lane opposite the pub and parked the car. As they got out, Bruissement looked at the ancient building.

'The Red Lion? But I though you said that was the name of the inn in Appledore – the one the smuggler runs.'

Russell smiled. '*That* is *another* Red Lion. The name is quite common although it is unusual to have two quite so close. Perhaps they will change it one day.' He shrugged. 'Come on. Let's see if the church is open.' They walked along the lane then up the brick path into the churchyard.

St Dunstan's sat squat and solid, anchored between the gravestones by a beefy square tower at the western end. The ridge, running along the top of the roof, was distinctly hump-backed, the result of the building settling over the centuries it had been standing. Turning the iron ring, Russell pushed the heavy wooden door open. Although not a hot day, inside was cooler with a soothing calm. Out of the corner of his eye he noticed Bruissement cross himself as they stepped on to the tiled floor.

'*Tres magnifique*,' the Frenchman exclaimed, his voice hushed.

Russell was quietly amused at the other man's piety. Since he had discovered Buddhism he was rarely awed by Christianity. 'Yes, it is a lovely church, around 800 years old. But look, this is what I wanted to show you.' They walked towards the north aisle. On the wall was the painting of a ship. 'Apparently it dates from the end of the 15th century and is a *great ship*, a four-master that was the successor to a carrack. It's believed it was put there to signify that church was a safe place to store smuggled goods – which is why I think Jack Mills may have used it.' They looked around but there were no cases or boxes piled up. The tiled and stone floor was bare. 'I expect if he had moved them here from the pub, it wasn't for long.'

'Perhaps we should have arrived earlier?' Bruissement suggested.

'Maybe.' The terrier had trotted in behind them and was now snuffling about in the shadows. Suddenly she gave a sharp yelp. 'What is it, Aggie?' Russell moved to where she was standing, excitedly wagging her tail. He crouched and reached behind a pillar. 'Well I'll be…' he said, standing and holding out a piece of card. There was enough lettering to see that it was from a carton of **LUCKY STRIKE**.

'American cigarettes!' Bruissement exclaimed. 'What are *they* doing here?'

Russell explained about the similar piece of card he had found stuck to the tarpaulin in the cellar of the Appledore pub. 'I would imagine the carton got damaged and this piece got torn off too. By itself it doesn't prove anything but it does seem to point towards Mills being deeply involved in smuggling contraband. Sadly, I think that's all the evidence we're likely to find here.' They had a good look round the rest of the church, with Bruissement marvelling at the antiquity, but found nothing else.

Finally the Frenchman said: 'Sonny. All this searching has made me thirsty. Do you think we can get a drink at the pub across the road?'

Russell slid back his cuff and looked at his wristwatch. 'I should think it will be open by now. Let's go and see.'

Differing from its namesake in Appledore, this Red Lion was small and dark but inviting. There was an L-shaped, marble topped bar. On its corner four beer pumps stood sentinel. The ceiling was low and nicotine-stained; on the wall a large clock ticked away the minutes. Seated on a high stool behind the bar was a small, round man. A stubby roll-up protruded from his stubbly jaws; his thinning hair was combed back over an almost spherical head. He grinned.

'What can I get for you, gentlemen?'

'I'll have a pint of your best bitter, please,' Russell said, then turned towards his companion.' I know you're not a fan of English beer, how about cider?'

'Ah, *cidre*! Yes, I would like that.'

'It's rather strong,' the landlord said.

'Pff! I think I can manage. Can I have a glass with an 'andle please? As you can see I am a leetle – 'ow you say – indisposed.' Bruissement nodded towards his plastered right arm.

'Of course.'

'And one for you?' Russell asked.

'Don't mind if I do. I'll have a half.'

When they had their drinks and the money had been put in the large ornate till, the two policemen sat down on the bench with their backs to the window. The landlord returned to his stool, struck a match and tipping his head to one side, lit the stub of a roll-up, being careful not to singe his nose hairs.

'Cheers,' Russell said, raising his glass.

'À *votre santé*.' Bruissement replied and took a deep draught. He immediately spluttered and tears came to his eyes.

'Are you all right, my friend?' Russell asked, concerned.

Bruissement coughed and wiped the back of his hand across his eyes. 'Ah *oui*. I am okay. It went, as you say, down the wrong

’ole.’ He took a pack of *Gauloises* out of his pocket. ‘Do you mind?’

‘Of course not.’ As a non-smoker Russell didn’t enjoy the smell of normal tobacco but he didn’t object to the more fragrant smoke from French cigarettes. He wasn’t averse to the smell of cigars either although he couldn’t bear the stench of Superintendent Stout’s cheroots. He drank from his glass then looked towards the landlord. ‘A nice pint – Alf, isn’t it?’

Alf grinned and nodded his head. ‘Glad you like it. I try to look after my beer. What brings you two gentlemen here?’

‘Well, it’s a bit delicate. We’re actually policemen. This is my colleague from France.’

Alf’s grin widened. ‘Thought as much.’

‘We’re interested in Jack Mills – landlord of the Red Lion in Appledore.’

‘I know who he is – shifty character. Now he *don’t* know how to look after his beer.’

‘I’ll remember that.’ Russell saluted with his glass.

‘He came down from London, after the war. Thinks ’e knows it all. And do you know what? He knows bugger all.’

‘You’re not a fan then?’

Alf snorted. ‘No I ain’t. And I don’t want to see ’im in ’ere again.’

Russell looked quizzically at him. ‘Has he visited recently then?’

‘He was ’ere yesterday.’

‘On his own?’

‘No ’e was with a skinny bloke – ain’t seen ’im afore. Oh and Angus Goodyear. Thick as thieves, they was.’

Who is Angus Goodyear?’

‘’E farms just up the road.’

‘I see.’

Alf tutted. 'Well, 'e's got a bit of land and a few scraggy sheep. Seems to scratch a livin' – don't know 'ow.'

'What were they talking about?' Russell asked.

'Dunno. Kept their 'eads together and their voices low.'

'He's got a farm nearby, you say?'

'Yes, on the way to Brookland. Easy to miss. Just a shack and a barn – if you can call it that. Don't know 'ow it's still standing.'

~O~

Nettie made her way back to what was left of the funfair. Where the stalls and sideshows had stood there were patches of yellowed grass and, round them, areas flattened by dozens of feet. A generator, on the back of a large Scammell lorry, thudded rhythmically and figures scurried back and forth with ropes and bundles of canvas. Spotting Weeks in conversation with a thin man she made her way towards them. When the man saw her uniform his eyes widened, he shook his head and shot off between two vans. Weeks gave a wry smile.

'Nobody knows anything, apparently. Or else they don't want to tell me. I hope you had more luck with young Duke.'

'Well sort of. We seemed to be getting on well and I'm sure I was on the brink of a breakthrough. Then suddenly, he decided he couldn't tell me any more and dashed off.'

'What *did* he tell you?'

'Only that he knew his father didn't kill Ivy Rose.'

'Why did he say that?'

Nettie paused and considered. 'He said it was somebody else.'

'Who?' Excitement at the revelation filled Weeks's face.

'He wouldn't say,' Nettie answered sadly. 'I think he wanted to but he said whoever it was, that it wouldn't be fair.'

Week excitement evaporated. 'That's a nuisance.'

'It's worse than that. If we knew, we could probably wrap up the case *without* the help of Bonnie Parker. Now we're no further forward.'

'Can't we haul him into the station for questioning?'

'We could – if we could find him. But I don't think he'd say anything else. He's got a stubborn streak, inherited from his father, I expect.' She thought for a moment. 'What about his mother? Could she get him to talk?'

'I'm afraid not,' Weeks said. 'She ran off with a casual who worked on the dodgems a few months ago. That was about the only thing I *did* find out.'

'So who's been looking after him – while his dad's been in the cells?'

'That's a point. If we know that, whoever it is might be able to get him to talk.'

'Maybe.'

'Although I suspect not. The fairground folk are not the most forthcoming. Besides, by the way he wolfed down that hotdog I suspect he's been running wild.'

~O~

The two detectives eventually came out of the Red Lion and were about to cross the road to the car. Russell suddenly pulled on Aggie's lead and put his hand on Bruissement's arm. 'Hang on. We don't want to get run over.' They stepped back as a convoy came trundling up the road from the north-west. Leading the procession was an ex-army truck, towing a large, cream-coloured caravan. Half a dozen cars were strung out behind it, waiting until the road widened enough to get past the slow vehicle. 'Looks like the fair is on the move,' Russell said. The convoy had soon passed and they made their way over to the Ford Popular. When they were settled in their seats Bruissement spoke.

'Sonny. I 'ave been thinking. If your man Mills 'as moved the goods from the church, 'e would not move them far, would 'e?'

Russell, gripped the steering wheel and stared ahead. 'You may be right.' He turned to the Frenchman. 'What are you suggesting?'

'Perhaps there is an old building where 'e would 'ave moved the free of duty brandy and cigarettes – in a 'urry.'

'Do you mean Angus Goodyear's barn?'

'Perhaps…'

'Yes, that's a thought. Maybe we should try to find it.'

Russell reversed the car out of the lane by the church and they drove slowly up the road until they came to a turning. It was just a dirt track that didn't appear to lead anywhere, closed off with a broken five-bar gate. It was so deeply rutted that it seemed prudent to leave the car at the roadside. With difficulty he pushed the gate open enough to get through. The two men walked for a hundred yards between unkempt hedges, the blackthorn laden with creamy-white blossom. There was a sharp bend in the track and these petered out, replaced on either side with pasture that was more weeds than grass. Half a dozen pathetic-looking sheep stood around, miserably chewing the cud. It was likely that they had never been properly shorn; clumps of wool had just fallen off them, leaving bare patches. A little farther, past a stand of elders, a building came into sight.

'Alf wasn't wrong,' Russell said. The barn was a patchwork of rusty, corrugated-iron sheets in various shades of red and orange, many with holes and some flapping gently in the breeze. It looked as if a strong gust of wind would blow the whole structure over. He and Bruissement walked up to it and could see there was a rickety wooden door with a length of timber wedged against it, keeping it shut. Russell leaned forward and was just about to pull the wood free when there was a shout from behind them.

'*Oi*! What do you think you're doing?' They turned to see a man, as threadbare as his sheep, pointing a double-barrelled shotgun squarely at them. 'This is private property. Get orff my land. And take that bloody mutt with you. I don't want it worrying my sheep.'

Russell called Aggie to heel then said: 'I hope you've got a licence for that.'

'What's it to you?'

Russell slipped his hand into to his pocket and produced a warrant card. 'I could have you for threatening a police officer – Mr Goodyear.'

The man looked slightly surprised but went on: 'I don't care *who* you are, you've no right to trespass. If you want to look around, come back with a warrant.'

'We might well do that.' Russell was not intimidated by the farmer, but knew he was on shaky ground. 'What have you got in your barn? What is it that needs guarding so carefully?'

The man looked startled. 'What? In the barn? The usual – farming equipment.' Then he glowered. 'Not that it's any of your concern.'

Russell tried another tack. 'Do you know Jack Mills, landlord of the Red Lion in Appledore?'

'Maybe I do. Not that it's any of your business either.'

'I just wondered if you were storing anything for him.'

Goodyear's face darkened. 'I've had enough of this. Time you went.'

'You'd better be able to produce a licence for your gun when we come back though. Come on Guillaume. We don't want to waste any more of this gentleman's time.' They turned and made their way back along the track, the terrier trotting obediently at their heels. Once in the car, Russell sat quietly, before starting the engine. 'Well, what do you make of that?'

''E was 'iding something, that is for certain.'

'That's what I thought, too. I reckon Mills's contraband is stored in that rickety barn.'

'So 'ow are we going to find out? He seemed ready to use that shotgun.'

'I doubt if he would have done. I'm sure he knows it could be a hanging offence. But yes, we need to find a way of having a look in there. Not now though; we'll have to come back.'

Chapter 11

A Waltzer is a *fairground ride* consisting of a number of cars which spin freely while *rotating around a central point, in much the same way as a carousel. As they revolve, the floor of the ride undulates* over a track so th*at the cars rise and fall and the offset weight of the riders causes each one to rotate. The riders experience varying levels of g-force from the constant spinning.*

'SO I was right all along. I knew it!' Parker sat back in his chair, a triumphant grin lighting his smug face.

'Looks like it.' Lewis's expression was far from triumphant. It stuck in his craw to admit it.

On the DI's insistence he had reluctantly gone back to Boswell's caravan, not expecting to turn up any further evidence, but he was wrong. On his original inspection, which he was sure had been thorough, he'd found nothing incriminating. So this time he'd virtually turned it upside down. He'd emptied all the cupboards, shining the beam of a powerful torch into the recesses. The cushions had been pulled off the settee and the boards forming the base lifted. The bed had been stripped of its linen, the mattress upended and the wooden frame examined minutely. Even the carpet had been rolled back. Nothing. Lewis had stood in the middle of the van scratching his head. He was still convinced that the man was innocent of the murders. Looking round one final time his eyes stopped at the cast-iron range. 'I wonder…' he thought and crouched in front of it. He opened the door to the firebox and shone the torch. His eyebrows rose in disbelief as the beam picked out a small packet. Carefully he retrieved it, shaking the ash off as he did so. The corner had been burned but the rest of the box was intact. He recognised it immediately as a deck of cards. With rising astonishment he slid them out of the pack and began carefully laying them out on the small table. This was no ordinary deck – these were Tarot cards.

Since the beginning of the investigation he'd made a study of them and knew the pack almost intimately. He went through them twice, but the result was the same each time – four cards, *Death*, *the Lovers*, *Justice* and *The Tower* were missing from the major arcana. Judging by the designs and the intricate blue and white pattern on the backs, he was pretty sure they were the same set as the cards found in the mouths of the two fortune tellers. The absence of *Justice* and *The Tower* was a bit of a mystery, but that would have to wait for now. It seemed that, for once, DI Bonnie Parker had got it right.

'You say you found them in the stove?'

'That's correct.'

'I suppose he was trying to burn the evidence.'

Lewis could only agree. 'So it seems.'

'Right. Let's see what the pikey has got to say about this.'

~o~

'You can't keep me here any longer – I know my rights,' Boswell growled.

'Is that so, sunshine?'

'Yes, it bloody well is. You know you haven't got any evidence against me so you're going to have to let me go.' He started rising.

'Not so fast. Sit down!'

Parker's menacing tone took the man by surprise and he flopped back in his chair.

'I *was* prepared to give you the benefit of the doubt. You really took me in. But things have changed.'

'What do you mean? Boswell's brows were knitted together; suspicion written across his features.

'We've *got* the evidence.'

'Oh yeah? Where?'

'Here.' The DI slipped the pack out of his pocket and placed it on the table between them.

'What's that?'

'As if you didn't know.' Parker grinned, shook the cards out and spread them out in a fan.

Boswell stared uncomprehendingly. 'They've got nothing to do with me.'

'That's just where you're wrong.'

'What do you mean?'

'They were found in the stove in *your* caravan. How do you account for that?' Parker sat back in his chair, arms folded across his chest, a fixed Cheshire cat-like grin plastered across his face.

'Listen. I've never seen them before.'

'A likely tale. See where they're charred?' Parker prodded the nearest card where the corner had been burned away.

Boswell stared but didn't speak.

'You obviously tried to get rid of the evidence but didn't succeed.' Parker's voice was joyful. He celebrated by lighting up.

Boswell shook his head disbelievingly. 'You cannot be serious?'

'You'd better believe it. This is damning evidence. On its own it might not prove conclusively that you did for both those fortune tellers. But I can tell you, I'm expecting more of the same.'

'How's that?'

'We're going to take your lovely caravan and your smart pickup apart, until we find what we need,' Parker said triumphantly.'

'How *dare* you!' Boswell hissed and lunged forward.

The DI was just quick enough to jerk back before the other man could grasp his throat. There was a scuffle as Weeks and a constable standing by the door leapt in and thrust him back in his chair. Parker let out a breath. 'Easy sunshine! No point in losing your rag. You know I'm right. I'm afraid you're not going anywhere in a hurry.' He nodded to the constable. 'Take him down to the cells. I've got evidence to find.'

~o~

Russell and Bruissement trudged back to the car and slumped into their seats. 'Well,' Russell said, 'there's not much point staying here. Goodyear is obviously determined to keep us *orff* his land.'

'What do you suggest we do then, Sonny?' the Frenchman asked, wincing. He'd banged his plastered arm on the door.

Russell frowned and looked thoughtful. After a pause he said: 'I think we should try to meet up with Johnny Weeks and find out what's been going on – what blunders Bonnie Parker has managed.'

'Blunders? What is this?'

'Foolish mistakes – miscarriages of justice – generally ignorant behaviour – that sort of thing.'

Bruissement chuckled. 'I think I understand.'

'Plus, I ought to see if Johnny needs his car back.'

'Yes. That is something I am not understanding.'

'What's that?' Russell asked, as he manoeuvred the Ford out of the gateway and on to the road.

'Why you do not 'ave a car of your own.'

Russell smiled. 'Yes, I suppose it is a little strange.'

'I mean, 'ow do you get anywhere? *Notamment* when there is an emergency?'

'I suppose that's the privilege of being an Inspector. My DC, Johnny Weeks, lives close by or they'll send a man with a car from the station. If necessary I can borrow one from the car pool. It doesn't seem to be a problem.'

'Hmm, I see – I think.' The Frenchman took a deep breath and let it out noisily. 'Anyway, that *cidre, agréable* as it is, 'as made me, 'ow you say, peckish. Is there anywhere we can get something to eat?'

They were nearing Appledore and Russell said: 'We could try the Red Lion. I'm not sure how good it would be but it could be interesting.'

'You mean the pub of Jack Mills – the man you 'ave suspicions of?'

'That's the one.'

'Why not? It might be *amusant*.'

Russell parked the car in the main street and they entered the pub. The bar was empty, although it was still lunchtime. There was no sign of Mills but Russell was pleased to see Edna standing behind the counter, smiling. He introduced her to the Frenchman who reached over, took her hand and held it up to his lips. The customary blush spread from her throat to the rest of her face.

'W-what can I get you, gentlemen?' she stammered.

'We'd like some food. Is that possible?'

'Jack's not here so I'm afraid the kitchen's closed.' Bruissement's face fell; his moustache drooped even lower; his eyes were as sad as a spaniel's. Edna took pity. 'I might be able to rustle something up.'

'I'm afraid I don't eat meat,' Russell said. 'But my friend will eat anything,' he grinned.

'Can I get you a drink first?' Edna asked. Russell suggested that Babycham would be no match for Alf's cider so they opted for two pints of best bitter. They took their drinks over to a table by the window.

Bruissement took a sip from his glass, and, pleasantly surprised that it wasn't as bad as he'd expected, followed it with a deeper draught. 'She is a nice girl.'

'She certainly is.'

'Why is she working for such a bad man?'

'She needs the money, apparently.'

'Ah, *je comprends.*' He took another drink. 'Do you know, Sonny. I could get used to this!'

'That's one thing in Mills's favour. Despite what Alf said – he keeps a good cellar.'

'Let us hope that 'e keeps a good kitchen, too.'

It wasn't long before Edna appeared carrying a tray. There was cold pork pie for Bruissement, hard-boiled eggs and cheese for Russell along with crusty bread, tomatoes, sliced cucumber and home-made chutney.

'Ah, a feast!' the Frenchman exclaimed.

'Better not eat too much. Don't forget we're dining with Isobel this evening.'

Bruissement patted his ample stomach. 'You do not 'ave to worry about me, Sonny. My appetite is *tres* 'ealthy.'

When they had finished, Edna came over to clear the table.

'Where is Jack today?' Russell asked.

'He *was* here. But he had a phone call and had to dash off – no idea where. It was just before you arrived.'

Oh, I see,' he said mildly. Then when she had disappeared back to the kitchen, 'I thought I recognised his pickup, Guillaume. We passed it on the way here. Now I wonder where he was going.'

Bruissement raised his eyebrows. 'Perhaps to move some of that *contrebande* in farmer Goodyear's barn?'

'I wouldn't be surprised.'

~o~

They drove back to Nottery Quay and, as Russell had hoped, a vehicle he recognised from the car pool was parked by the Salts. He grinned knowing it was the Ford Pilot that his DC hated. Stopping behind it they made their way into what was left of the funfair where they found Weeks and Nettie Sharpe talking to a very large man next to the Waltzer. He was wearing an army battledress jacket, tight over his wide shoulders, and a pair of threadbare suit trousers, held up with a thin leather belt. The trousers were obviously too small as the fabric strained over his massive thighs which bulged below the belt. His eyes were small – piggy-like; a dark, bushy moustache covered most of his mouth; a greasy cap was tipped towards the back of his head.

'So you hadn't noticed that the fortune teller was missing?' Weeks was asking.

'No. Far too busy working on this.' He had the voice of a man who gargled with razor blades. He sniffed and pointed his thumb towards the part-dismantled machinery.

'Any idea when you last saw her?'

The man shook his head. 'Don't have much to do with them in the caravans.'

'What about the one before – Petulengro?' Nettie asked.

'Him? He was all right. Bit of a strange bloke, but he kept himself to himself.' The man let out a huge sneeze then wiped snot from his nose and moustache with the back of his hand.

'Did you know he was queer – a homosexual?'

The man shrugged. 'Didn't know and don't care,' he growled. 'There's all sorts here – working on a funfair.'

'Any idea why he left?'

'The thing about working in a fair is that you're always on the move – always new places to go and new faces to meet. People come and people go. That's the nature of travelling folk.' After that surprisingly eloquent statement the man sneezed again and shrugged. 'Sorry. Can't help you any more, I don't feel great. I've got to go – need to pack up as we're moving on.' He was just turning when Russell touched his arm.

'Where are you going next?'

'North of here. Tenterden, I think it's called.' Another shrug and he walked away. Picking up a large spanner he started undoing an equally large nut. In his oversize hand it looked small.

'Do you think you're done here?' Russell asked Weeks.

'I reckon so, Sir. Either no one knows anything or they're reluctant to tell us if they do. Been a bit of a waste of time.'

'I expect you could do with a cuppa then?'

Nettie smiled. 'I could, Sir. I'm parched.'

'Right. Let's see what Terry can offer.'

As they made their way across to the lay-by Russell introduced her to Bruissement. For a change he didn't kiss her hand but took it in his and shook it gently.

'*Enchanté, mademoiselle*. It is a pleasure to see such a pretty lady in a uniform of the police.'

'Don't you have them in the *Gendarmerie*?'

'Perhaps. But not in my *departement*.'

Terry served them with four steaming mugs of strong tea which they took over to the table and sat down.

Russell took a drink from his mug. 'Well, Johnny, can I ask how the investigation is going?'

Weeks pushed his hair off his forehead. 'As well as can be expected' He grinned. 'With Bonnie Parker in charge.'

'Has he found a suspect yet?'

'He has.'

'And it is?'

'Vado Boswell.'

Russell was just taking another swig from his mug. At Weeks's words he spluttered, spraying tea from his mouth. '*What!* I thought he'd have had to let him go?'

'Parker made Lewis look in his van again and he found some evidence to link him to the murders.'

'Which was?'

'A pack of Tarot cards.'

'Pah! That's hardly evidence.'

'They were found in the ashes in the stove.'

'Mmm, I suppose that's something.'

'That's not all.'

'Oh?'

'The Lovers and Death cards and a couple of others were missing from the deck.'

Bruissement, who had been listening carefully, spoke. 'Is it not possible that cards were, 'ow you say, planted?'

'I suppose that's possible. But who by?' Weeks replied.

'Someone who wants to implicate him – shift the blame. Presumably the actual murderer.' Nettie suggested.

'But maybe he is guilty,' Russell said.

'Well that's what Parker thinks. And he's insisted that Lewis finds more evidence.'

'The poor man. I bet he's cross that he missed the cards in the first search. Bonnie Parker must have been delighted.'

'You know how he likes to gloat.'

'I certainly do.' Russell drained his mug and put it down on the table. 'Anyway. Did you get *anything* from the people at the fair?'

Weeks looked at the WPC. 'Nettie? Do you want to tell him?'

'Of course. Well, Sir. I talked to Boswell's son, Duke. Inside that tough, streetwise exterior is a rather sensitive and frightened little boy.'

'What makes you say that?'

'I talked to him – on his own – and he began to open up. Did you know that his mother ran off with one of the casual workers?'

Russell shook his head. 'I didn't. That would explain his grubby appearance and gruff manner. But you said you thought he was sensitive.'

'Yes, Sir. He was almost in tears. I'm sure he's covering up for someone – someone he cares about.'

Russell looked towards Weeks. 'Any idea who?'

The DC shook his head.

There was a pause. Nettie looked thoughtful then spoke. 'I could be wrong but I got the distinct impression that the chap we were talking to earlier – the big bloke – was nervous.'

'The huge one dismantling the Waltzer?' Weeks asked. 'I thought he was just a bit shifty – keen to finish the job and move one.'

'Perhaps…' the WPC said slowly. 'Maybe he just wasn't well.' She paused. 'Did you notice how he shot off when we first arrived – when Duke came running across to confront us?'

'Now you come to mention it, I did. And maybe you're right about him appearing nervous.'

Russell had been listening to their conversation with interest. 'Perhaps you'd better speak to him again,' he said.

'I'd better check in with Bonnie Parker first,' Weeks said. 'You know what he's like…'

'Before you go. I wanted to ask about your car. Is it okay if I keep it a bit longer – so Guillaume and I can get about?'

'Of course, Sir. I'm delighted to be driving this wonderful motor instead.' Weeks gave a wry smile.

'Thanks, lad.'

~o~

'What do you mean? You've found another suspect!' Though the speaker was small and tinny Parker's voice echoed around the car. 'I've got the *only* suspect here – Vado bloody Boswell!' he thundered.

'But Sir…' Weeks said meekly. 'What about evidence?'

'*Evidence*? I've got the bloody evidence! Get your arse back here now. I need you in the interview room.'

~o~

'*Who* did you say turned up?' Jack Mills's eyes blazed.

'He was a copper. Short, with a big chin. Nattily dressed.' Angus Goodyear stood in front of the barn, his shotgun over his arm, the breech broken.

'What was 'is name?'

'I dunno. He didn't say.'

'Bet it was that nosey DI Russell. Didn't he show you any identification?'

'Er… oh yeah, he did. A warrant card.'

'Well, what was on it?' Mills demanded.

Goodyear bristled. 'Oi! Don't you have a go at me. I'm doing you a favour.'

Mills backed down. 'Yeah, well. You're going to be paid, ain't yer?'

'That's not the point. If he *does* come back with a search warrant and finds the stuff…'

''E won't come back. An' if 'e did 'e wouldn't find nothing.'

Goodyear furrowed his brow. 'How's that?'

'Cos I'm going to shift it. All right? Come on. Give me a hand to load it up.'

The farmer looked even more puzzled. 'Where will you take it? You've already moved it once.'

'Never you mind. Just be 'appy you won't 'ave to worry no more.'

'But if you're taking it away, what about me?' Goodyear could see some easy money slipping through his fingers.

'Waddyer mean, what about you?'

'You said you'd pay me for storing it, and if it's not here…'

'Don't worry, I'll see you're all right,' Mills grumbled. 'No come on, let's get it shifted. I want it out of 'ere.'

Once the pickup was loaded, Mills gave the farmer some cash. It was not as much as at first promised and Goodyear grumbled but he was glad to see the back of the stuff. Mills drove along the track and stopped the truck in the gateway. He was in a quandary. Where should he take the boxes? He'd thought the church would have been a safe place – luckily he'd moved them in time. But transferring them to the barn had obviously been a bad idea.

That blasted copper. He was fed up with him and his meddling. Why couldn't he leave him alone? Mills thought that after he'd thumped him the other morning he'd stop looking but it seemed it had made him even more determined to continue. He couldn't take the stuff back to the pub – that would be too obvious. So where? He sat for a long time, his hands on the steering wheel, his forehead resting on his knuckles. There was nothing for it. He'd have to take it back to Dungeness. Albert Stern would not be pleased.

~o~

Mills was relieved to see that Stern's van was parked outside Prospect Cottage but still approached the house with a feeling of trepidation. Stern had made it patently clear that he wanted nothing more to do with his smuggling operation. He'd said this before, on more than one occasion, but Mills got the impression that he really meant it this time. It was annoying as the man's boat was swift and seaworthy, which meant the collection of the goods had always gone smoothly.

He was at a loss as to where he could find another willing boat owner and he was blowed if he was going to give up on the trade. Running the pub was okay but it was long hours for a relatively small reward. Whereas bringing cigarettes and brandy across the channel – without the burden of paying duty – and selling them on the black market was much more lucrative. Perhaps he should buy a boat of his own? Now, that was a thought. He was turning this over in his mind as he knocked on the door. It was a while before it opened a crack and Stern's face appeared round the edge. When he saw who it was, the skinny man's face darkened – thunder clouds filling a summer sky.

'Waddyer want?' he said, his voice coming out as a menacing growl.

Mills held his hands up in supplication. 'Don't be like that, my friend.'

'Don't you *my friend* me. Turning up like this can only mean one thing – you need my help.'

The landlord chuckled. 'You know me too well. Aren't you gonna invite me in?'

'*No*, I'm not. I told you I want nothing more to do with you or your schemes. Every time I hear a knock on the door I'm expecting it to be a visit from the rozzers, after you thumped that copper.'

Mills's arms spread. 'Don't worry about that. No one knows it was us...'

'*Us*...? You mean *you*! I don't want nothing to do with it – or with you. Now bugger off!' With that he shut the door firmly and Mills heard the bolt being shot.

He stood on the step for a few moments, debating whether to try again, but seeing Stern in such a mood he doubted he would change his mind. Mills trudged back to the truck, climbed into the driver's seat and just sat, thinking. He couldn't take the stuff to the pub – that would be an obvious place for the coppers to look. Besides, he was growing suspicious of Edna. That blasted detective, Russell, seemed to be one step behind him and he wondered how he managed it. The barmaid could well be telling him more than she should. He would have a stiff word with her when he got back. But that didn't help with his present dilemma.

He had backed the truck into Stern's drive so it would be easier to unload the boxes. He stared out through the windscreen, his eyes half-focused on the boats pulled up on the distant shingle bank. Then he noticed the shed next to the little railway track they'd used a couple of days before. 'I wonder…' he thought. He started the engine and drove across the road and on to the shingle. Keeping the truck in low gear he bumped across the stones, hanging on to the steering wheel as he was thrown from side to side. Luckily it wasn't far and shortly he pulled up beside the semi-derelict building. He switched off the engine and climbed out of the cab.

The door to the shed was firmly shut. He pulled it open, the woodwork complaining as the bottom was dragged across the pebbles. He scanned the interior, unaware that it had been Russell's hiding place. It looked to him like no one had been in there for ages. It would have to do. He rolled back the cover, spat on his hands and lifted the first box out of the back of the pickup. In a few minutes he had transferred the goods into the shed. He dragged a couple of pieces of moth-eaten canvas over the stack he had made and piled some broken boxes on top. After shutting the door he kicked a pile of shingle against the bottom, hoping no one would be curious enough to look inside. He was due to meet one of his contacts who could shift the stuff so it wouldn't have to be there for long. After one more glance at the shed he climbed back into the truck and reversed out on to the road.

Chapter 12

Canadian Military Pattern (CMP) trucks were a range of military vehicles, made in large numbers, and in numerous variants, by *Canada* during *World War II. They were built to British Army* specifications, primarily intended for use in the armies of the *British Commonwealth.*

AFTER BOSWELL had been sent down to the cells, Parker returned to his office. He lay back in his chair; feet on the table; one scuffed brogue crossed over the other. A cigarette dangled from the corner of his mouth, a thin column of smoke spiralling towards the grubby ceiling. He was feeling disgruntled. His usual sidekick, DC Clyde Barrow, was sick – again. Parker enjoyed using DC Weeks as he knew it annoyed Russell, but, in his opinion, the man was useless. He found him surly and uncommunicative, unlike Barrow, who always agreed unquestioningly with him. But that wasn't the only reason he was out of sorts. He was concerned about the case. Although the discovery of the charred deck of Tarot cards seemed to implicate Boswell, he had a feeling in his water that it wouldn't be enough.

He was annoyed that Lewis had missed the cards on his first search and wondered if he'd missed anything else. But he doubted it, the blasted man was rarely wrong. If he didn't turn anything further up there wasn't much of a case and he'd have to let Boswell go. He loathed the gypsy, especially after he'd been nearly assaulted by him and he was buggered if he was going to let him walk free. He sat, turning things over in his mind. The forgotten cigarette burned down and a long column of ash fell and peppered his lapel. Then he had an idea… He grinned. Yes, he had an idea and it was a good idea. In fact, it was a *very* good idea.

~o~

'Wickstead, my friend,' he said, 'how are you today?'

The desk sergeant was taken aback. Bonnie Parker was *never* this convivial. 'I'm fine, thank you.'

'That's good, that's good,' the DI said, nodding sagely. 'Tell me, what happened to the clothes Boswell was wearing when he was arrested?'

'His clothes?' Wickstead was even more confused. 'They're in a box in the store. You won't find anything on them though; Lewis has been over them with a fine-tooth comb.'

'Oh, I don't doubt that. He's very thorough,' Parker said, spreading his arms in a magnanimous gesture. 'I just thought I'd take a look, get a feel for the man.'

'Right.' Wickstead's eyebrows joined in a frown.

'You say they're in the store?'

'That's right. You'll have to search as the boxes are in rather a muddle.'

'Don't worry. I'll find them.'

'Do you want a hand?'

'No. *No*! I can manage – thanks,' he said, trying not to sound alarmed. The last thing he wanted was anyone with him.

'Well if you're sure…'

'Perfectly.' Parker tapped the side of his nose with a nicotine-stained finger; his eyes narrowed. 'Listen. Keep this to yourself, will you? I don't want to upset our flash and dab man if I find anything he's missed.'

~o~

He made his way to the basement, where evidence-filled boxes were stored. It was a narrow room, made narrower by floor-to-ceiling wooden racking down each side. A single 60 watt lightbulb hung from the ceiling, casting deep shadows. A selection of cardboard cartons, in a variety of shapes and sizes filled the shelves. Some remained intact while others were crumpled and split, their contents spilling out. Looking at them he wished he'd got Wickstead to show him where the box he wanted was. He considered going back to ask him but decided against it – he certainly didn't want to raise the man's suspicions. He sighed. He'd have to find it himself. After 10 minutes of looking he was on the verge of giving up. His jacket, already spotted with cigarette ash, was now covered in a fine dust from the coating on boxes that had lain untouched for years. He sneezed several times. 'Bugger this for a game of soldiers,' he muttered. 'I don't know why I bloody bothered.'

Deciding it was a stupid idea after all, he was just turning to leave when his eyes alighted on a new-looking box. It was on a high shelf, out of reach. He looked around for something to stand on. Crouching he searched the lower shelves in the gloom in case there was a wooden box but there was none – only cardboard. Standing upright and groaning at the effort, he cursed. There was nothing for it. He would have to trying climbing. Grasping a wooden upright he placed his left foot on the bottom shelf. He pulled himself up and put all his weight on the shelf. There was a creaking sound but it held. With an effort he lifted the other leg and put his right foot on the next shelf.

As he hauled himself upright the edge of the shelf splintered and a piece of the wood came away. His foot slipped but his toe just held. Bracing himself he managed to grip the corner of the box. He pulled; it slid over the edge and crashed to the floor. More of the shelf he was standing on broke away; he lost his grip and fell heavily with a resounding thump.

He lay on his side on the floor for some minutes. Panting he raised himself on his hands and knees. Nothing appeared broken but he was badly shaken. He stayed in that position, listening, expecting someone to appear at any moment. But all remained quiet; dust motes spiralling round the dim lightbulb. He stood upright and got his breath back. After a few moments he bent and lifted the lid off the box. Inside were Boswell's clothes: a collarless shirt, a pair of corduroy trousers, a thick belt and, what he was looking for – a red spotted neckerchief. Smiling gleefully he thrust it into his pocket. Bundling the rest of the clothes into the box, he shoved it on to a shelf. He made a half-hearted attempt at brushing the dust off his jacket, but it made little difference. As he re-emerged back in the reception area Wickstead looked up from reading the racing results in the paper.

'Find what you wanted?' he asked.

Parker quickly pushed his hand into his pocket, making sure the scarf was out of sight. 'Yeah, I found Boswell's stuff okay. But you were right. Lewis is far too canny to miss anything.' He nodded. 'I'm going out for a bit. I'll be back later, if anyone wants me.' With that he left the station.

~O~

He set off on the road to Nottery Quay but took the fork by the Peace and Plenty and headed through the village of Iden, just as Russell had done a couple of days before. He wound through the bends, down the hill and, just over the river, turned right. He bumped along the track, past the rusting vehicles and pulled up in front of Petulengro's caravan. Knowing the van would be locked he'd taken the precaution of picking up a key before he left the station and it was an easy job to unlock the padlock on the chain securing the entrance.

Once inside he shut the door and stood looking round. Little had changed since he'd last been in there. There was a light coating of white dust on some of the surfaces where Lewis and his men had been looking for fingerprints, but that was about all. The blood that had soaked into the sofa and rug had dried to a rusty brown. He cursed. He was hoping to find some that was still damp. Lifting the corner of seat cushion he peered beneath. The wood had been varnished to a high gloss; blood had run under the fabric on to the surface and formed a film. He smiled. This would suit his purpose admirably.

~O~

Sometime later he was sitting in his office with the door open so he could see who passed by. As luck would have it, it wasn't long before the suave figure of the fingerprint man appeared.

'Ah, Lewis,' he called out. 'Could I have a word?'

Lewis's heart sank but he had no alternative but to enter the fusty room. 'Is it about the search of Boswell's caravan?' he asked. 'We still haven't turned anything else up, I'm afraid.'

Parker smiled. 'No, don't worry. I'm sure you've done your best. Please, sit down.' He gestured to the vacant chair. Lewis sat, wondering what was coming. Parker lit a cigarette and by way of concession, blew a cloud of smoke out of the side of his mouth. 'Listen, my friend,' he began. 'I know how thorough you, and your lads, are. Missing the cards was an easy mistake,' he said magnanimously. 'Anyone could have done it.'

Lewis was becoming increasingly suspicious. Parker was never this friendly.

'Let's forget about Boswell's caravan. Instead, I think *we* should concentrate on the other one.'

'What, Ivy Rose Lee's?' Lewis was baffled. That had been thoroughly searched some time before.

'No, the other fortune teller – Pilgrim what'sisname.'

'Petulengro?'

'That's the kiddy.'

'But we've already done that one. We went over it as soon as it was found.'

Parker nodded knowingly. 'Yes, I'm sure you did. But… I don't like to bring it up again. You did miss the cards, didn't you?' He folded his arms, the cigarette dangling from his lip.

Lewis couldn't argue that one, although he was still baffled as to how it had been missed. So, to placate the man he said: 'Of course, I'll take another look.'

'There's a good chap. Let me know if you turn anything else up.'

~o~

Pint-sized Charlie was not well. One minute he was shivering with cold, the next he was sweating like a pig. He felt constricted by his clothes and just couldn't get comfortable. In fact he felt like death warmed up. He reckoned one of the punters at the fair had passed on something to him. Normally he prided himself on having the constitution of an ox – a creature he closely resembled – but whatever it was that he'd picked up made him feel terrible. He'd been sneezing so much that his eyes constantly streamed, blurring his vision, and he'd had trouble concentrating on driving. It was starting to grow dark and he didn't know the way to Tenterden very well.

To compound his misery he'd taken a wrong turning, driving the truck and caravan up a lane that was far too narrow for them. The lane became a track with grass growing along the centre; thick bushes either side restricted the width even more. Finally the headlights of the lorry showed that it ended in an open gateway, leading into a fallow field. Cursing, he tried turning the vehicles, making numerous manoeuvres, but a combination of the narrow lane and his weakened state meant he ended up with the caravan solidly wedged against a tree. Normally he would have persevered until he'd freed it but he was feeling so rough he just gave up. Switching off the engine he sat for several minutes with his head on the steering wheel. He realised he was drifting into a feverish sleep, but couldn't help himself.

He woke several hours later. It was pitch black, his body was stiff and he was shivering with fever. With an almost superhuman effort he hauled himself out of the cab, stumbling and nearly falling as he stepped on to the ground. Purely by luck it was the back of caravan that was jammed against the oak tree and he was relieved as he felt his way along the body and his hand found the door handle. He knew the interior so well that was able to locate a drawer and take out a box of Swan Vestas. As he slid the tray of the box open his hands were shaking so badly that most of the contents scattered across the floor. He was just able to save one, and with difficulty, struck it. By its light he could see a stub of candle stuck on a worktop and managed to light the wick before the match burned right down to his fingers. Just the effort of doing this was too much and he slumped down on the sofa. He had just enough strength left to swing his legs up before he slipped into a deep, dreamless sleep.

~o~

Lewis had arrived in the Morris J-type van. When the engine was switched off there was just the sound of nature: the bubbling chatter of a reed warbler; the cooing of wood pigeons. He made his way to the caravan and mounted the steps.

'Blast!' he exclaimed out loud. 'I've forgotten the bloody key. Now I'll have to go back.' In his annoyance he shook the chain. Unexpectedly the padlock fell open. 'Strange. I thought I'd locked it securely when we left. Ah well, Parker's right, I must be losing my touch.' He entered the caravan and stood, hands on hips, looking round. He knew they'd been thorough before but after the gaffe with the pack of cards he was starting to doubt himself. So, with a sigh, he began another meticulous search.

After half an hour and finding nothing he was about to give up. Then he realised he hadn't looked inside the stove – again. He knelt in front of the range. Several days of neglect, and the damp riverside atmosphere, had dulled the metal surface and spots of orange rust were beginning to show. The door opened with a creak. Inside, the grate was covered with a thick layer of cold, grey ash. He looked about for a poker so he could prod around inside. He could just see a brass handle sticking out from under the stove.

As he pulled, it disturbed a piece of fabric lodged in the narrow space. Carefully, he pulled it free.

'What the…?' It was a red spotted scarf. He unfolded it and saw it had rusty marks on it, faint but clear on the white spots. He sniffed. A faint but distinctive metallic smell of blood. A shiver ran down his spine. He was baffled. How the hell had they missed that? There was nothing for it but to go back and test for the blood group. Then, he supposed, he would have to grovel to Bonnie Parker. He wasn't looking forward to another humiliation.

~O~

After they left the Salts Russell drove Bruissement back to his railway-carriage home at Shinglesea. Sitting on the little bench in the shingle garden, drinking tea and enjoying a slice of Joan Spratt's renowned fruit cake, they discussed what they'd heard.

'I wonder if there's any truth in what Nettie said?'

'About the man working on that piece of equipment – what was its name?' Bruissement asked.

'The Waltzer. It's a kind of carousel with moving cars.'

'I see. It does not sound like the sort of thing that would make me 'appy.'

Russell gave a little chuckle. 'No, I doubt if it would. I don't see you on any fairground ride.'

The Frenchman took a sip from his cup. 'Well, perhaps the carousel *ordinaire*.'

The chuckle turned into a laugh. 'Maybe we should visit the fair in Tenterden and we can both go on it.'

'Perhaps…'

They sat in companionable quiet, drinking tea and eating cake. Wisps of white drifted lazily across the azure sky; a pair of common blue butterflies performed an intricate whirling dance over the newly emerged creamy-white flowers of the sea kale. The mournful, rising note of a curlew's call came floating across from the beach; a wren perched on the chestnut fence, tail bobbing.

'Anyway, what do you make of her idea?'

Bruissement dabbed his moustache with a handkerchief. 'It is perhaps possible, I suppose. Is there not another person – as you say – inside the frame?'

'I don't think so – no one comes to mind.'

'What about the man Bonnie Parker has in custody?'

'Boswell? Pah! I don't think so.'

'*Mais pourqoi pas*?'

Russell frowned and thought for a moment. 'I've never actually met the man – only seen him at a distance. But, from what I've heard, I don't think he's got it in him. He might seem tough, but I would imagine the fair, and running it, is his life. And he wouldn't want to jeopardise that. Plus I get the feeling that he and Petulengro were good friends.'

'But I thought 'e told Weeks and Nettie that 'e did not like the man so much.'

'He did, but I don't think that he was telling the truth – maybe covering up.'

'*Pourquoi*?'

'I don't know but I reckon they were actually mates.'

'Well, if you are right, the man who is from the Waltzer seems to be a suspect most likely.'

Russell nodded. 'That's right.'

'But Bonnie Parker does not think so.'

'No, he doesn't.'

'Is there not something that can be done about it by you?'

'I don't think so. I'm off the case and if I interfere, the Super won't be pleased.' Russell collected the tea things and put them on the tray. As he picked it up to take it inside he said: 'We've got a couple of hours before we need to leave for Isobel's. Do you fancy a walk to the beach?'

'But of course. It would be a pleasure.' Bruissement leaned forward and stroked the terrier's head. 'I expect Aggie will be delighted to 'ave a run.'

~o~

The tide was out a little way, leaving a strip of sand below the shingle bank where Aggie could dash about. The two men sat on a tree trunk that had been washed up by the winter storms. They took it in turns to throw a stick which the terrier delighted in retrieving, bringing it back to drop at their feet and wait expectantly for the next throw, tail wagging. The wind was from the land, causing waves to heap up, several dozen yards offshore. Gulls sat on the water, rising and falling with the swell. Every now and again a wave crest broke just behind them and they rose lazily in the air, then just as easily settled back on the smoothed surface until the next wave.

After he had thrown the stick again Russell said: 'So your boss did not think you should have confronted the smugglers?'

Bruissement snorted. 'That is, as you say, an understatement! He does not think that men who try to make a little extra money by avoiding taxes are *particulièrement* illegal.'

'But what about the injury to your arm?'

'Pff! That was my fault. I should not have challenged the man. Then 'e would not 'ave pushed me and I would not 'ave fallen.' He lifted his arm in the sling. 'It is not so bad. And anyway, it 'as given me the chance to spend time with *mon bon ami*.' His face formed a huge grin, the moustache lifting at the corners.

'Are you not going to do anything about it?'

The Frenchman shrugged. 'What can I do?'

'Don't you know who they are – the men you saw on the beach?'

'Perhaps. Wissant is a small town. *Ce ne serait pas difficile* to find out who it was.'

'Why don't you then, my friend?'

Another shrug. 'Even if I did, my boss would not be willing to prosecute. 'E would not think it to be worth the while.'

'That's a shame. Mind you, I suspect my boss, Superintendent Stout, would probably feel the same.'

'So why are you pursuing Jack Mills?'

Russell shrugged and gave a wry smile. 'I'm not sure. I suppose I like to be busy. And as I'm off the murder case it gives me something to do.'

The Frenchman put his free hand on Russell's arm. 'You should learn to be relaxed, *mon ami*.'

''I am, really,' Russell laughed. 'Especially in your company.'

'You are too kind.' Bruissement bowed his head.

They sat for a while, watching Aggie try unsuccessfully to chase gulls, dabbling at the water's edge. The birds took off before she got anywhere near them; the terrier unworried, happy just to run.

Russell pulled back the cuff of his jacket and looked at his watch. The face was still cracked but it was going again. 'It's still a bit early to go to Isobel's. Shall we have a look round Nottery Quay?'

'I would like that very much. I understand it is a very nice town.'

He smiled. 'Well, I think it is, but then I would.'

~o~

An ex-army truck towing a twin-wheeled, cream-coloured caravan turned on to the Dungeness estate. The purposeful vehicle was still painted in its wartime khaki livery; the canvas back had faded but still looked to be in good condition. After half a mile the driver changed down to a low gear, took a sharp left and bumped off the metalled road and on to a rough, stony track. The truck took the surface in its stride but the caravan rolled precariously from side to side, like a yacht running before the wind. The track ended on a shingle ridge above the beach and the truck came to a halt. The driver switched off the engine, climbed down from the cab and stood looking out to sea. The only sounds were of the waves rolling in, the insistent piping of an oystercatcher and the *slap, slap, slap* of a halliard as it flapped against the stubby mast of a fishing boat, pulled up on the beach. The man held his arms out, stretched and sighed deeply. This would do nicely.

''Ere! What are you doin'? A figure had appeared from behind the boat. He was wearing the tan smock of a fisherman. 'You can't park that 'ere. This is a private beach.' He folded his arms across his stick-thin body.

'I don't see a notice anywhere,' the man answered. He looked around, swivelling his head in an exaggerated manner.

'Maybe you don't, but it's still private, reserved for us legitimate fishermen.'

'And what if I was to park here? What would you do about it?' The man had taken a few paces forward and was face to face with the fisherman, a couple of feet between them.

The fisherman stood his ground. 'Now listen. I don't want no trouble. I suggest you turn that thing around and go back where you came from.'

The stranger gave a sharp laugh. He was more than twice the size of the other man. Putting his hands on his hips he spoke. 'As I said, what are you going to do about it?'

The fisherman took a pace backwards. 'I'm not alone,' he said.

The stranger made a show of looking round again. 'Ha! You're bluffing. I don't see anyone coming to your rescue. I suggest you toddle off and leave me in peace. I'm parking here.'

Emboldened the skinny man stepped forward, reached out and prodded the stranger in the chest. 'Don't come it. I want you gone.'

'Oh you do, do you?' the stranger returned the prod, but he was much so much bigger and stronger that it knocked the fisherman off balance. He stumbled, his heel caught on a piece of chain lying on the ground and he fell backwards. His head hit the upturned rusty fluke of an anchor with a sickening crunch.

~o~

Back at the station Wickstead was troubled. Bonnie Parker's unnaturally friendly manner had put him on edge. It just wasn't like the man to be so pleasant. He was so used to the DI being sour and bad tempered that the cheerful demeanour just didn't sit right.

The sergeant had known him for many years, seen him rise up through the ranks from humble PC and remembered that, even then, he wasn't a very good copper. He'd cultivated a knack of doing very little and making it look like a lot. He had been good at passing the buck and getting other, more able beat bobbies into trouble when they didn't deserve it. But somehow he'd wormed his way into the CID, first as a detective constable then rising far too swiftly to his present status as a detective inspector.

His nickname, *Bonnie* Parker, after the infamous American gangster, had stuck. Wickstead knew he was secretly proud of it, although he pretended to be annoyed if anyone used it in his hearing. The sergeant smiled to himself. Parker obviously didn't realise that the real Bonnie was the female half of the notorious pair and it was *his* sidekick, DC Clyde Barrow, who was the male half. Also that the US pair were highly successful in an unpleasant way whereas the British Parker and Barrow were, at best, inept.

Wickstead knew very little about Parker's life outside the station. He knew he was married and rumour had it the wife was as sour as the husband. He'd visited their house once to deliver a message when Parker was sick. The front garden of the semi in a backstreet in Collinghurst was weedy and overgrown; the front-room window was streaked with grime; the curtains looked like they could do with a wash. He'd knocked on the door and, after a while, it had been opened by Mrs Parker. She was wearing a grimy wrapover housecoat. Obviously a heavy smoker like her husband, a part-smoked cigarette dangled from her mouth. When she spoke the inch of ash fell, peppering the grubby fabric. The sergeant had relayed the message as quickly as possible, eager to get away from the unpleasant smell that wafted out of the gloomy hallway of the house. It was no wonder that Parker spent so much time at the station.

~O~

Lewis the fingerprint man had not long returned. Normally he would have stopped for a few minutes, exchanging pleasantries, but today he'd stalked in, barely acknowledging the sergeant. He'd gone straight down the corridor and into Parker's office. Wickstead wondered what was going on. The DI's demeanour was so out of character he couldn't help being suspicious. All was quiet in the station so, lifting the flap on the counter, he headed out of the room and down to the cellar. Knowing how gloomy it would be he had taken the precaution of taking a torch. Switching it on, he swept the powerful beam around the cramped room. Almost immediately it picked up the shard of broken wood on the floor. He crouched down and he picked it up. One edge was dull with age, the other creamy white from a recent break. As he stood he ran the beam along the shelves immediately above where he had found it and saw the splintered edge. He held the piece of wood up to it. It matched. Playing the beam higher he could see a space. He was sure that was where the box containing Vado Boswell's clothes had been. He spent a few more minutes searching the other shelves until he found the new-looking carton, wedge between two older boxes. He slid it out. Boswell's clothes were there as he remembered. It had been his job to log what went in the box. He was puzzled. Something seemed to be missing. He went through the garments again. He would have to check them against the inventory.

~O~

'I'm surprised at you, Lewis. You must be losing your touch,' Parker chuckled. The spotted neckerchief was on the desk between them where the forensics man had laid it.

'I really don't understand,' Lewis said. 'I could have sworn we searched everywhere.'

Parker's lips formed a smile that wouldn't have disgraced a cat that had got the cream. 'Tut tut – first the cards and then this.' He pointed at the scarf with a stubby forefinger. 'Now we have proof.'

'We-ell,' Lewis said slowly. 'I'm not so sure.'

'What do you mean?' The smile had vanished, replaced by a snarl. 'I thought you said the blood was a match for the nancyboy Petulengro?'

'Yes, I did.'

'And it was on the pikey Boswell's scarf?'

'It would seem so.'

'What's the problem then?'

Lewis was quiet for a moment.

'Well?'

'It just seems strange that the scarf turned up in Petulengro's caravan.'

'What are you suggesting?'

'I'm pretty sure he was wearing it when he was arrested.'

'No, he couldn't have been,' Parker said quickly. 'All his stuff was put in a box in the basement. Wickstead should have the inventory – you can check.'

'Yes, I will.'

'You do that.' Parker started shuffling papers on his desk, being careful not to touch the scarf. After a few moments he looked up, his face a picture of innocence. 'Aren't you going to check then?'

'I suppose so.' Lewis was far from happy.

Parker pointed at the neckerchief. 'And take this please. I don't want anyone accusing me of tampering with evidence.'

~O~

Russell parked the Ford Popular at the bottom of Seahorse Street and they got out of the car. Bruissement stood, one hand on his hip, the other across his chest in the sling, looking up the road. '*Mon Dieu*! That is *une rue magnifique*!'

'It is pretty, isn't it?'

The street rose steeply, its surface paved with rounded cobbles. As they climbed they passed black and white, half-timbered houses, some cloaked with hanging pegtiles or faced with Tudor brick. Towards the top, on the left, they stopped in front of the handsome façade of the Seahorse Inn. On the wall next to the steps leading up to the front door was written:

The Seahorse
Rebuilt 1420

'Rebuilt?' Bruissement said, puffing after the effort of climbing the hill.

'Yes, your lot kept coming over and burning it down.' Russell chuckled.

His companion looked baffled.

'In the days when our countries were at war with each other, they took it in turns. One year our men would go over and sack Boulogne, burning and pillaging – the following one the French would come over and do the same here. Thankfully that's a thing of the past. You'll get a warm welcome now.'

'Shall we have an aperitif then?' Bruissement's eyes twinkled. ''Opefully *they* keep a good cellar.'

The two men entered the inn and walked along the narrow, beamed corridor and down into the bar. They took their drinks and sat down in a pair of plush armchairs next to the Giant's fireplace. This deep inglenook was lined with Tudor brickwork and stretched the whole width of the room. A couple of large logs smouldered on top of a pile of ash in the centre; an elaborate iron crane hung over the fire with a soot-blackened pot suspended on a chain.

Bruissement sipped at his glass of claret. 'Yes, the landlord does keep a good cellar,' he said. 'À *votre santé*.' He clinked glasses with Russell.

'Cheers,' Russell returned. 'How long do you think you'll be able to stay?'

'*Pourqoi*? 'Ave you 'ad enough of me?'

The DI laughed. 'Of course not, my friend. You are welcome to stay as long as you like. I was just thinking about what else you might like to do.'

It was the Frenchman's turn to laugh. 'I do not think I need to do anything very much. I am just enjoying 'aving the company of you and making a visit to your delightful part of *Angleterre*.'

'As long as you're not bored.'

'Pff! Never!'

'Good. Then drink up. We should make our way to Isobel's.'

They drained their glasses, left the inn and carried on up to the top of Seahorse Street and turned right into another cobbled road. A turn to the left and St Mary's church came into view. The medieval structure stood in the centre of the citadel at the highest point, surrounded by equally old houses – a sturdy stone mother hen with her half-timbered chicks gathered round her.

As they approached, Bruissement stopped in his tracks. '*Merveilleuse*!'

'It is rather splendid, isn't it?' Russell agreed.

'So is this where the *délicieuse* Isobel lives?'

'Over there,' Russell said, pointing to the row of black and white houses, just beyond the wall round the graveyard. They made their way past the church and along the path between the ancient moss-covered tombstones. A few more paces and they reached a row of half-timbered buildings. Each one had blackened beams framing whitewashed panels decorated with simple pargeting. Tradition had it that many of the oak beams had come from sailing ships, wrecked along the coast. They certainly looked as if they had weathered many storms. Between the beams the windows were small, with lead strips framing diamond panes of glass. Each house had a substantial oak front door, once a defence against marauding Frenchmen and smugglers, as well as the revenue men seeking them out. But these threats belonged to a past long gone; the doors now concealed homely interiors. Russell led Bruissement down an alleyway between two of these dwellings. The passage was narrow with a low ceiling but they soon came out into a more open space. On the right was another cottage. Russell lifted the brass anchor-shaped knocker and sounded a rat-a-tat-tat. No sooner had the last knock faded than the door opened and Isobel stood there, smiling at the men. She looked stunning. Her flame red hair was swept back and twisted into a sophisticated chignon at the nape of her neck. She was wearing an emerald green silk dress with a dropped waist – more 1920s than 1950s – but it suited her colouring perfectly. Her makeup was light and subtle and Russell could smell a waft of floral perfume.

He leaned forward and, taking her hands in his, kissed her lightly on the lips. 'You look marvellous.'

'Thank you, kind Sir.' Letting go of his hands she turned to Bruissement. 'Lovely to see you again, Guillaume.'

The Frenchman put his good arm lightly round her waist and kissed her on both cheeks. He stood back and beamed. 'Sonny is a very lucky man.'

A blush rose up her neck. 'Enough of your Gallic nonsense. Come into my humble abode.' She turned and led them into the cottage.

They had just sat down at the table and Isobel had placed bowls of soup in front of them when there was a hammering on the door. 'Who on earth could that be?' she said. 'Excuse me for a moment; I'll get rid of whoever is disturbing us.'

A few seconds later DC Weeks burst into the room, his mop of curly hair looking more dishevelled than ever. 'There's been another death!' he stammered.

'Easy lad. Slow down – take your time.'

'Sorry, Sir. I didn't mean to burst in on you. It's just I can't get hold of Bonnie Parker and I didn't know what else to do.'

'What's happened? Can't be another fortune teller, can it?'

Weeks couldn't resist a smile – then was serious. 'No, it's a fisherman.'

'Oh? Where?'

'Dungeness. Found dead in a boat.'

'What, drowned?' Russell asked.

'No, the boat was on the shore. Seems he's got a head wound.'

'Any idea who he is?'

'No, the local bobby just rang it in. That's all I know.'

'I suppose you want me to come with you and see what's happened?'

Weeks looked sheepish. 'I hate to intrude on your party…'

'Don't worry. I'm sure Isobel will enjoy Guillaume's company.' He looked at her.

Isobel gave a wry smile. ‘I suppose this is something I’ve got to get used to – my chap going off at all hours.’

‘I’m afraid so – but not too often, I hope.’

~O~

In less than half an hour they were approaching Dungeness. Weeks had finally got the hang of the gears in the Ford Pilot so the journey had been relatively smooth. While they were travelling he had brought his boss up to date with what had been happening.

‘After we had left you at the Salts we had to drive straight back to Collinghurst.’

‘Didn’t you get a chance to interview that chap on the Waltzer again?’ Russell asked.

‘No, we didn’t. Bonnie Parker insisted we go back immediately.’

‘Then he didn’t think there might be another possible suspect?’

‘Far from it. He’s convinced that Boswell committed both the murders.’

‘What happened when you returned to the station?’

‘He told Nettie to go off and do some paperwork – he’s such a dinosaur – and wanted me to sit in while he carried on interviewing Boswell.’

‘How did that go?’

Weeks gave a little laugh. ‘As I’m sure you suspect – not well. Boswell kept insisting that he’s innocent. He even accused Bonnie of trying to frame him.’

‘I bet that went down like a concrete glider.’

‘Funnily enough, Parker hardly reacted. Just sat there with that knowing smile on his face – the one he does so well.’

'Is he any further forward?'

'Not really. The evidence is pretty thin – just the burnt pack of cards and the spotted scarf with bloodstains.'

Russell sat in silence for a while as the Ford hummed along. Then: 'I'm not so sure. If they both link to Boswell, there *could* be a case to answer.'

'That's what Parker reckons, but I don't think so.'

'Why's that, lad?'

Weeks took a large gulp of air. 'If there were fingerprints on either the cards or the scarf then I'd agree – it would be pretty conclusive. Parker hasn't let on to Boswell that there aren't any but I've spoken to Lewis.'

'And what did he say?'

'Well, although he'd conducted some pretty exhaustive tests on the cards, the only prints were smudged and even the partials weren't a match for Boswell.'

'What about the scarf?'

'Nothing. *And* he's convinced it wasn't there when he searched Petulengro's caravan the first time.'

'Then how did it get there?'

'That's a mystery.'

Russell paused in thought again. 'Someone planted it?'

'It's possible.'

'But who?'

'That's another mystery.'

'This case is full of mysteries. But then that's not surprising, considering it revolves around fortune tellers.'

'Anyway, that's why I came looking for you.'

By now they were on the Dungeness estate and Weeks had turned off the road. It had grown dark as they had journeyed from Nottery Quay and the headlights flashed up and down and from side to side like wartime searchlights as the car bumped along the rough track. Shortly they pulled up beside an open fishing boat on the shingle ridge.

The local PC was standing there, the lights picking out his bike propped against the hull. He saluted. 'Evening Inspector.'

'Evening…constable?'

'Fishwick, Sir. PC Fishwick.'

'Right. Who found the body?' Russell asked.

'A local fisherman, Georgie Oiler. He'd come down to check his boat and found the dead man in it.'

'Let's have a look then.' All three men had powerful torches and the combined beams lit up a body, lying on the bottom boards of the boat. Russell reached in and lifted a piece of canvas that was partially concealing the man's head. His hair was matted and dark with dried blood. Carefully the DI turned the head to reveal a deep gash in the skull. 'It appears to be the cause of death, but I'd rather John Crooks confirmed that before we jump to any conclusions.'

'Oh, I took the precaution of ringing him before I left the station, Sir,' Weeks said.

'I bet that didn't please him. Being called out in the evening.'

'Funnily enough he didn't seem bothered.'

'Strange. He usually doesn't like being disturbed when he's gone home.'

Russell was carefully lowering the man's head when he said: 'Hang on! I know who this is.'

'Sir?'

'If I'm not mistaken he's a friend of the landlord of the Red Lion in Appledore. Let me think.' He paused. 'Yes I'm sure. It's Albert Stern. Lives over there.' He pointed back towards the land. 'In Prospect Cottage.' Russell winced at the painful memory of waking after having been bashed on *his* head. Luckily the injury *he* had sustained wasn't so serious.

'The one involved in smuggling duty-free goods?'

'The same – which is strange.'

'Why's that, Sir?'

'It doesn't make sense that this has happened – unless he and Mills fell out…'

The sound of an engine could be heard coming closer, headlights growing brighter. In a few moments a Morris J-type van pulled up beside the Ford Pilot. The elegant figure of Lewis unfolded itself from the driver's side, closely followed by the more rotund shape of the pathologist from the passenger side.

Crooks arched his backed and groaned. 'Not my favourite form of transport but it saved me driving, I suppose.' He walked across to the boat. 'What have we got here then?' he boomed.

'A dead fisherman with a nasty head injury. Just want to make sure he didn't do it himself.'

Crooks had to stand on tiptoe in order to reach into the boat. 'Not much chance of his doing this to himself – unless he was a contortionist. Looks like someone bashed him with a heavy, pointed instrument and then dumped the body in here.' He shone his torch around the inside of the hull. 'There's nothing obvious that could have inflicted such a wound.'

While he and the others had been engaged in observing the dead man, Lewis had been shining his torch on the various objects scattered about the beach. The beam lit up a tangle of worn and sea-stained rope, some rusty chain, a pile of wooden fish boxes and a jumble of rotten fishing nets. Then he spotted something. 'John!' he cried. I think I've found it.' The others turned to look. Lewis's torch beam was shining on an old anchor, the sharp fluke pointing heavenwards.

Crooks walked over and knelt on the stones. He looked closely at the rusty metal spike. 'I think you're right. Looks like blood. And fairly fresh at that.'

'What do you think happened, John?' Russell asked.

'I reckon he must have fallen and ended up bashing his head on this. Judging by the dent in his occiput, death would have been pretty swift, if not instantaneous.'

'Would just falling have been enough to kill him?'

The pathologist considered. 'Hmm, probably not. I suppose he could have been pushed.'

'By the person who dumped him in the boat?' Weeks added.

'Yes, most likely. Help me up lad.' Crooks held his hand out and the DC pulled him to his feet. 'I don't see we can do much here tonight. Any idea what the forecast is – any rain in the offing?'

'I don't think so, John,' Lewis answered. 'As long as no one tramples over the site it should be okay until the morning.'

'How do you feel about standing guard for a while, Fishwick?' Russell asked.

'That's fine, Sir. I only came on at six.'

'Good man – we'll get someone to relieve you later.' He turned towards the pathologist. 'Thanks for coming, John. I know how you hate being disturbed at home.'

Crooks snorted. 'Normally, I'd agree but tonight I was glad to get out of the house. We had a lawyer and his wife to dinner – both tediously boring. This is much more enjoyable. However, I think we've finished here for the evening. Fancy having a drink?'

'I'd love to, but I've got a dinner party to get back to – if I'm still allowed in.'

'Ah, the fragrant Isobel.' Although he couldn't see his face in the gloom Russell could hear the chuckle in the man's voice. 'Better not keep her waiting any longer.'

'That's all right – she's got Guillaume for company.'

'You'd better rush back then, you know what they say about the French!'

Chapter 13

Dungeness *is one of the largest expanses of shingle in Europe. There is a collection of unusual dwellings. Most are wooden weatherboarded beach houses, but there are approximately 30, built in the 1920s, constructed around old railway coaches.*

PARKER WAS in a foul mood. When he'd heard that Weeks had summoned Russell to the incident at Dungeness he was apoplectic with rage.

'Why the hell didn't you try to get hold of me?' he demanded. Before the DC could reply he went on: 'Russell is on leave! *I'm* the senior detective in the station.'

'I did try,' Weeks said mildly. 'But no one knew where you were.'

'I was with the Super!' he thundered.

'But I tried him and he wasn't at home.'

'That's because we were at the golf club – not that it's any of your business.'

Standing in front of the DI's desk, hands clasped in front of him, Weeks remained silent.

'You've been nothing but a nuisance since I generously took you under my wing. I can't wait for DC Barrow to get back to work. At least he knows how to behave.'

'Like a lackey,' Weeks said under his breath.

'What was that?'

'I just said he was lucky – to work with you…Sir.'

'Hmm. Glad you appreciate it. Now, bugger off, I need to talk to the Super. Bring him up to date with this latest development.'

'Er, I think he's busy right now.'

'What do you mean?'

'DI Russell is with him. I'll leave you in peace, Sir.' Weeks scooted out of the office before he was subjected to the broadside he knew would be coming.

~O~

'I told you to take some leave.' Superintendent Vic Stout said. He was sitting behind his large uncluttered desk, one of his customary cheroots smouldering in the glass ashtray.

'I did, Sir.'

'I meant for at least a week.' Russell could see the colour rising in Stout's puffy cheeks.

'But Weeks needed a senior officer last night.'

'He should have found DI Parker.'

'He tried to – with no luck.'

'Couldn't have tried very hard.'

'Sir, DC Weeks is a very diligent officer. He tried very hard to find Parker but he wasn't anywhere to be found.'

'Enough!' Stout banged the flat of his hand down on the desk making the ashtray jump. 'He was with me, if you must know. Discussing the case he took over from you *and* has made progress with. Something you were unable to do.'

'Sir?'

'He's got the murderer in the cell. Going to charge him this morning.'

Russell was dumbfounded. 'Charge him? Has he got sufficient evidence?'

'Enough to pin both murders on the man.'

'But Sir. As I understand it the only evidence is a pack of cards and some bloodstains on a scarf. And it's not certain how they got there.'

The colour in Stout's cheeks had spread to the rest of his face and was fast turning a shade of beetroot. 'Inspector!' he snapped. 'If DI Parker thinks he's got enough evidence then I'm happy to let him go ahead.'

'I think you're making a mistake.'

'*What did you say?*' he snarled. 'How *dare* you question my authority! I suggest you leave Parker to get on with his job and as a concession I'll let you continue with the investigation of the death over at Dungeness. Shouldn't tax you too much – probably a brawl that got out of hand.'

'But what if the deaths are related?'

'What? Preposterous! How could the accidental death of a fisherman, miles away, have anything to do with the deaths of a couple of gypsies over here?'

'I don't know at the moment, Sir. I just have a feeling…'

The cheroot had gone out so Stout stuck it in his mouth and lit it with his Zippo lighter. He sucked hard then blew out a column of smoke. 'You and your blasted *feelings*.'

'What if I'm right?'

'Then you'll have proved me – and Inspector Parker wrong. And I think that's about as likely as men landing on the moon. Now get out before I suspend you indefinitely.'

~o~

Russell left the room, muttering as he walked down the corridor. 'Bloody Bonnie Parker. How does he always manage to get round Stout? How can such an idiot appear at all credible? After all the cock-ups he's made in the past… I just don't get it.'

'Sir?'

While he'd been talking to himself his feet had led him into the open office. Weeks was sitting at his desk, the teetering stack of files threatening to tumble to the floor at any moment. 'Oh, lad. Take no notice.'

'Sounds like someone's really upset you.'

Russell grinned. 'Perceptive as ever. Listen. Does DI Parker need you at the moment?'

'He told me to "bugger off" a while ago, so probably not.'

'How do you fancy coming back over to Dungeness with me? See if we can get any clues as to what happened to Albert Stern.'

'I'd be delighted, Sir.'

'Lewis and Crooks should be there already. We can go and talk to the locals – see if anyone saw or heard anything.'

~o~

'*Weeks? Weeks? **WEEKS!***' Parker's bellowing brought not the DC but Sergeant Wickstead.

'You after DC Weeks, Sir?' the desk sergeant said, leaning round the open door.

'Course I bloody am. That's why I was yelling his name. Where is he?'

'Out, Sir. Gone off with Inspector Russell.'

'*WHAT? WHERE?*'

'Dungeness, I think.'

'I thought Russell had been told to take some leave?'

'Apparently the boss said he can investigate the death over there.'

'First I've heard of it. Doesn't give him permission to pinch my DC.'

'Ahem. Weeks is actually *his* DC.'

'What? Oh yes, I suppose so. Don't expect he'd be much use, anyway. Who else is in the station?'

'Constables Beaumont and Lee are both here, Sir.'

'Good. I want that gyppo, Boswell, brought up from the cells. You'd better hang around too. After last time I've got a feeling he may cause trouble. Stick him in the interview room.'

'Will you wait there for him, Sir?'

'No. *I'll* keep the bugger waiting.'

Boswell was led into the interview room by the two PCs. He'd had little sleep and it showed. There were dark circles under his eyes, his curly blond hair needed a wash and was flattened greasily on his skull. He was wearing a borrowed police shirt and dark blue serge trousers, neither of which fitted, the shirt too tight and the trousers too short. He sat, slumped in the chair, arms folded – chin on chest. He'd been sitting for a good ten minutes. 'When are you going to let me go?' he rasped.

Wickstead was standing by the door with the two constables. 'I'm sorry, Sir. You'll have to wait until DI Parker gets here.'

Boswell looked up. 'Where is he?'

'He's on his way.'

'What's keeping him?'

'I don't know, Sir. I expect he's got some important business to attend to.'

'Ha! *I've* got important business too. I've got a fairground to run.'

They waited a few minutes longer – the silence becoming increasingly uncomfortable. Then the door burst open and Parker strode into the room, a Capstan Full Strength clamped between his smirking lips, a cloud of ash trailing behind him. He sat down heavily opposite Boswell and plonked a file on the table between them.

The fairground owner sat up and looked the policeman straight in the eye. 'So can I go now?'

Parker sat for a long while before answering. 'You're not going anywhere in a hurry, matey.'

'What do you mean?' Boswell's eyes were half-closed, his whole body tense. The words came out as a growl.

'I'm afraid I've got some bad news for you.' Parker was obviously relishing every moment.

'What?'

The DI opened the file and read from a sheet of paper: 'Vado Boswell. You are accused of the murders of Ivy Rose Lee and Pilgrim Petulengro. You will be taken from here and held in custody until…' He got no further as Boswell leapt up, sending his chair flying. He reached across the table, scattering the papers, and tried to grab Parker's throat. In a flash Beaumont and Lee were on him. His arms were pulled back and handcuffs snapped on his wrists.

'Why, you bastard…!' he shouted. 'You haven't got any evidence.'

'Oh yes we have, plenty. And it's probably the hangman's rope for you.'

The chair had been righted and the two constables forced Boswell to sit. 'You can't be serious. I admitted I'd moved Rose

Lee's body – I told you I didn't kill her. *And* Pilgrim was my friend. I didn't kill him – why would I?'

'I don't know but the evidence against you is damning. I suggest you own up to it and hope the judge is lenient.'

Boswell shook his head violently. 'No, no, *NO!* It's not true – you can't pin this on me – it was someone else.'

Parker decided to play the game a little longer. He really was enjoying this. 'Okay. So tell me – if it wasn't you, then who was it?'

'I don't know. I only know you've got the wrong man.'

'I don't think so. You're not going to wriggle out of this now.' The DI started gathering the papers together. 'Take him down. I've got a case to prepare.'

~O~

As Weeks and Russell headed over to Dungeness they chatted. 'Tell me again what Parker said about the worker on the Waltzer,' Russell said.

'Nettie and I tried to get him to let us go over to Tenterden, where the fair had gone, and interview him again. But he's adamant that Boswell is guilty of both murders. And he seems to have persuaded the Super, too.'

'I'm surprised. Despite his faults, Stout usually likes everything cut and dried before he allows any of us to make a decision – especially one that might mean the death penalty.'

'Between you and me, Sir, I think the Super has the same opinion of travellers as Parker. I reckon he wants him to be guilty.'

'But that's terrible. We could be sending an innocent man to the gallows.'

'I know, Sir. But what can we do about it?'

'I'm not sure, right now. But we have to try to do something.' The car hummed along the road. Russell was thoughtful for a while. 'Listen, Johnny. I know it might sound fanciful but I've got an odd feeling that this death – the one we're going to investigate – is somehow linked to the others.'

'Really?'

'Yes. Don't ask me how. Hopefully all will become clear before too long.'

Weeks felt no need to comment. He had become used to his boss's hunches and *feelings* and he knew, however unlikely they at first appeared, they often bore fruit – eventually.

By now they had reached the turning to the beach where the body had been found. 'Park here, lad,' Russell said. 'There's no point in bothering Lewis and Crooks. We'll go over and see if any of the locals can tell us anything.'

On the other side of the road, half a dozen dwellings were spread out. None had a discernible boundary with its neighbour, it was just continuous shingle. In fact there was shingle as far as the eye could see. In this desert of a place wild plants grew in surprising profusion: Santolina, all spindly glaucous leaves and yellow button flowers; Valerian in rich pink, with occasional white blossom; Vipers bugloss with electric blue flowers on upright stems. The first home they came to was a converted railway carriage, not unlike Russell's own, except this one was much more careworn. The structure was essentially the same – a redundant Victorian carriage, but the paint was peeling and a couple of the windows had wooden slats instead of glass. Russell smiled as he knocked on the door. After a few moments it was opened by a wizened figure dressed from head to toe in dark-blue, shapeless clothing. A battered felt hat was rammed down on the small head. It was difficult to tell the sex until the figure spoke.

'Yes?' The croaky voice announced it to be female.

'Hello madam, we're police officers. I wonder if you can help.'

'*What*? You'll have to speak up – I'm deaf.'

Russell raised his voice. '*We're from the police*.'

Alarm crossed the woman's face. 'You can't accuse me of nothing. I ain't left the house for a week.'

'No, we're not accusing you of anything,' the DI said patiently.

'I should think not! What do you want then?'

'I wondered if you'd seen or heard anything – anything unusual in the last day or so?'

The woman frowned, her nut-brown face wrinkled like a walnut. 'I told you, *I'm deaf*! I don't hear anything.'

Russell tried once more. '*But have you seen anything*?'

'What?'

'*Have you seen anything unusual*?'

'Seen anything? No, I broke my glasses.' She cackled, a sound that wouldn't have disgraced one of Macbeth's witches. 'Can't see farther than the end of me nose.'

Russell admitted defeat. '*Thank you anyway*,' he said loudly.

'Don't mention it,' she answered, and closed the door.

'I hope they're not all like that,' Weeks said, as they walked back to the road.

The next house looked more promising. It was a single-story dwelling, the weatherboard-clad exterior tar-black under a tiled roof. An attempt had been made to create a garden with circles of larger stones round trimmed shrubs. The front door looked as if it had been newly painted. From a hook to one side hung a loop of fishing line, threaded with hagstones.

Russell rapped with his knuckles. This time the door was opened by a man who appeared to be a fisherman. He looked to be in his mid-fifties but could have been younger. His face was so weather-beaten it was difficult to tell. He wore a traditional smock, tan coloured like the sails on an old fishing boat, and a Breton cap sat on his head at a jaunty angle. He took the clay pipe out of his mouth and viewed the two policemen with suspicion.

'Yes?'

'Hello, we're making enquiries about an incident on the beach.'

The suspicious look softened. 'Oh, Albie Stern. I 'eard about that.'

'Was he a friend of yours?'

'A friend?' the man snorted. ''Don't think 'e was friends with anyone. Sorry to speak ill of the dead but 'e was a miserable sod.'

'Then you didn't have much to do with him?'

'Well… I sometimes gave 'im an 'and to launch 'is boat. And 'e did the same for me, from time to time. We fishermen tend to 'elp each other out – it's an 'ard life, you know.'

'I imagine it is. I wondered if you'd seen or heard anything in the last couple of days – anything unusual.'

'Let me think.' The man stuck the pipe back between his teeth and sucked hard. The tobacco in the bowl must have still been glowing as after he'd inhaled he blew out a gout of smoke from the corner of his mouth. 'Now you come to mention it there was something a bit odd.'

'Oh? What was that?'

'A caravan.'

'A caravan?'

'Yeah. Big bugger – twin-wheeled job. Had one of them ex-Canadian army trucks towin' it.' The man's eyes glazed over as he relived the memory.

'Where was this, Sir? On the road?' Weeks prompted.

'Well that was the odd thing. It came bumpin' along the track

– away from the beach. Goin' like the clappers – much too fast – rockin' all over the place. Wonder it didn't turn over. Dunno what it was doin' there anyway.'

Russell had a sudden flashback. He felt he'd also seen something like that recently but the exact time and place eluded him. He shook his head. 'When was this, Sir?'

The man sucked on his pipe again. 'Must 'ave been yesterday. He paused. 'Yeah, yesterday – late afternoon I think.'

'Did you see which way it went?'

'It was odd. I thought whoever was drivin' it would 'ead back off the estate.'

'And he didn't?'

No. 'Eaded towards the light'ouse. Obviously didn't know it's a dead end.'

'And that was the last you saw of it – it didn't come back?'

'Dunno. I went indoors to make me tea. Didn't see nothing else.'

Russell looked at Weeks. 'We'd better go and have a look.'

They returned to the Ford Pilot, settled inside and Weeks drove out towards the end of the road. As they approached the impressive structure of the old lighthouse a figure ran out into the road and waved them down. Weeks stood on the brake and the car skidded to a halt. Russell wound the window down as the figure stumbled up to them.

''Ere! You the police?' The man wore a ragged jacket and trousers held up with a length of rope. His thin, straggly hair flew around his head in the breeze and his cheeks were speckled with grey stubble.

'Yes. Is there a problem?'

'There was – but you're too late – as usual!'

Weeks switched off the engine and the two detectives got out of the car. 'What are we too late for, Sir?' Weeks asked.

'Come and look. I'll show you.'

They followed him as he led them along a track and towards another converted railway carriage. His shambling gait and ragged appearance reminded Russell of Ben Gunn in *Treasure Island*, a book he'd loved as a boy. He half expected the man to ask for a piece of cheese. When they reached the dwelling he was surprised to see that it was in a much better state than the one they'd seen earlier. The paintwork looked fresh, the windows sparkled and the bronze door handles gleamed. It even had a neat picket fence around the garden.

The man noticed the policeman's admiring glances. He beamed. 'Proud of me home, I am. Looks after it proper-like. I used to work on the railways. Bought it when I retired. Lived here ever since.' His face darkened. 'Hate it when anyone disturbs me peace.'

'Who disturbed your peace, Sir?' Russell asked gently.

'Bloody idiot with a caravan – 'scuse my French.'

'Oh yes?'

'Yes. Came roaring up here – towing it with an old army lorry – bashed into me gatepost. Look.' He pointed to one of the timbers, leaning at a drunken angle. 'And he left this behind.' They followed him along the fence to a large clump of Euphorbia, the mat of glaucous leaves topped with acid-yellow florets. Tangled up in the plant was a wheel. The tyre had very little tread and when Weeks lifted it upright and rolled it they could see that part was shredded. 'Had the cheek to change it here and leave his rubbish behind.'

'When was this?'

'Yesterday. Getting on for six before he went off.' The man chuckled – Ben Gunn again. 'Drove off a lot slower than when he arrived.'

'Did you speak to him?'

'Me? Not likely! Stayed indoors. Don't like strangers.'

'How come you flagged us down then, Sir?' Weeks asked.

'Ah, that's different. You was driving careful like – knew you was respectable.'

'Did you see the man clearly?'

'See him?' The chuckle became a cackle. 'Couldn't miss him. Built like a Bulleid Pacific.'

'I'm sorry, Sir – a what?'

The man stared at them as if they were gormless. 'A Spam Can.'

The two detectives looked at each other.

'Blimey, don't you know anything? It's a 4-6-2 Southern engine – streamlined. You must have seen them.'

Realisation dawned. Russell chuckled. 'Oh, I see what you mean – a big fellow. I don't suppose you could describe him?'

The man screwed up his eyes and scratched the stubble on his cheek. 'Can't say I took much notice. Just glad when he went away. Wouldn't want to meet the likes of him in a narrow alley on a dark night though.'

'Are you sure you can't remember anything about him?'

The frown deepened and he paused for thought, rubbing his chin. 'He might have had a moustache. Can't be sure.' Suddenly he looked up. 'Anyway. What are you going to do about it?'

'About what, Sir?'

'About me gatepost, of course!' The look he gave suggested they were the idiots not to understand.

'I'll see what I can do,' Russell improvised. 'If there's nothing else you can tell us, we'll be on our way and leave you in peace.'

As they drove back along the road Russell sat slumped in his seat, deep in thought.

'Penny for them,' Weeks said, as he steered round a pothole.

The DI took a while to respond. 'What? Oh, I was just thinking. Something's bugging me.'

'What's that, Sir?'

'That caravan – the one that both he and the fisherman saw. Something's nagging at the back of my brain about it and I just can't bring it to the front. I've got a vague notion that it might be important.'

Before long they'd arrived at the beach. Weeks parked the car next to the familiar shape of Lewis's Morris J-type van. Crooks had apparently suffered the indignity of travelling with him again as he stood next to the boat, fists on hips with his ample stomach bulging.

'Morning, John. Found anything of interest?'

'Apart from a dead body?' He shook his head. 'Afraid not.'

'Do you know how he died?'

'As I suspected – it was the anchor what did for him.'

'And did he fall or was he pushed?'

'Difficult to be certain but I would think the latter.'

'So deliberate or accidental?'

'That I can't say. You find whoever did it and you might discover the truth. Now, if no one minds, I'd like to get back.' He turned to the forensics man. 'Are you ready to go Lewis?'

'I'd quite like to hang around. I still haven't made a thorough search of the area.'

'And *I'd* quite like to have a better look here,' Russell said. 'Weeks, why don't you take John back? I'll hitch a ride with

Lewis later. Then you can find out what's been going on in our absence.'

'Oh good!' Crooks said, rubbing his hands together. 'A ride in a proper car.'

~O~

Jack Mills could feel panic rising when he saw a policeman standing guard outside Prospect Cottage. Instead of slowing, he drove on past it, keeping his speed steady and his eyes straight ahead. He carried on to the end of the road and brought the pickup to a standstill by the lighthouse. With the engine ticking over he sat in his seat, sweat dripping off his forehead and a trickle rolling down between his shoulder blades. What the hell was going on? Why was there a rozzer at Stern's place? Had they found the goods already? 'Think logically,' he said to himself. 'If they've found it, wouldn't they be on the other side of the road, near the derelict shed? Of course they would.' So why was there a policeman outside the cottage? Fear gripped him.

Had Stern ratted on him – told them about the operation to bring fags and booze into the country without paying duty? He couldn't believe Albert would do that – he'd have to implicate himself too and the man wasn't fool enough to do something so stupid – he hoped. So why was the copper there? The trickle of sweat on his back turned to ice. Had something happened to him? He daren't go and enquire – it would look too suspicious. There was nothing for it but to turn round and return to Appledore – hoping no one would spot him.

~O~

Back in Collinghurst DI Parker's mood had quickly gone from pleasure to anger. Initially he'd been cheered by the reappearance of his loyal sidekick, Clyde Barrow. 'Welcome back, son. Are you feeling better now?'

'Much better thank you, Sir.'

'Good. Now I won't have to put up with that waste of space, Weeks.' This pleasure was short lived when the Barrow challenged his motives for charging Vado Boswell with the double murders.

'Sir,' he'd said. 'What if the gypsy *didn't* do it? What if it was someone else – someone with a grudge?' His period of rest while he convalesced had obviously emboldened him.

'Are you questioning my judgment?' Parker's eyes narrowed and the words came out as a growl.

Barrow back-pedalled. 'Er, no. It's just that…

'Just what exactly.'

The DC stood wringing his hands, fearing that he'd gone too far, but decided to press on anyway. 'The evidence is a bit flimsy,' he said, then added, 'Sir.' When the DI didn't respond he continued: 'Just a bit of blood on a scarf and some burnt cards. It's not much, is it?'

There was a pause while Parker took a Capstan Full Strength out of a battered pack. His hands were shaking. 'Now listen, *constable*. If I say there's enough evidence, then there's enough evidence. Savvy?' He rammed the cigarette into his mouth, lit it with a Swan Vesta and sucked hard, making the end glow cherry red.

Defeated, Barrow gave an almost imperceptible nod of his head.

'So. I want you to go over the case and write up a report, making sure everything points to Boswell being the murderer. I want to see that pikey at the end of a rope. I hate the bastard and all his kind. *Now get on with it*!'

Unused to this level of vehemence being directed at him, Barrow was only too happy to leave the room. Perhaps he should have stayed longer on sick leave.

~O~

The body of Albert Stern had been taken away to Collinghurst for a post mortem examination. Lewis was carefully going over the boat where the fisherman had been found. Russell walked round the site, being mindful not to get in the forensic man's way. Normally Aggie would be scampering at his feet but, on this occasion, he had left the little terrier with Guillaume. The Frenchman had been happy to remain in Russell's railway-carriage home. The previous evening he had enjoyed a very pleasant time at Isobel's house and when both men had got back he had regaled Russell with details of the dinner that he'd missed. The DI had felt an unexpected pang of jealousy. Bruissement was an attractive man – and French to boot. Plus he was charming. But, Russell rationalised, he was a good friend and he knew there was really nothing to be jealous of. Even so…

'Sonny!' An excited shout from Lewis broke into his reverie. Russell joined him peering into the boat. 'I think I've found something – look!' He pointed to where two bottom boards met. Wedged in the gap was a piece of card. It appeared to have a blue and white pattern on it. With a gloved hand Lewis eased it out and carefully unfolded it.

'It's another Tarot card!' Russell exclaimed.

'*Justice*. Another of the absent cards.'

'Sorry? Have I missed something?'

'Didn't you know?'

'Know what?'

'There were four cards missing from the pack that was in the stove.'

'Oh, I didn't realise that. I thought there were only two.'

'Of course, you hadn't been told. Two matching ones were found in the mouths of the fortune tellers but there were two further cards.'

'So you think this is one of them?'

'I can't be certain, but it certainly looks like it.'

Russell stood upright and rubbed his back with his knuckles. 'You know what this means?'

'What's that, Sonny?'

'That this death can't be attributed to Vado Boswell. And… it's got to throw doubt on his guilt over the other deaths.'

Lewis stood up and stared at Russell, a serious look on his face. 'And… I need to have a talk with Sergeant Wickstead.'

Chapter 14

***Don Francisco Fonseca** founded his brand in the 1890s. Made using a delicate blend of filler and binder tobaccos from the Vuelta Abajo zone his cigars are dressed in silky tissue paper.*

'I JUST don't understand.' The desk sergeant shook his head slowly from side to side, a perplexed look clouding his features. 'I *always* make a list of the contents before the boxes go down to the cellar.'

'Is there a chance it's in another book?' Lewis was equally baffled.

'No, this is the current one. See? We're only halfway through it.'

'Let me have a closer look.'

Wickstead passed him the ledger. Lewis laid it on the countertop, open between the date before the day Boswell's effects were put into store and the date after. He smoothed the pages flat and leant down, peering closely at the book. He moved even closer and ran his finger down the centre. 'Hold on. Something's not as it should be. I think there's a page missing.'

'What?'

'Look'

Wickstead put on a pair of horn-rimmed spectacles. 'You're right. There's a very faint ridge!'

'Someone's cut it out. And so carefully you can hardly see it. Must have used a razor. Who on earth would do that?' It was Lewis's turn to shake his head.

Wickstead took time to remove his spectacles. 'I think you'd better sit down. I've got a horrible feeling I know what's happened.' When they were seated he explained about DI Parker's interest in Boswell's effects. 'I thought it strange at the time. Why would he be so concerned about some clothes?' He puffed out his cheeks and exhaled noisily. 'But that's not the worst of it. I *know* that Boswell was wearing the spotted scarf when he came in. I remember it quite distinctly.'

'You realise what you're saying is extremely serious?'

'Yes, I do.' The sergeant's voice was low, with a quaver in it. 'I know that Parker was determined to find the gypsy guilty – and maybe he is – but I don't hold with twisting the truth to get a result.'

'I agree. What on earth was the man thinking of?'

'He's desperate to get a result. He's made no bones about the fact that he loathes the gypsy and his kind, especially since Boswell has tried to assault him on several occasions while in custody. Plus, his success rate has been pretty low of late…'

'Not that it was ever wonderful,' Lewis said wryly.

'Quite.' Wickstead stroked his moustache. 'What do you think we ought to do?'

'We could take it straight to Superintendent Stout.'

'Trouble is, I think he's of the same opinion as Bonnie Parker.'

'What's that?' Lewis asked.

'That all gypsies are guilty of something and they need putting in prison.' Wickstead's tone made it clear that he didn't agree.

'Hmm. That certainly makes it tricky.'

'What *do* we do then?'

Lewis looked thoughtful. 'Does Sonny Russell know about this?'

'No. you're the only person I've told.'

'Perhaps we should tell him.'

'That's a thought.'

'Then he could approach the Super.'

'Trouble is he's not Stout's favourite person at the moment.'

'But he can be quite persuasive – more than you or I could.'

~O~

For once Russell had been invited to sit – and had been sitting for some time before the Super spoke. He'd had to wait while his boss carefully selected a cheroot from the tin on his desk and rolled it by his ear, as if it was a Fonseco Churchill cigar. He then took his time to light it with his Zippo lighter, suck the smoke deep into his lungs and hold it for a surprisingly long time before blowing out a blue cloud. 'Let me get this straight,' Stout said finally. 'You're suggesting that DI Parker falsified evidence?'

'I'm afraid so, Sir.'

'You do realise that this is a very serious allegation.' It was a statement, not a question. 'If there is any truth in this, I will have to take action. Do you actually have any hard evidence?'

'There's the log.'

Stout flicked through the pages of the ledger. 'Wickstead could just have forgotten to enter the details.'

'You know how conscientious he is, Sir.'

'Yes, yes,' the Super said, waving his arm, scattering ash from the cheroot he was holding.

'And you can see where the page has been cut out.'

'I'm afraid I don't agree. It just looks like part of the book binding.'

'But what about the neckerchief?'

'Again, it's just Wickstead's word against the DI's.'

'But why should he lie?' Russell could feel his temper rising.

'Calm down, Inspector. I'm not suggesting he lied, just that he was mistaken.'

Russell realised he wouldn't get anywhere if he continued in this vein so he changed tack. 'What about the card we found in the boat?'

'The Tarot card?'

'That's right.'

Stout took one last drag of his cigar and stubbed it out in the heavy glass ashtray. 'Coincidence.'

'But it matches the others – the ones found in the fortune tellers' mouths and in the pack that was discovered in the stove in Boswell's van.'

Stout tipped his chair back and linked his fingers across his chest. 'Tell me. Is it a particularly special deck of cards?'

'How do you mean, Sir?'

'Could I buy a pack – just like that?'

'I should imagine so. I don't think it was especially rare or anything.' With a sinking heart, Russell could see where this was going.

'Then is it not possible that the card you found could have come from another, similar deck?'

'I suppose so, Sir.'

'So it could be pure coincidence that it was there.' Another statement. 'I'm afraid I'm inclined think there's no connection and that DI Parker is still on the right track.'

'But Sir…'

'Listen, Inspector. I was prepared to give you the benefit of the doubt but you've given me no good reason to change my mind.' He sat up and straightened the papers on his desk. 'The charge still stands against Boswell. I suggest you get back to investigating the death of the unfortunate man in Dungeness and leave Parker to carry on with his good work. Understand?'

'Yes, Sir. But I'm not happy about it.'

Colour started rising from Stout's collar. Russell recognised the signs. The next sentence came out as a growl. 'You're not here to be happy – you're here to do police work. Now get on with it!'

~O~

Lewis wore a troubled look. 'So the Superintendent is prepared to go along with Parker's deductions?'

'And allow a probably innocent man to stand trial for murder – yes.' Russell agreed.

'Are you sure there's nothing we can do?' Wickstead asked. Russell shrugged and shook his head.

The three men were sitting in Russell's compact office. He'd outlined what Stout had said and they'd discussed what options there were. 'He won't allow me to be involved so *my* hands are tied.'

'What about DC Weeks?' Wickstead asked.

'I'm not sure. Parker has got his faithful sidekick Clyde Barrow back so Johnny will be surplus to requirements.'

They sat in silence for some moments until Lewis looked up and spoke. 'Listen. Could you get Weeks to suggest that it would be a good idea to talk to the fairground people? Find out what Boswell was like – how he treated them, that sort of thing.

Chances are Parker won't want the bother of doing the interviews himself and will probably suggest that Weeks does it.'

Russell rubbed his chin. 'Hmm. That might be a way to find out more.' He nodded. 'Yes, I think it's worth a try.'

~o~

There was a light tap on the door. '*Come*!' Parker commanded. Then, seeing it was Weeks: 'Oh, it's you. I thought you were back with Russell?'

'No, Sir. He doesn't need me at the moment.'

'Right. And neither do I. I've got my own DC here, who at least is capable of following my orders.' Barrow sat opposite the DI, smirking. 'So if there's nothing else, you can bugger off again.'

'There is one thing,' Weeks said, quietly.

Parker let out a heartfelt sigh. 'I suppose you'd better tell me. You're obviously not leaving until you do.'

'It's just a suggestion, Sir. I've been thinking about how you could make a stronger case against Boswell.'

'Go on then – spit it out.'

'Well, if you were to talk to the people who work in his funfair you might find out if he was unpopular. Perhaps they hold grudges against the man.'

Parker nodded slowly. 'It's a thought, I suppose. Trouble is I'm tied up here with Boswell himself.' He pulled back a grubby shirt cuff and consulted his watch. 'He's due in the interview room shortly.'

Weeks looked pointedly at Barrow. 'Perhaps you could send *your* DC?'

'No, I want him with me.' Parker's reply was abrupt.

'I could go – if you like,' Weeks volunteered.

'I suppose so – if I can trust you not to hash it up.'

'Yes, you can, Sir.'

'All right. And take that wopsie with you again.'

'WPC Sharpe?'

'That's the one. Those fairground types are bound to like a bit of skirt. Might make them more talkative.'

'Right, Sir.'

When the DC hesitated, Parker said: 'Go on then. Get your arse over to Nottery Quay.'

'But the funfair was on the move when we were there earlier.'

Parker gave a huge sigh. He spoke slowly, as if Weeks was a small child. 'There might be some stragglers left. If not, find out where they've gone and go there.'

~O~

'Well done, Johnny. I knew you could do it.' Russell had a huge grin on his face.

'I didn't think he'd go for it so easily. I was quaking in my boots.'

'Oh I had faith that he would. He's a lazy sod – anything for an easy life. I wish I was going with you but I don't think that would be wise, under the current circumstances.'

~O~

Weeks stopped the Ford Pilot by the Salts.

'Oh heck,' Nettie said. 'They've nearly all gone.'

'Just as we'd expected. Look, Boswell's truck and caravan are still there.'

'That's strange. I thought if they hadn't been impounded someone would have driven them on to the next site.'

The two walked across towards the vehicles. Just a couple of caravans and some part-dismantled stalls stood forlornly in the flattened field. Where dozens of feet had milled around, the grass was bruised and battered. In a number of places it was scorched brown where fires had been lit; in others it was stained black, from oil that had leaked on to it.

Nettie felt a wave of sadness wash over her; that feeling you get when the fair has left town. Nostalgia for a fleeting and false gaiety. Candyfloss and hamburgers. Eager faces, hoping to win some tacky reward. "Roll up! Roll up! A prize every time!"

'Look,' Weeks said suddenly, 'there's someone in the van!' A curtain twitched and fell back into place.

'I bet it's his lad, Duke.' Nettie turned to the DC. 'Listen, why don't you go off and chat to anyone who's left. He might respond better if I see him on my own.'

'Good idea. I'll do that.'

While Weeks went off Nettie climbed the steps to the caravan. She knocked tentatively on the door. There was silence from inside. She tried again, a little harder. Still nothing. Set in the door was a polished brass letterbox. She crouched and pushed the flap open.

'Duke,' she called. 'I know you're in there. Could we have a chat?'

'Go away!' The voice was muffled but had a distinct tremor in it.

'I only want to talk.' Nettie tried to sound her most calming and persuasive.

'I don't wanna see no one. I just want my dad back.'

'That's what I want to talk to you about.'

'*You're lying*!' The words came out as a shout.

The WPC tried a different approach. 'You must be hungry.'

'So?'

'I'll buy you a hotdog.'

'Yeah, you say that. Then you'll take me to an 'ome.'

'No, I won't.'

'Promise?'

'I promise.' Nettie's face twisted in anguish; her fingers crossed behind her back. She heard light footsteps crossing the floor. A key turned in the lock; the door opened a crack.

A grubby face peered out. 'You on your own?' the boy asked suspiciously.

'Yes, only me.'

'Right. Just a hotdog then I can go back?'

Nettie slowly let out the breath she'd been holding. 'Of course.'

The door opened farther, just enough to let Duke slide out. He closed the door and locked it firmly. Without much hope the WPC held her hand towards him. Automatically his grubby mitt closed in hers. They walked over to Terry's van. She ordered a hot dog, chips and a Tizer for Duke and a tea for herself.

'When did you last eat?' she asked while they waited.

'Dunno.' Duke had taken his hand back and thrust it in the pocket of his grimy shorts. His chin was on his chest; he kicked idly at the ground with a booted foot. 'Found some cheese and a crust in the van.'

'You must be starving.'

He gave a non-committal shrug. When the food appeared they took it over to a table. Almost before they'd sat down Duke had grabbed the hotdog and started stuffing it in his mouth, followed by the chips. In less than a couple of minutes it was gone and he was sucking greedily on the straw sticking out of the top of the Tizer bottle. The contents of that too disappeared in a matter of seconds. He sat back in the chair, let out a loud belch and wiped the back of his hand across his mouth.

'Would you like another?'

Again the shrug. 'Don't mind.'

'Stay there then.'

Praying that he wouldn't run off, Nettie went back to the tea van. Surreptitiously she watched the boy as she waited. She was relieved to see he was making no effort to abscond. He was just sitting, staring into space and idly biting the skin on the side of a finger. When she returned with a further course he hadn't moved. This time he ate more slowly, savouring the food.

'Tell me why the funfair people didn't take you with them,' she prompted.

'Why?'

'Yes.'

'Because I didn't want to go. I want to wait here 'til my dad gets back.'

'But that might be for a while.'

'Don't care. I ain't goin' nowhere.' He folded his arms, his face set in a belligerent scowl. 'An', the council ain't taking the truck away. I've 'id the key an' I ain't tellin' no one where it is.'

'Listen, if I could find you somewhere to stay – until your dad comes back – would you go?'

'Depends.'

'On what?'

'Who it is and where it is.' He looked up, a haunted stare marring his young features. ''Ere! It ain't an 'ome, is it?'

Nettie thought furiously. Where the hell could he go? 'No, it won't be a home. Can I trust you to stay here for five minutes?'

The boy grinned suddenly. 'If you get me another drink – an' a doughnut.'

~O~

'Johnny. I've told Duke that I'll find him somewhere to stay. I'm racking my brains to think of where he can go.'

'I can't take him. My place is far too small and besides, I'm hardly ever there. Let me think.' The DC's shoulders slumped and he rubbed his chin, thoughtful for a while. Then he looked up and pushed his thick fringe off his forehead. 'I've just had a thought.'

'Oh yes?'

'He trusts you, doesn't he?'

'He does.'

'And your brother is about the same age as him?'

'Michael? Yes, why?'

'I wondered if they'd get on.'

'I hadn't thought of that.' Nettie glanced back towards the tea van. Duke hadn't moved. He was still sitting at the table, showing no sign of wanting to run off.

'Do you think your mum would put him up?'

'She might. There's enough room in the house for him.'

'It would only be for a short time – until his dad is released.'

'*If* he's released.'

'He will be,' Weeks said confidently. 'DI Russell thinks he's innocent, and so do I.'

'Me too,' Nettie agreed. 'But we've still got to find the real killer.'

'I know, but I don't think he's here,' Weeks said. 'The few people who are left all say that Boswell is a good boss – treats them fairly and never cheats them.'

'So nothing to back up Bonnie's hopes that he was unpopular or difficult?'

'Far from it.'

'I suppose we'll have to go over to Tenterden and talk to the others.'

'Looks like it. Do you think we could drop Duke at your mum's on the way?'

'I suppose so. I just hope he's willing to go – and she's happy to have him.' She stood looking thoughtful for a few moments, then made up her mind. 'All right, let's get on with it.'

They were walking back across the battered grass when Weeks suddenly stopped. He looked round and scanned the site. 'That's odd.'

'What is?' Nettie asked.

'Gypsy Rose Lee's caravan has gone.'

'So it has. Perhaps the other travellers took it.'

'Probably.'

'Why don't you ask the stragglers while I talk to Duke? He might be suspicious if you're there when I put our proposal to him.'

~O~

'You tryin' to trick me?' Duke's brows were lowered, making him look like a young bull about to charge.

'Of course not. We're friends, aren't we? You do trust me, don't you?'

The brows lifted and the boy sighed. 'S'pose so. Ain't no one else I can trust.'

'Right then.' Nettie was business-like. 'How d'you fancy a ride in a police car?'

Duke's eyes lit up. 'Can we 'ave the bell goin'?'

The WPC chuckled. 'Not sure about that, but it should be fun. Shall we go and find Johnny?'

'Has *he* got to come?'

'I'm afraid so. He's the driver.'

'Right. But no funny business. I *ain't* goin' in an 'ome. Okay?'

'Of course. I wouldn't dream of it.'

~O~

Nettie's family lived in a large, detached house on the outskirts of Collinghurst. Weeks was surprised to see a gravel drive curving round in front of the building with two exits.

'Don't get too excited,' the WPC said. 'We don't own it. My dad's a vicar and it goes with the job. It's not as grand as it appears.'

'Looks all right to me,' Weeks said as he pulled up outside the house. Duke was obviously impressed too although he was trying hard not to show it.

Nettie got out of the car first. 'Stay here while I speak to mum. Don't want to give her too much of a surprise.' She disappeared inside the front door, returning shortly with an elegant-looking woman; an older version of her daughter. She stood on the step with Nettie, smiling warmly while Weeks and Duke made their way towards them, the boy dragging his heels and scowling. As soon as they reached them the woman crouched so that she was on the boy's level and spoke to him.

'You must be Duke. What a lovely name.'

'S'alright.' He stared at the ground, hands in pockets, one toe kicking the step.

'Would you like to come in and have a look round?'

He shrugged. 'Don't mind.'

'I'm afraid that my son Michael isn't home from school yet. But he shouldn't be long.'

Duke looked up alarmed.

Mrs Sharpe touched him lightly on the shoulder. 'Don't worry, he must be about the same age as you. He's very nice. Come on. There's some lemonade in the kitchen. And I've just baked scones.'

~O~

'That went better than I'd expected,' Nettie said, as they travelled towards Tenterden. 'I thought he might run off again.'

Weeks smiled. 'Your mum seemed to reassure him. He even turned and gave a smile as we were driving off.'

They were back in the Ford Pilot which Weeks now quite enjoyed driving. Leaving the Sharpe household they were motoring cross-country to Tenterden. They dropped down Mackerel Hill; past hopgardens where the new growth was starting to twine round the strings; meadows dotted with sheep and fields of emerging spring crops. Soon they reached Blackwall Bridge.

'Oh, stop here, please,' Nettie said. Obediently Weeks pulled over to the side of the road. 'I just wanted to look at the water. We come here in the summer. We like to think we're swimming from Sussex to Kent, although the border is actually a bit further over. It's fun though,' she beamed.

'Are you a good swimmer?' Weeks asked.

'I was a junior champion. Got my lifesaving badges and everything. Still enjoy it when I get the chance.'

While she looked upstream Weeks was staring downriver when something caught his eye. 'Hello. Looks like there's a big fire down there.' In the distance a pall of smoke was climbing into the blue sky, carried north-eastward on the gentle breeze.

'Too early for stubble-burning,' Nettie observed. 'Wonder what it can be. Hope it's not someone's home.'

'I'm sure we'll find out soon enough,' Weeks said, putting the car smoothly into gear and setting off. They passed through Wittersham and, rather than carry on through Smallhythe, Weeks took the slightly longer route towards Rolvenden. They were held up at Wittersham Road station as a tired-looking Stroudley Terrier tank locomotive came puffing over the level crossing, pulling a handful of wagons.

'It's a shame they shut the line to passengers a couple of years ago,' he declared. 'It's such a pretty route.'

'I know. Dad's a bit of a steam buff and loved taking us on it when we were kids.'

The signalman shuffled down from his box at the side of the road. After he'd made a big show of pushing the gates open they were on their way again. Ironically, when they reached the dip at the bottom of Rolvenden Hill where the railway crossed the road, the gates were closed again and the train they had seen earlier clattered over the level crossing on its way to the town. They weren't delayed for long and were soon climbing the hill up to Tenterden. The road levelled out and they drove along the wide, tree-lined high street. On the left, sitting a little lower than the road, were shops and on the right, behind mature gardens, were elegant Georgian houses and traditional Kentish tile-hung cottages. As the road narrowed it was lined with shops on both sides. Finally, the recreation ground came into view. They could see a bustle of activity as the rides and stalls were erected. The funfair had come to town.

Chapter 15

***Ben Gunn** was a former member of Flint's crew in Robert Louis Stephenson's Treasure Island. He became half insane after being marooned for three years, having convinced another member of the ship's crew that he was capable of finding Flint's treasure. After Dr Livesey gives him what he most craves, cheese, Gunn reveals that he has found it.*

RUSSELL LEFT Weeks's Ford Popular behind the station as there was a spare police Wolseley. He returned to his home and collected his French friend along with Aggie.

'So do you think we will be finding this Jack Mills in his pub?' Bruissement asked, as they drove along the Military Road.

'I do hope so. I want to question him about the death of Stern. Somehow, I don't think he was involved but I need to talk to him.'

''Ave you any *idée* who did kill him?'

'None at all – it's a mystery. And I'm still puzzling over that caravan.'

'Ah, the one that was seen by the funny old man with the broken gatepost. Tell me again what 'appened.'

Russell steered the car round one of the jinks in the road that followed the route of the canal. 'Okay. First the neighbour saw the truck and caravan going like a bat out of hell along the track away from the beach. That, presumably, was when the tyre was damaged. Then, Ben Gunn…'

'Pardon ? Who is this man you speak of?

'He was a character in a book by Robert Louis Stevenson. Marooned on a desert island for several years.'

Bruissement laughed. 'I see why you are calling him that – he was very, 'ow you say, scruffy.'

'He was a character. Just a shame he wasn't able to give a better description of the man.'

'Could 'e not tell you anything about him?'

'Not really. Just said he was large.'

'Pff. That's not much 'elp, is it?'

'None at all. Could be anyone.'

They passed the pillbox where the body of Ivy Rose Lee was found – where it all started. Russell turned off the Military Road, drove up the High Street and parked outside the Red Lion. 'You stay in the car, my friend. This shouldn't take long.' As he had hoped the landlord was there, standing behind the bar, polishing a glass with a checked tea towel. He looked up as the DI crossed the room – a welcoming smile quickly replaced by an expression that was a cross between a frown and look of disbelief as he recognised Russell. He quickly regained his composure.

'What can I get for you?' His voice was oily with charm.

'Nothing to drink, thank you. But I'd like some answers,' Russell said brusquely.

'Oh?'

'You have a friend over at Dungeness – Albert Stern.'

'You know I 'ave.'

'And I know that you've been over there recently.'

Mills's eyes narrowed. 'Oh yeah?'

'Yes, I saw your pickup there a couple of days ago.'

'Did you?' he said, his face a picture of innocence.

'Yes. And it was full of cartons of cigarettes and cases of brandy.'

Mills shook his head, incomprehension clouding his face. 'Don't know what you're talkin' about.'

'I'm talking about goods you've smuggled from France. Goods that duty hasn't been paid on.'

'I've really no idea what you're on about,' he said mildly.

'Oh yes you have,' Russell hissed. '*And* I expect it was you who thumped me over the head.'

'You've lost me.'

The DI struggled to keep his voice level. 'I was there. I saw you bring the goods ashore and load them into your truck.'

'And you 'ave proof?' Mills asked.

Russell regained his composure. He *knew* that he couldn't prove that it was Mills who had hit him, and the man knew it too. He decided to go for the jugular.

'I should say, you *had* a friend.'

A cloud crossed the landlord's face. 'What do you mean?'

Russell rested his hands on the bartop and leaned forwards. 'Your friend is dead – but I expect you already knew that.'

'*What*? *No*! *He can't be*! How would I know?'

'I'm afraid that he is. And I suppose you're going to tell me that you had nothing to do with it?'

'Of course I didn't!'

'Hmm. We'll see about that. I'm sure some evidence to implicate you will turn up.'

The panic returned. 'What do you mean – evidence?'

'Evidence that you did for him.'

'I don't believe what I'm hearing.'

'Try this for size: you went over to Dungeness to see him – discuss what you were going to do with the stuff you smuggled across the Channel. The discussion got heated – turned into an argument – perhaps he didn't want to participate any more. You struggled; he fell and bashed his head. Maybe you didn't mean to hurt him but he ended up dead. How's that for a scenario?'

Mills face turned as white as a sheet. 'You are joking,' he said, his eyes wide.

'No, I'm deadly serious.'

Somehow the landlord recovered his bravado and folded his arms across his chest. Despite Russell's best efforts he wasn't going to be drawn. 'So come up with the so-called evidence.'

'Leave it to me to find it.' Russell turned on his heel. As he reached the door he looked over his shoulder. 'Don't worry, I'll be back.'

Almost before the door had closed Mills grabbed a glass off the shelf and helped himself to a brandy – a very large one. In one swallow it was gone and he refilled the glass. He lifted the counter flap, took the drink round to the other side of the bar and sat down heavily on a stool. Sweat beaded on his forehead. This was a real blow. He wasn't overly fond of Stern – he just found him, and his boat, useful. But he wouldn't have wished him dead. What the hell had happened? He wasn't aware that Stern had any friends, let alone enemies. Who an earth would want to kill him? Maybe it was an accident. He took a smaller sip from his glass.

And that bloody policeman. He had it in for him – would probably say anything to rile him. So if it had been an accident, how had it happened, and where? Hell's teeth! How could he find out? As he was pondering this dilemma another thought barged its way into his head. He gulped down the last of the brandy. If the police were investigating around Stern's house they could easily discover his secret hoard in the wrecked shed. Oh God! He wasn't worried about losing the goods – it was too late for that. He was more concerned that the rozzers would trace them to him. Then his whole world would come tumbling down. That bloody copper, Russell, would know he was right and probably be able to prove who had thumped him. There was nothing for it. He would have to risk going over to Dungeness and clear the stuff out. The trouble was he knew he should wait until after dark and could only hope and pray that his hoard hadn't already been discovered.

~O~

The Waltzer was already well on the way to be being fully constructed. A couple of men were manhandling one of the gaudily decorated cars into place. Sideshows were erected and there was the thump-thump-thump of diesel generators. The chairoplanes were being hung from their chains; dodgem cars were pushed on to the steel deck, their metal poles thrusting upwards to connect electrically with the overhead metal grid. Weeks and Nettie walked across the fresh green grass towards it.

'We're looking for one of the men we talked to in Nottery Quay,' the DC said.

'So are we,' one of the workers muttered.

'He's a big man – wears a battledress jacket,' Nettie added.

'You mean Pint-sized Charlie,' the other man said as he heaved a roll of canvas on to the roof timbers.

'Pint-sized? But he's huge.'

'That's the joke,' the first man guffawed.

'It's *because* 'e's 'uge,' the second one said. 'A gentle giant.'

'Is he around?'

'No 'e bloody ain't. The bleeder 'asn't turned up.'

'Do you know where he is?' Weeks asked.

'Not a bloody clue. 'E left a day before us and 'e ain't been seen since.'

'Why did he go off early?'

'He said he weren't feeling too good. Must've picked up a bug or something,' the first man said.

'Left us in a right mess,' the second one added.

'Why's that?'

''E's got our billet.'

'Your billet?'

'Bloody great caravan. Where we all kip down. Tows it with an old army lorry. 'Ad to sleep under a truck last night. Dunno where we're gonna sleep tonight if 'e don't turn up soon.'

'Thanks for your help,' Weeks said. He gripped the WPC by the elbow and quickly steered her away from the men. When they were out of earshot he said. 'Did you hear that? "A bloody great caravan". It's got to be the same one that was seen in Dungeness. The funny old chap said it was a big man driving the truck. It's got to be him – Pint-sized Charlie.'

'So where is he now?'

'Who knows? I'd better radio it in. Put out an alert out for him. He's obviously dangerous.'

Chapter 16

***The Lucky Strike** brand was introduced in 1871 by the company R.A. Patterson, the brand's founder, who was inspired by the era's rush for gold searching. Very few of the gold diggers were fortunate enough to find gold and if they were, this was often referred to as a 'lucky strike'.*

RUSSELL STOMPED back to the Wolseley, a frown on his face. He got into the car and sat in the driver's seat, staring out through the windscreen. He felt rattled. Mills had got under his skin – the man was smug but there was nothing Russell could prove.

'What is it, *mon ami*?' Bruissement asked.

'That blasted man really gets to me. I *know* he's been smuggling stuff from France and I'm pretty certain it was him who thumped me. I just can't prove any of it, and he knows that. It's so galling.'

The Frenchman nodded sagely. '*Oui*, I can see that. So what can be done? There must be some way we can, 'ow you say, trip 'im up.'

Russell sat quietly, pondering. After a few moments he slowly shook his head. 'No, I just can't think of anything.'

'Listen. I 'ave an idea.'

Russell turned to his companion. 'Go on. I'm listening.'

'Perhaps we should go over to Dungeness – talk again to the people there.'

'But Weeks and I have already spoken to a number of them. And the local bobby, PC Fishwick, and a couple of other constables have been knocking on doors and talking to the rest.'

'Ah yes, but what is the question they 'ave been asking?'

'I suppose they've been enquiring about the mysterious caravan and whether anyone saw anything else suspicious.'

'That is just as I thought. Perhaps they should be asking about the landlord Mills. Whether 'im or 'is pickup truck 'ave been seen around.'

'That's an idea. Good thinking. Yes, we should go over there now.' Russell started the engine and turned the car.

As they approached the other Red Lion at Snargate, Russell had a sudden flashback. 'The caravan! This is where we saw it!'

'*Mais bien sûr*! It was leading a convoy along the road.'

'And heading towards Dungeness. If only we'd seen who was driving.'

'Too late now, I fear.'

They'd travelled only a few hundred yards when a battered Landrover came barrelling out of a gateway, veered across the wrong side of the road before heading off in the opposite direction. Russell had to swerve to avoid it, mounting the verge. '*What the…*?' he said, wrestling the car back on to the road.

'Sonny! Did you not see who was driving?'

'No. Who was it?'

'I 'ave a conviction it was that farmer – Angus Goodyear.'

'Really?'

'I think so.'

Russell drew to a halt. 'I have an idea.' He put the car in reverse and looking over his shoulder, backed it up the road to the gateway. Stopping, he said: 'If he's gone we can have a look in that barn.'

This time they reached the building without being challenged by an angry, shotgun-wielding farmer. And this time, the pair of large doors to the barn were open. The hinges were obviously shot as each hung at a crazy angle. There was enough light streaming in through the doorway and the holes in the corrugated cladding to see the interior clearly.

Bruissement let out a sigh. 'Pff. It is as the man said – just full of *matériel agricole*.'

'More like junk,' Russell said.

The barn contained a tangle of old broken boxes and hessian sacks, so decayed they would hold nothing; unidentifiable worm-eaten tools and pieces of rusted metal that might once have belonged to farm machinery. But no sign of duty-free goods. Russell took a few steps inside and kicked unenthusiastically at a stack of old newspapers, secured with baler twine. The string was so rotten that it gave way, the stack toppled and the papers cascaded on to the dirt floor.

The Frenchman crouched down. '*Un moment*, what is this?'

Russell's action had revealed a piece of card. Bruissement turned it over. The black capital letters **LU** above **STR** were visible on a red background. 'Yes! he cried. It's our old friend Lucky Strike! The box must have disintegrated. I knew I was right.'

The Frenchman was kneeling and pushing the papers aside – the pages disintegrating into flakes. Suddenly he stood, moving with surprising speed, considering his bulk. '*Regardez*!' With eyes gleaming and a huge grin breaking beneath his moustache he held aloft an intact carton of Lucky Strike cigarettes.

Smiling, Russell congratulated him. 'Well done! That proves the stuff was here.' Then his face fell. 'But where is it now?'

Bruissement leaned forward and brushed the dirt from the

knees of his trousers. ‘That, I do not know.’ He frowned. ‘I am wondering if that is the reason the farmer was driving away in such an ’urry.’

‘I suppose that’s possible,’ Russell said slowly. ‘So where was he going?’

‘Back to the pub of Mills?’

Russell rubbed his chin. ‘Perhaps, but somehow I don’t think so. Mills must have told him that the police had been keeping an eye on him and I would have thought that our friend Goodyear would keep his distance. No, I reckon him rushing off like that was just a coincidence – and a bit of luck for us to have a nose round here. I think we should carry on to Dungeness. Hopefully that will be more productive. Plus, I’d rather he didn’t find us here – I suspect he’s quite handy with that shotgun.’

The two men hadn’t travelled more than a mile when the radio crackled into life. ‘*Calling all cars, calling all cars. Keep a lookout for a large, cream-coloured caravan being towed by an ex-army lorry – possibly a CMP truck. Location: somewhere between Rye and Tenterden. Driver is a large man and believed to be dangerous. Approach with caution. If discovered, radio for reinforcements.*’ The broadcast ended and Russell glanced at his companion.

Bruissement’s eyes were sparkling with excitement. ‘It is our killer, *non*?’

‘Maybe.’

‘Oh, come on, *mon ami*. It ’as to be.’

‘Well if it is, we have to find him first.’

~O~

Weeks had spread an Ordnance Survey map of the area across the bonnet of the Ford Pilot. He and Nettie leaned over it, studying the possible routes Pint-sized Charlie may have taken.

'Bearing in mind the fact that he was towing a large caravan, the most straightforward way would be to travel along the Military Road and up through Appledore,' the DC said. 'That way the only hill would be after Ebony church, going up Reading Street.'

Nettie stood up. 'Let's follow that route then. Perhaps he's broken down.'

'Or hiding.'

She gave a sharp laugh. 'You'd struggle to find anywhere to hide anything as big as that caravan.'

'I don't know. There must be any number of narrow lanes where it could be concealed.'

'Let's see.' The WPC bent over the map again and traced her finger along the route. 'If he is hiding it's unlikely that it would be anywhere close to Rye, or Tenterden. Too many people and too many houses around. It has to be deeper in the countryside – away from habitation.'

'Yes, you're probably right. I'll radio through to the station and tell them that we'll start from here and get them to send a car from the Rye end.'

~o~

'Hello, It's Wickstead here.'

PC Andrew Gold, holding the phone to his ear, was gripping the handset tightly. He didn't like using the telephone – found it an unnatural instrument – much preferred face-to-face communication. He was a big lad, tall and broad, young and newly married. As well as Appledore being his first solo posting he was still getting used to the job and was worried about being out of his depth. The excitement of finding the body of Gypsy Ivy Lee in the pillbox had proved almost too much and he'd been hoping that things would settle down into the steady routine he preferred. 'Hello Sergeant. What can I do for you?' he said.

'You probably won't have heard but there's a shout out for a wanted man.'

'Oh yes?'

'You know that fisherman who was found dead over at Dungeness?'

'Albert Stern?'

'That's the one.'

'Yes, PC Fishwick told me about it.'

'DC Weeks called it in. Apparently they think the man who did it is driving an ex-army truck, towing a big caravan. He set off from Nottery Quay yesterday and should have arrived in Tenterden. But he hasn't shown up. Weeks and WPC Sharpe are starting the search from the Tenterden end and PCs Beaumont and Lee are setting out from this end. As you're about halfway it might be an idea if you keep an eye out.'

'Okay,' Gold said slowly. He could feel himself starting to shake. Sweat prickled on his skin.

'There's a warning that he's dangerous so, if you see him, be careful.'

The PC gripped the handset even tighter and pressed it hard against his ear. 'Right Sarge, I will.'

He put the phone down gingerly, as if it might explode, and let out a huge breath that he'd been holding. This was all he needed. He knew he could just have a cursory look round the village and no one would be any the wiser, but he wasn't like that. He was an officer of the law and he took it seriously. He felt duty bound to get on his bike and cycle round the lanes. After carefully securing his trouser cuffs with bicycle clips he put on his helmet, checking the strap was tight under his chin. Once satisfied he mounted his trusty Rudge, swinging his leg over the crossbar. He settled into the saddle and headed down The Street.

As Gold pedalled he thought about the places where a caravan might be concealed. He enjoyed being in the countryside, one of the reasons why he had applied for the post. During his spare time he liked to explore the surroundings and in the short while he had been there he'd got to know it well. He had a pretty good mental map in his head and was thinking about where he would look first. There was little point in going along the Military Road. The canal, on the left of the road, made concealment impossible. There weren't any turnings on the other side for a couple of miles until Knock Hill so he'd leave it to the PCs coming from Compass Point. He could go down the road towards the station but didn't think it was a likely choice as it was dotted with houses, sparse, but close enough to make things tricky. Instead, he decided to cross over the canal and turn sharp right along the lonely lane that made its way eventually to Brookland, following the meandering New Watering Sewer.

The sewer was one of the many drainage dykes that criss-crossed the Marsh. The road was narrow and twisting with, he recalled, several farm tracks leading off it. After the first tree-lined right-angled, bend to the left, the countryside opened up to the flat landscape, so typical of the Marsh. Fertile fields, reclaimed after the great storm of 1287, spread evenly on both sides as far as the eye could see. Overhead a huge dome of sky made the scene appear like a giant snowglobe. PC Gold felt slightly intimidated and not a little anxious, the regular creak of a chain that needed oiling the only sound as he pedalled steadfastly on. Within a few minutes he had reached the first farmstead. A grainstore stood elevated, like a featureless cathedral, with a smaller farm building to one side. Nowhere to hide a caravan here, and besides, Farmer Ashby would soon chase an interloper off his land.

Without pausing he pressed on, the lane now crossing Five Watering Sewer. A few scrubby bushes lined the route but none was large enough for concealment. In a short time he came to the railway level crossing and paused to look both ways – north towards Ashford – south towards Nottery Quay. He stopped, one foot on the polished railhead, and consulted his watch. The trains ran only once an hour, none was due for some time. He knew that a little farther along the road was the delightful St Thomas à Becket church. A tiny gem, it sat alone on a slight hummock in a large meadow, surrounded by sheep, the one-time village of Fairfield long confined to the mists of time. When the land flooded in winter the water came right up to the church door. The officer was pretty sure there wouldn't be anywhere for the man to hole up anywhere near it because the site was so exposed. With a sigh, he decided there was little point in continuing. His hunch that this remote area was where he was most likely to come across the caravan had been proved wrong. Turning his bicycle round he set off back towards Appledore.

~O~

PCs Beaumont and Lee were having no luck either, even though they were able to cover the ground more swiftly in the police Wolseley. They had driven up a number of rutted farm tracks that petered out in ploughed fields. Lee, who was driving, had had to reverse to extricate the car, something he was not very good at, causing great merriment in his companion.

After another manoeuvre where he'd backed into the hedge several times he asked: 'Why don't you drive, if you can do any better?' The words were spoken through gritted teeth.

'No mate,' Beaumont said, chuckling. 'I'm enjoying this.'

When, once again, they were back on the Military Road, Lee said: 'This is bloody hopeless – a complete waste of time. Why would anyone want to hide a caravan in this godforsaken place? If it was me, I'd be miles away from here by now?'

'Orders is orders, mate. We're just going to have to keep going until we meet up with the others coming from Tenterden. Then we'll know for sure that he's not here.'

The others – Weeks and Nettie – were doing no better. After the first dead-end track they'd driven up Weeks had got in such a muddle with the Ford Pilot that he decided they'd explore any others on foot. Nettie had found it hard not to laugh when she'd had to stand at the side of the car and guide him in reversing. That was after he'd wedged it securely against the hedge for the umpteenth time. So they'd walked up a few more winding rutted paths and, apart from a rusting plough and an empty tumbledown barn, they'd seen nothing of note.

As they trudged back over tussocks and puddles after another fruitless search Weeks confessed: 'I'm beginning to wonder if I've got this all wrong. If he is the man who killed Stern then maybe he won't bother to join the fair and his colleagues – just disappear.'

Nettie stopped and stared across the scrubby hedge towards the sheep that were munching the short, dry grass. 'Maybe,' she said. 'But then again, he may not know that we're looking for him and might reason that returning to the funfair will provide an alibi for him.'

'Possibly. You could be right. But… If he *was* at Dungeness, he might be holed up somewhere on the Brookland Road.'

'True.' Nettie pulled up a piece of long grass and chewed thoughtfully on the end.

'I reckon we're going to have to widen the search. I'll call in again when I get back to the car.'

'Ah, Johnny,' Wickstead said, his voice crackly down the line. 'Inspector Parker would like a word with you. Just a moment.'

The DC's heart sank. He feared the worst.

'Weeks?'

'Sir.'

'I'm not sure what's going on but I suspect you've been wasting your time, as well as that of several PCs.'

'If I could explain…'

'No, let me explain. Do you have any evidence that this, what's he called…?'

'Pint-sized Charlie.'

'That this "Pint-sized Charlie" was actually involved in the death of the fisherman at Dungeness?'

'Well no, but the caravan…'

'Yes, the caravan. Has it not occurred to you that all these bloody gyppos live in caravans of one sort or another?'

'I suppose so.' Weeks could feel a wretched sensation of doom deflating his earlier enthusiasm.

'So is it not possible that it could be *any* caravan with *any* greasy gyppo towing it?'

'But the distinctive lorry…'

'Hang on. There are any number of *distinctive* lorries – mainly ex-army – out on the roads. All you've got is the word of some deranged loony who doesn't even live in a proper house, just some shitty old railway carriage on a beach. Remind you of anyone?'

Weeks refused to take the bait and kept silent, the radio crackling with static.

'I suggest you pack up now and get back here. There's proper police work to be done.' With that the connection was cut.

'Bloody Bonnie Parker. Bang goes my chance of widening the search.'

Nettie touched him lightly on the arm. 'Don't worry Johnny, he doesn't know where we are so there's no need to rush back. I'm sure we can explore one or two other lanes.'

Chapter 17

The ***half crown*** was a denomination of *British money, equivalent to two shillings* and sixpence, or one-eighth of a *pound. It* was first issued in 1549, in the reign of *Edward VI.*

BY THE time Edna was due to turn up for the evening shift the brandy bottle was down to a couple of inches and Mills's mood was as sour as the taste in his mouth. He sat at the bar, the fingers of one hand massaging his brow, those of the other wrapped tightly round his glass. There was a tap at the door. He heaved himself off his seat and walked across the room. Drawing the bolt he pulled the door open.

'Afternoon Jack…' Edna began cheerily, but stopped when she took in the lowered brow and scowling mouth. She knew that the landlord had developed a temper lately and had upset a number of the locals. But she hadn't been on the receiving end of it – until now.

He grabbed her wrist. 'Get in 'ere!' he growled and pulled hard.

'Let go, Jack. You're hurting me!' she pleaded, trying to twist away from him.

But his grip was vicelike and he dragged her across the room. 'Waddyer mean, talking to that bloody copper?'

'*Who*?' Her voice was breaking; big fat tears welling in her eyes.

'Russell. That interfering DI with the mangy dog.'

'No, I didn't…'

'*Liar*! It was you. 'Ow else would 'e know about the stuff in the cellar?'

'Oh, Jack. I'm sorry.'

'Too late for that. Thanks to you I'm up shit creek an' my mate is dead.'

Edna brought her free hand up to her mouth and her eyes widened. '*Dead*? Who?'

'Albert Stern.' His grip slackened and Edna wrenched her hand away. She backed off, massaging her wrist.

'What happened?' Her voice was hushed.

'Someone killed 'im – over at Dungeness. That's where the stuff is now.' The last sentence was spoken so quietly Edna had to strain to hear him.

'Who killed him? Why did they do it?'

Mills stalked back to the bar and slumped down on the stool. 'I don't know – but it weren't me.' He drained his glass. 'Anyway, that's not my problem. But bringin' the stuff back 'ere is.'

Edna approached cautiously. 'Why don't you share it with me?'

Under normal circumstances he would never have shared anything with her but the effects of the brandy and the news of his friend's death made him less careful. He cast caution to the wind and said: 'Listen, I don't want this to go no further – and I certainly don't want that nosey copper to know about it.'

She put her hand lightly on his arm. 'You can trust me, Jack. I won't say anything.'

'You'd better not.' The words came out as a snarl but she stood her ground. He let out a huge sigh. 'The pub's been struggling for some time.'

'I thought it had been quiet.'

'Well, that's 'ow things are at the moment. I dunno know why but the punters seem to prefer to go into the Railway 'otel when they get off the train. Or drink in The Swan, up the road.'

'Maybe you've upset some people,' she ventured.

'*What*?' Another growl. Then his voice softened. 'I suppose you could be right. Whatever, it means that the pub's been losin' money. If I 'adn't done something, the brewery would 'ave taken it away from me.'

'So what have you done?'

'What 'ave I done?' Mills looked up, his eyes bloodshot. 'I've broken the law, that's all.'

'Oh, Jack.'

'It was the only way to keep the business afloat.'

Edna had slipped on to the stool beside him. 'Do you want to tell me about it?' she asked gently.

'Hmm? I suppose so.' He held his glass out. 'Get me another drink, would you?'

'Don't you think you've had enough?'

'*What*?' His mood changed instantly – a bull cornered. He stood up and hurled the glass at the fireplace where it shattered into a thousand pieces. 'Why the hell am I talking to you? *You* sold me down the river. *Get out*! You're sacked!' When she hesitated he pushed her hard. 'Go on – get out! Go!' Edna stumbled across the room, the tears flowing now, and ran out.

Mills went back behind the bar and rummaged around under the counter until he found a piece of card and a pencil. He scrawled PUB CLOSED and underlined it twice. He weaved unsteadily across the floor, went out though the door and slammed it hard behind him. On the second attempt he got the key in the lock and turned it closed then pushed the card under the knocker. It was still light but he was beyond caring as he got into the pickup, started the engine and drove off.

~O~

PC Gold pedalled back along the New Watering Sewer road, wondering where to look next – or even whether it was worth continuing to look. The man was bound to be long gone. He felt he'd done his bit and if, by any chance, the suspect was still around, someone would have come across him by now. He pushed on, reached the last sharp right-hand bend before the end of the road and realised there was a lane that ran off the corner, along the canal. How had he missed it on the way out? His pulse quickened. Some sixth sense told him to be careful. Dismounting he pushed his bicycle along the track. This was one of the few areas on the edge of the marsh that was fairly heavily wooded with scrubby alders, self-sown sycamore and ash. On the right was the canal. The water was still; a willow, its roots barely anchored in the bank, hung over it, the tips of the branches trailing in the surface. Swallows, newly arrived from Africa, skimmed the surface, catching insects on the wing. Gold could see a heron on the farther bank, standing sentinel, alert for the movement of fish in the shallows. There was a splash as a minnow broke the surface. The heron's head shot forward into the water and came back up with a silver, wriggling body in its beak. Gold shuddered and carried on.

Another track curved to the left and as he rounded a clump of bushes he was brought up short. There, tucked away among trees was a large, cream caravan hitched to the distinctive shape of a CMP truck. His heart was in his mouth as he carefully lay the bicycle down on the grass. He knew he should return and call for backup but something pushed him on. He was by nature a fairly timid man but uncharacteristically he just couldn't help himself. Slipping his truncheon out of his pocket he tiptoed up to the caravan. Automatically he put his hand on the handle of the door and was just about to press it down when it flew open, knocking him off balance. He staggered backwards, his arms flailing, the truncheon dropped, until his heel caught in a tree root and he landed on his back with a thump that knocked the breath out of his body.

'What do you want?' His light voice was at odds with his appearance.

Gold looked up. A huge man, almost as broad as he was tall, towered over his prone figure. 'I'm looking for you,' he said. He had no idea where the words came from but something inside said 'don't let him slip away'.

The next instant the man had reached down, grabbed him by the front of his tunic and hauled him to his feet. Gold was by no means small but the man handled him as if he were a rag doll. He pulled the policeman close until their faces were only a few inches apart. 'You've found me. Now what are you planning to do?'

The acrid smell of the man's breath filled Gold's nostrils. He tried to struggle but was held too firmly. 'Let me go,' he said, through gritted teeth.

The man laughed in his face. His voice was high-pitched; he sounded like the villain in a theatrical melodrama. 'And then what? You'll get on your bike and cycle off for reinforcements? Not likely! You're staying here with me.' The PC tried again to struggle free but the man was far stronger. Before he knew what was happening the huge man let go of his tunic and swung his fist round hard, connecting with Gold's jaw and sending him flying. He crashed to the ground in a heap. He tried getting up, raising himself on his hands and knees. He was just about to push himself upright when the big man kicked out with a booted foot. It caught the policeman on the side of the head and he saw stars – then blackness. He was unaware of the man dragging him into the caravan.

~O~

Nettie and Weeks trudged along another lane – much longer than the others they'd checked. Little was said as they walked and the WPC thought about her companion. They got on well – made a good team – but there was no chemistry between them. Nettie wondered at this. The DC was an attractive man – his mop of dark hair and his boyish good looks made him appear younger and more innocent than he was. She knew that his parents lived somewhere in the north of the county and that he had his own house, near DI Russell's railway-carriage home. She knew that he liked puzzles – regularly completed cryptic crosswords – and that he had an eidetic memory. She'd known him recall whole conversations – word for word although he always made comprehensive notes for the sake of clarification. Perhaps he would become one of those *confirmed bachelors* like a favourite uncle of hers. She sighed. He noticed.

'Something up?' he asked.

She shook her head. 'No, nothing important.' Then: 'How long *is* this lane?'

'It's got to end soon – somewhere.'

What had begun as a tarmacked road – easily wide enough for a car or even a truck – was turning into a rutted track, with bushes encroaching on both sides and grass growing up along the centre. Weeks noted the broken twigs and scattering of leaves along the lane. 'Looks like something big has been down here recently.'

'Yes, I think you're right,' Nettie agreed. A bend in the lane ahead had obscured their view forward but as they turned the corner she let out a little gasp. There, 100 yards ahead, was the distinctive form of a large, cream-coloured caravan and the dull khaki of an ex-army truck.

'It's him!' Weeks said in a whisper. 'What do we do now?'

'We're supposed to call for reinforcements.'

'I know. But the car's a good half a mile back. What happens if he decides to move while we're gone?'

'I'm not sure he's going anywhere in a hurry. Look, the caravan is wedged tight against that tree.'

'True. But we don't want to lose him now we've found him.'

Nettie gripped his arm. 'Why doesn't one of us stay while the other goes back to the car and radios base?'

'That's an idea – but which one?'

'We'll toss for it.' The WPC reached into her tunic pocket and brought out a half crown. 'Heads you stay, tails, it's me.' She flipped the coin, caught it and placed it on the back of her hand. 'Tails!' she said, triumphantly.

'Will you be okay?'

'Of course I will. Go on.'

Weeks knew she could be impetuous. 'You won't do anything daft – anything heroic, will you?'

'Of course not. I'll just stay here and observe.'

Weeks set off at a trot and Nettie watched him until he was out of sight. She really had intended to just observe, but something inside, some little voice, made her want to know more and, after only a moment's reflection, she started walking slowly towards the caravan. When she reached it, she hesitated. Perhaps she should just wait for the others to turn up. The man was supposed to be highly dangerous – and probably armed.

When she was little she was always getting into scrapes. Her parents said she was a tomboy, and probably she was: climbing trees, scrumping apples and scraping her knees. She'd devoured Enid Blyton's *Famous Five* stories and Arthur Ransome's *Swallows and Amazons* was her bible. Despite being brought up in a vicarage, where church on Sunday was mandatory, she was allowed free rein the rest of the time. She was also a loner.

She remembered growing up during the war. Her father had gone off to Portsmouth as part of his ministry, to comfort people that had been bombed out of their homes and to give the last rites to the dying. Mother had stayed at home busily immersing herself in village life, making friends so that they were never short of fresh vegetable and eggs. Her brother was a good deal younger so there were no older boys around when she was growing up to go on adventures with. But it didn't matter. She was quite happy in her own company and would set off exploring, with just sandwiches and a bottle of pop in a knapsack, not returning until the light was starting to drain from the sky.

So the independent child had grown strong and fearless and, after she finished school, had been drawn to the police force. Nettie loved being a WPC but really wanted to be a detective. She knew this just wasn't possible, although there was talk of women joining the CID – sometime. But, until it happened, she would have to be content with her lot.

She was grateful that DI Russell could see potential in her even though those dinosaurs, Superintendent Stout and DI Bonnie Parker, thought she was fit only to make tea. Pah! She'd show them. With that thought she tried the door handle on the caravan. It was unlocked. Cautiously she pulled the door open. The curtains were drawn and it was dark inside. The air was heavy with the stench of sweat and unwashed male bodies, stale cooking smells and damp. She gagged then held her breath. Suddenly there was a great snort which made her jump, but she kept her nerve. Then a sharp exhalation followed by loud snoring. Whoever was in there was asleep. Emboldened she stepped inside. In the gloom she could just make out a figure, sprawled on the sofa. He was so large that he was pressed right up against the wall with one arm dangling over the side. Nettie took another step forward. Her foot caught on the corner of a rug and she stumbled. Reaching out to stop herself from falling, her hand bumped the man's shoulder and he woke with a start.

'*What*? *Who?*' he exclaimed. Suddenly he half sat up, twisted and stared at Nettie. The effort was obviously far too much and he slumped back. 'Go away! Leave me alone!'

'Are you Pint-sized Charlie?' Nettie asked.

'What if I am?' came the groggy reply.

'We've been looking for you.'

He struggled to sit up again. 'Who has?'

'The police.'

'*The police? Why?*' He was puzzled rather than angry.

Nettie was taken aback by his apparent calmness. She had assumed that he would react violently. 'It's with regard to the death of a fisherman in Dungeness.'

'What?' he snorted.

'The death of a fisherman…'

'I haven't heard of bleedin' Dungeness,' he broke in. 'Nor ever been to the hellhole.' He let out a bark of a laugh which transformed into a hacking cough. He doubled over convulsed, the cough coming at regular intervals like the spluttering of a recalcitrant engine, reluctant to start. When it finally subsided he looked up, his eyes streaming and spittle dribbling down his chin. He wiped it away with the back of his hand. 'Well if you've quite finished, Missy,' he croaked, 'I ain't well and I need to sleep.' With that the conversation was finished. He lay back down and turned to face the wall.

Nettie was nonplussed. She expected aggression and confrontation, not a poorly man who wanted to do nothing but sleep. What should she do? Her initial bravado was replaced by a sensation of doubt. Perhaps Parker was right when he had spoken to Johnny. Travelling folk did indeed tend to live in caravans. Maybe this wasn't the one that had been seen at Dungeness. The man was certainly large, but somehow Nettie didn't think he was dangerous. He started snoring again. Baffled she turned and left the caravan and stood outside, waiting for reinforcements.

~O~

PC Andrew Gold came to with a thumping headache. Wincing, he opened his eyes and discovered he was lying on the floor of the caravan. He tried to move but his hands and feet were tied. In a panic he looked around. There was no sign of the other man. He was alone – for now. What the hell had he got himself into? Sergeant Wickstead had told him the man was dangerous – that he should be careful – but did he listen? And here he was, trussed up like a chicken with a head that felt as if it was about to split open. He tried to wriggle free but the bonds were too tight. By shuffling across the floor he managed to sit upright, his back against the edge of the sofa. The effort caused the pain in his head to escalate to such a high level that he just sat, panting, his eyes squeezed tight shut. After a few minutes it had reduced just enough to enable him to start thinking again. He had no idea how long he'd been there. There was a chink in the curtains and he could see that although it was still daytime the light was starting to drain from the sky. Also, he had no idea how long he'd be alone. He shuddered. When the man came back he wondered what he would be in for. He didn't have long to wait.

The door burst open and the man mountain strode in. He grinned, his eyes shining with menace. 'Ah! Good to see that you're awake then.'

~o~

Nettie didn't have long to wait until relief arrived. Russell had been *en route* from the visit to Jack Mills in Appledore when he'd received the 'all cars' alert. He'd decided to head back in the direction of Tenterden and was travelling towards Reading Street when Weeks's call for reinforcements had come in. As he was only a couple of miles from the location he was the first on the scene.

'Right lad. What have we got?' he asked as he stepped out of the car.

'We've found the caravan!'

Russell looked along the track. 'Where is it?'

Weeks pointed. 'It's about half a mile up there.'

'So why is your car here?'

'Ah.' Weeks coloured.

Russell chuckled. 'You don't like that Ford Pilot, do you?'

Weeks shook his head.

Then alarm crossed the DI's face. 'Hey, where's WPC Sharpe?'

'Don't worry, Sir,' Weeks said reassuringly. 'She's keeping watch – from a distance.'

'Are you sure?' The alarm had spread to his voice.

'Well, she said she would just observe…'

'Mmm. That young lady is brave. She's got an adventurous streak. Come on, get in the car. Let's see what's happening.'

Russell drove fast along the tarmacked section of the road and didn't slow when it degenerated into a track. The Wolseley bucked and rolled and poor Bruissement had to hang on for dear life so his arm didn't get jolted. They reached the bend and could see Nettie standing calmly, her arms folded, the caravan just beyond. The car came to a halt and they piled out.

'Hello lass. Well done for waiting.'

Her colour rose just as Weeks's had. 'I, er…'

Russell let out a huge sigh and shook his head slowly from side to side. 'Don't tell me you've been up to the caravan?'

'Afraid so, Sir.'

'I don't know.'

'Um – *and* I had a look inside.'

'You were told *not* to approach – the man is *dangerous*.'

'I know, Sir. I just thought I'd take a peek.'

'And?' Russell stood with his fists on his hips.

'He's in there all right. But I don't think he poses a threat. Plus… I don't know whether I should say this.'

'Say what?'

'I've got a feeling he's not our killer. He was genuinely surprised when I said we were looking for him. Also I think he's got some sort fever and was sleeping when I left him.'

Russell knew about instincts. He'd been castigated enough times by Superintendent Stout when he'd expressed *feelings* – feelings that had proved right on more than one occasion. Often he would sense that something wasn't quite as it should be, when everyone else was convinced of the opposite. He was aware that he might not have the monopoly when it came to some sort of sixth sense and was prepared to overlook the WPC's rash behaviour and trust that she might be right.

While they were talking there was the sound of an engine. Another Wolseley came along the track and skidded to a halt in a cloud of dust. PCs Lee and Beaumont tumbled out and stood waiting for instructions.

Russell nodded towards them. 'Okay. Let's go and take a look. There are enough of us here in case he cuts up rough.' He started leading them toward the caravan, then stopped, holding his hand up. 'Is he armed?'

'I didn't see a weapon, Sir,' Nettie answered. 'And besides, I don't think he is in any state to put up a fight. I reckon he really is quite poorly.'

They continued walking and on reaching the caravan Russell held his hand up again. 'Stay here while I take a look. I'll yell if I need you.' He opened the door and stepped inside. After a few seconds he reappeared. 'Weeks, Beaumont and Lee. Come here with the cuffs and read him his rights. I don't think he's going to cause us any trouble but best be on your guard.'

As Nettie had intimated he put up little resistance and they were able to get him into the PCs Wolseley – with difficulty. This wasn't caused by his reluctance to get in the car but purely because of his bulk. PC Beaumont was staying behind to guard the lorry and caravan until a breakdown truck turned up to retrieve them. Once the prisoner was settled, Lee, who was driving, reversed a few dozen yards back along the track until he was able to turn the car in a farm gateway. Russell repeated the manoeuvre with his car. When they got to the end of the lane, Weeks and Nettie transferred to the Ford Pilot and the cars travelled in convoy back to Collinghurst. On arrival, Russell, who should have been jubilant at the arrest, was troubled by misgivings. Nettie had sown the seed with her comments and Pint-sized Charlie's demeanour was not that of a guilty man. Either that or he was a very good actor – and Russell doubted that. But the caravan – and the ex-army lorry – were they the ones that had been seen at Dungeness – after Albert Stern died? Weeks had told him what Bonnie Parker had said about gypsies and caravans. He hated to admit it but the blasted man could well be right.

Pint-sized Charlie was led to reception, flanked by Lee and Beaumont, although he didn't look like he was going to cause trouble. In fact he looked cowed. His head was bowed, his handcuffs hands linked together in front of him, making him look like he was in prayer. Sergeant Wickstead asked his name. The reply was so mumbled to be incoherent and he asked him to repeat it.

He lifted his head a fraction and said: 'Charles Atcost.'

'Do you understand why you're here?'

'Not really.'

'You're accused of being involved with the death of a man in Dungeness.'

His head came up a little further. 'I've already said – I've never been to the blasted place.'

'That's something we'll have to confirm. Meanwhile, you'll be held in custody while further investigations are carried out.'

His voice was low – washed out. 'Look, I don't care about your investigations. I just need to lie down.' Almost in slow motion his legs started to buckle beneath him and it was only the two constables, either side, who stopped him from crumpling to the floor.

'Take him down to the cells,' Wickstead said. 'He's making the place look untidy.'

Russell was just about to go into his office when the Superintendent's door burst open and he yelled down the corridor: '*Inspector*! Get your arse in here – and bring Weeks with you!'

Wickstead rolled his eyes. 'Sorry, Sonny. I was going to tell you that he was on the warpath.'

Russell gave a wry smile. 'Ah well. I'm used to him by now.' He turned to Bruissement. 'Guillaume. You'd better stay here. The sergeant will look after you.'

'Do not 'ave concern for me. I will enjoy the company of this gentleman. You go and see your boss.'

'Right.' Russell was business-like. 'Come on Johnny, let's go and face the music.' Before they entered Stout's office he stopped and put his hand lightly on Weeks's arm. 'Listen. You're not to blame for any of this. I'm your boss so I'll carry the can. Leave me to do the talking.'

The Superintendent's room was wreathed in more smoke than Russell had ever seen before. The cut-glass ashtray was overflowing with cigar butts and there was a dusting of ash and two empty cheroot cartons on the normally pristine desk. As was customary, they were not invited to sit but treated to a wall of silence, while Stout appeared intent on some papers he was reading. After a considerable time, when more cigar smoke was added, he looked up – piggy eyes under a lowered brow.

'What on earth is going on?' he enunciated slowly and with precision.

'Well,' Russell began but faltered when Stout held his hand up.

'I was talking to Weeks.'

'Sir, with due respect, the DC was acting on my instructions. He's not to be blamed for this.'

'Is that so? In that case, I'll ask you. What *is* going on?' Russell opened his mouth but before he could speak Stout continued: 'No, let me tell you what's going on.' Maybe it was the quantity of nicotine he'd breathed in or maybe just his mood but the words came out as a low growl. 'Once again you taken all the staff away from the police station, without a word to me, and sent them off on a wild goose chase. I thought you would have learnt your lesson after last time.'

'But, Sir...' Russell protested.

'Quiet!' the growl became a bark. 'I'm amazed you bothered to leave Sergeant Wickstead to man the phones.' There was a pause while he lit another cheroot. Once it was going and he'd blown out the first blue cloud he continued. 'I'm trying to run an investigation into two murders here. They may only have been gyppos that were bumped off but we still have to be seen to following the letter of the law. I told you to investigate the death of a fisherman in Dungeness which, I might add, may have been an unfortunate accident. And what do you two do? Turn it into a full-scale man hunt.'

'But we think he may be responsible for all the deaths.'

'You think? You *think*? On what evidence?'

'The caravan.'

'Oh give me strength. How many more times do you have to be told, *most* travellers live in caravans. I said evidence.'

'The man who was seen in Dungeness was very large...'

Stout gave out a bark of a laugh. 'Is that it? You decided to go looking for a *large* man? Even for you that's a bit vague.'

Russell decided to press on. 'A large man, Pint-sized Charlie, disappeared somewhere between Nottery Quay and Tenterden, where the rest of the fair had gone.'

'You are kidding?'

'No, I'm not, Sir. He should have been there yesterday but didn't turn up. It's my belief he diverted to Dungeness, where Albert Stern was killed.'

'I've heard it all now. I suppose you're going to tell me that he killed those two fortune tellers, also.'

'Well, there's a good chance he was responsible – everything points to it.'

'Inspector. *Nothing* points to it. The real killer is already under lock and key. DI Parker has incontrovertible evidence against him.'

'Oh? I thought there was just a burnt deck of cards and a neckerchief.'

Stout put his hand to his mouth and harrumphed. 'So far, yes. But he said he's going to make a detailed investigation of Petulengro's caravan.'

Russell frowned. 'Strange. I thought Lewis had already done that.'

'Ha! He's supposed to have done, but he missed a vital piece of evidence.'

'That evidence was a bit fishy,' Russell muttered.

'What was that?' Stout said sharply.

'I said more evidence needs fishing out.'

'Hmm – maybe. Anyway, now I've got my officers back where they should be I suggest you charge this *large* man with the death of the fisherman in Dungeness. And don't you dare send anyone off on a wild goose chase again without consulting me first. *Do you understand*?'

'Yes, Sir.'

'Good. Now bugger off and do the job you're paid for.' Russell was just leaving when the Super called out: 'And tell DI Parker I want to see him.'

Chapter 18

*In **Romany Tradition** possessions such as clothes, bedding and the vehicle or trailer, if a traveller passed away in it, are traditionally burnt. This is done as a sign of respect to the person, so the possessions go with them to the afterlife and to aid the spirit to leave this world for the next.*

'I'M A bit concerned about the lack of concrete evidence implicating Boswell in this case.' Stout was leaning back in his chair, doubt clouding his face.

'I'm expecting to find plenty more later today, Sir.' Parker tried to sound more confident that he felt.

'You're going out to the caravan yourself then?'

'Yes. Me and DC Barrow are going with Lewis. I'm sure the man's usually thorough but I don't think he did a very good job last time he went. I want to make sure we find what I *know* is there. We're going to pull the van apart.'

Stout leaned forward and rested his elbows on the desk. 'Good. We need to get this case wrapped up. We can't keep Boswell here forever without more to go on.' There was a knock on the door. Without looking up Stout said: 'Come.'

The door opened and Wickstead put his head round. 'Sorry to bother you, Sir. But I thought you should know. I've just had a call from the fire brigade. There's been a blaze over near Iden.'

Stout looked puzzled. 'How does this affect me, sergeant? Surely they can deal with it.'

'Oh yes, Sir. The local brigade is very efficient.'

'I'm sure it is. But why are you bothering me with this information? Can't you see I'm in the middle of an important discussion?'

'Yes, Sir. But I thought it important enough to interrupt you.'

'A fire, that the brigade is dealing with, is no concern of the police force.' Stout was becoming increasingly tetchy.

'It's not that, Sir. It's what's *on* fire.'

'Well what is it? Spit it out man.'

'A caravan, Sir. Down near the river. The line was bad but I think it must be the one owned by Petulengro.'

'Why the hell didn't you say that in the first place?'

'Sorry, Sir. I was just coming to that.'

'Oh God. This is bound to complicate things. Parker Get over there immediately. See if there's anything you can salvage. If you don't get that evidence we're back to square one.'

~O~

When Jack Mills had left Appledore he was wound up and angry and drove like a madman. But he quickly realised that driving erratically might draw attention so he slowed down. As he approached Prospect Cottage he was relieved to see that there appeared to be no police presence. He turned the pickup off the metalled road and bumped along the shingle to the abandoned shed. With his heart in his mouth he dragged the door open. Inside was just as he'd left it. He let out a long sigh. He pulled the broken boxes aside and dragged off the piece of rotten canvas.

Breaking open one of the crates he took out a bottle of brandy, pulled the cork out with his teeth and, by way of celebration, took a long swig. Grinning he started loading the boxes into the bed of the truck. When he'd finished, he pulled the canvas tilt over the bed and tied it down firmly.

He then climbed back into the cab but, before starting the engine, he just sat, thinking. He needed to stash the stuff – but where? Angus Goodyear had made it plain he didn't want it in his barn and St Dunstan's was just too risky. If that blasted girl, Edna, hadn't been so nosey he could store it back in the cellar of the pub. Then he laughed. Of course – he'd sacked her, so there was no problem now. With that cheering thought he started the engine, ready to head back.

~O~

'What was all that about?' Russell was standing in the entrance lobby with Bruissement and Wickstead. Each had a steaming mug of tea that the sergeant had brewed. The Frenchman had four sugars in his. The DI had been more than a little surprised when Parker had come bursting out of Stout's office, yelling for Barrow. Russell had never seen him move so fast.

'He's going over to Iden. Apparently the gypsy's caravan has caught fire. He was *hoping* to get more evidence against Boswell.'

'Fat chance of that now.' Russell took a slurp from his mug. 'Hasn't Lewis already searched it?'

'Of course he has.'

'I doubt there would be anything he's missed. He's the most thorough man I know.'

'What about that scarf you 'ave told told me about?' Bruissement asked.

'Ha! That sounded more than suspicious.' Russell turned to Wickstead. 'Didn't you say you found Parker poking around in the store?'

'That's right. Said he was looking through Boswell's things. Wanted to get a feel for the man. It just didn't ring true.'

'So this evidence may have been, 'ow you say, planted?' Bruissement suggested.

'I wouldn't put it past Parker. He's a lazy sod and would do anything to cut corners and get a conviction.'

'That's a bit strong, Sonny,' Wickstead said.

'Yes, you're right. Sorry. It's just *I* don't think the fairground owner *is* guilty.'

'What about the man you've got in the cell – Pint-sized Charlie? Is he the one?'

'Somehow I don't think so either.' Russell looked gloomy and shook his head. 'But I've got to go through the motions – now we've got him.' Further conversation was halted by the telephone bell. Wickstead picked up the receiver.

'Hello, Collinghurst police station. Can I help?' There was a pause while he listened. 'I see.' Another pause. 'Yes, he happens to be standing right next to me.' He put his hand over the mouthpiece and turned to Russell. 'Sonny, I've got someone called Edna on the phone. She's asked to speak to you.'

'That's fine. I'll talk to her.' Wickstead passed the handset across.

'Hello Edna. What can I do for you?'

'Oh Inspector Russell. It's Jack.'

'What about him?'

'He's sacked me.' The girl sounded very distressed.

'That's a pity but I don't see how I can help.'

'I know you can't. It's not that.'

'What is it then?'

'He went off in his truck – I saw him. He was driving like a bat out of hell.'

'Oh?'

'And I think I know where he was going.'

'Do you? Where?'

'Over to Dungeness. I think that's where he stored all that stuff I told you about.'

'I see.'

'The thing is he's very drunk and I don't know what he'll do. He's become very violent lately – loses his temper easily.'

'Do you think he'll come after you?'

'Oh no. I doubt that.'

'Well that's good, anyway.'

'There's something else...'

'What's that?'

'I can't be sure but I have a feeling he may come back to the pub with the goods.'

'What makes you think that?'

'It was something he said – something about Albert Stern's death not being his problem but getting the stuff back was.'

'Right. Thank you for telling me, Edna. That's very helpful.' Russell passed the handset back to Wickstead and explained what the girl had told him. 'I think we'd better intercept him before anything happens. Our big friend will have to wait for now.'

'I wouldn't worry about him,' Wickstead said as he put the phone down. 'I looked in earlier. He's in no fit state to cause trouble. He was out for the count – snoring his head off.'

'Good. If we go to Dungeness via Appledore we're bound to bump into him.'

'Not literally, I hope,' Wickstead grinned.

'Oh, and not a word to the Super. I'm in enough trouble already. Johnny, you and Nettie follow me in your car. I'll go ahead with Guillaume. When we get to Appledore, you stop by the bridge in case I miss him or he doubles back across the Marsh. We'll carry on and see if we can cut him off.' They climbed into their respective cars and set off out of town.

~o~

The police car bumped along the track past the motor graveyard and arrived at the stand of elders. '*Bloody hell!*' Parker exclaimed. A Dennis fire engine was parked across the clearing – one hose snaking towards the river, another being held by two firemen clad in blue serge uniforms and wearing black leather, coal-scuttle helmets. They were playing a jet of water on to the charred remains of a caravan. Damp grey smoke curled lazily upwards.

A fire officer came up to the car. 'Afraid there's not much left of them,' he said.

'Them?' Parker questioned.

'Yes. There are – or rather were – two gypsy caravans.'

Parker hauled himself out of the car and stood staring, his hand on the open door. 'I don't understand. How come there are two?'

Barrow had come round to join him. 'I think I might know, Sir.'

The DI just stared – speech had deserted him.

'Apparently Ivy Rose Lee's caravan had disappeared from the Salts in Nottery Quay.'

'Was it a bowtop van?' the fire officer asked.

'I think so.'

'Well this might be it.' He pointed to a charred wooden carcass, just discernible as having once been some sort of vehicle.

'Why the hell would anyone set fire to them?' the DI asked. 'Kids I suppose.'

'Not necessarily,' the fire officer replied. 'I know a bit about travelling folk. Apparently it's tradition to burn a gypsy's wagon and possessions after death. Could be that's what happened here.'

Parker ran his hands through his hair. 'Hell's teeth! I was expecting to find vital evidence.'

'You'll be lucky mate. Whatever evidence there was has gone up in smoke.'

~O~

The big man picked up Gold as easily as if he were a puppet and threw him back against the cushions on the sofa. It winded the PC, he coughed, pain shot through his head and tears welled in his eyes. The man leaned in close to his face.

'Not feeling so good, eh?' The man's breath smelled of undigested food and unbrushed teeth. Gold tried not to gag.

'I feel terrible. Why did you have to hit me so hard?'

'Poor diddums. I can do worse than that, so don't tempt me.' He turned and paced the length of the caravan. It was only feet before he had to turn and retrace his steps then turn again. As he walked he spoke – almost to himself. 'Right. What am I going to do now?'

Turn.

'Get out of the country – that's the best thing.'

Turn.

'I'll have no trouble getting work as a strongman in another funfair.'

Turn.

He was silent for a while. The only sound was his footfalls as he walked. The caravan shook every time he put his foot down. At the mention of "strongman" it suddenly became clear to Gold. It was Charles Atlas! Wickstead had told him about the strongman and his arrest – and how they didn't have any evidence to hold him on, so Parker had been forced to let him go. The sergeant had also mentioned the black gloves he wore. Apparently he suffered badly from eczema and he liked to keep them covered. That would also explain the lack of fingerprints. How come Bonnie Parker hadn't noticed that? His thoughts were interrupted when Atlas spoke again.

'But what if I'm pulled up? I need some sort of insurance.' He stopped in front of Gold and stared hard at him. After a few moments a grin spread across his face, wrinkles appeared round his eyes and the corners of his moustache lifted. '*You'll* be my insurance.'

'Me? How?'

'I take it you know how to drive?'

'Why yes.'

'Good. Then you'll be my driver.'

'What if I refuse?'

The eyes narrowed and the grin disappeared. 'You won't,' he said threateningly.

'How are you going to make me?' The young PC tried to sound more confident than he felt.

Atlas swivelled round, surprisingly swiftly for one so large. He dragged open a drawer and pulled out a wicked-looking knife with an eight-inch blade. Turning back he brandished it close to Gold's face. 'I've killed before and I'll do it again.' He gave a bark of a laugh. 'I'll be hanged if I'm caught, so one more won't make any difference.'

'*What*?' There was a tremor in the policeman's voice.

I said I've killed twice before – they both deserved it. The third one was an accident but they won't see it like that.'

Gold couldn't keep the horror from his face. He knew someone had killed the two fortune tellers but he couldn't believe that he was here, with the murderer. And a third one? Of course! It was the fisherman, Stern, in Dungeness. Now he felt really helpless. The man was obviously deranged and would stop at nothing. What *was* he to do?

Think…

Talk…

Talk. Yes, that was the best thing. He took a breath. 'Okay. So if I agree to be your driver, what then?'

'Oh, you'll agree all right.' The knife was waved in front of Gold's face again. 'You're going to drive me to Dover.'

'And then what?'

The man pushed the tip of the knife against the policeman's chin. A drop of blood fell and rolled down one of his polished buttons. 'We'll cross that bridge when we get to it. Now – I'm going to untie you. But if you try anything…' Another scarlet dropped followed the first one.

Gold tried to ignore the stinging sensation on his chin. 'But shouldn't there be some sort of plan? We might get stopped by customs.'

Atlas looked thoughtful. He paused in untying the bonds. 'True. Maybe I should think more carefully about it.' Then he shook his head, like he was trying to dislodge something stuck on his ear. 'What am I saying?' His high voice rose even higher. 'Stop trying to trick me!' he screamed.

The more the man became worked up the calmer Gold felt. It was as if he had nothing to lose. 'Sorry,' he said quietly. 'I'm not trying to trick you – just trying to help.'

'What do you suggest then?' Atlas had moved in so that their faces were inches apart again.

'Well…' the young PC was struggling to think.

'Yes?' The man had tilted his head to one side, looking like a gargoyle made flesh.

Gold shook his head. 'I don't know. You're probably right – cross that bridge when we get to it.'

Atlas stood back and put his hands on his hips. 'Huh! You'll never make a detective.' His face twisted into a sneer. By now the light was draining from the sky and the interior of the caravan had grown gloomy. The man turned again and, taking a box of matches, lifted the glass and lit an oil lamp that was fixed to the wall. It cast a warm glow that did nothing to cheer Gold's mood at all.

A silence stretched between them. Gold thought furiously. All the time the man was talking he was safe and, hopefully, his colleagues would be out looking for him. Well, he hoped so. He didn't fancy his chances *if* they made it to Dover – Atlas wasn't going to let him go. He was sure of that. He would need to do something to stall him until the others arrived. Almost without thinking he said, in a quiet voice: '*Why* did you kill Ivy Rose Lee?'

Atlas looked up, Puzzlement on his face. 'Why?' He paused. 'Why? Because she was a cow,' he snarled.

'Killing her seems a bit drastic if that was all.'

Atlas seemed lost in thought and didn't answer for a while.

'What? No, that wasn't all. At first we were friends. She knew I was missing Pilgrim – it wasn't really her fault he went away.'

'Whose was it?'

'Bloody Boswell. He never liked him. Once he found out what he was he couldn't wait to get rid of him.'

Gold was puzzled. 'What do you mean, "*What* he was"?'

Atlas gave a snort. 'He called him a "nancyboy" and a 'Jessie". Said he was "as bent as a nine bob note". And much worse than that.'

'I see.' Again Gold was finding it hard to comprehend but was determined to keep playing for time. The cavalry would have to arrive soon – wouldn't they? 'So why the fortune teller and not Boswell?'

Atlas narrowed his eyes and his face darkened. 'I wish I had done for him. Would've been much simpler.'

'Why didn't you?'

Atlas's face softened and took on a wistful look. 'His boy.'

'What, the lad Duke?'

'Yes, we were friends.' Atlas had stood up and was pacing again.

Without thinking Gold said: 'Is he – you know – queer?'

'*Good God no*!' The man looked horrified at the suggestion. 'He's just a nice lad – troubled but basically decent. When his mother ran off he started to go a bit wild. His brute of a father didn't know how to deal with him – or didn't care. I'm not sure why he came to me but we just got on. It wasn't a father and son relationship, nor an uncle or nephew. We were just… friends.'

'I see.'

'That's why I planted the cards in Boswell's stove. Hoped he'd be accused of the murder. By the way, has it worked?'

'Well, he's in custody. I believe they're still trying to get evidence against him.'

'Serves him right, nasty piece of work.' He looked up, regret crossing his face. 'It's the boy I feel sorry for. He hated the thought of going into a home.'

'I think he'll be all right,' Gold said softly. 'I heard someone had taken him in.'

'That's good.'

A silence stretched between them again. The PC pushed his luck. 'So… why Ivy Rose Lee?'

Atlas returned to his seat, rested the knife across his knees and cupped his hands round his chin. 'She was all right at first, even cooked a meal or two for me.'

'What changed?'

'She did.'

'How?'

'She started to snipe at me – make nasty gibes – about me being queer. But it wasn't that. I've put up with that for years.'

'What was it then?' Gold wondered when his luck would run out.

'She made a horrible accusation about my relationship with Duke. That was a step too far. I saw red and lost my temper. I don't really know what happened. Just found a knife in my hand and when I looked round there was blood everywhere and she was dead.'

'What about Petulengro?'

At the mention of the fortune teller's name the man's face softened and in the lamplight Gold could see that he was close to tears. 'I didn't mean too.' His voice too had grown soft. 'I loved him.'

'Then why?' Gold asked gently.

'I don't really know. I was mad, I suppose.'

'What made you mad?'

The man started to look quite pathetic. His shoulders drooped and his head was bowed. He'd clasped his hands, turning one over the other in a washing motion. 'It just happened.'

As Gold watched Atlas's gloved hands he thought again about fingerprints but quickly cast the thought from his mind and pressed on. 'What did?'

'He said he didn't love *me*. That I was a bloody nuisance and that I should leave him alone.'

This was a long way outside Gold's experience. He knew men and women loved each other – he loved his wife and was sure that she loved him. But men loving men? His mind moved up a mental gear. 'You really loved him?'

'Of course I did,' the man's face twisted into a grimace.

'So why?'

'Why?' the man sat slumped on the seat opposite the policeman. One gloved hand massaged his stubbly chin; the other held the knife, its tip pointing towards the floor. 'I still don't know. He'd rejected me, but I still loved him – couldn't help it.' He seemed to be reliving the experience and was silent for some minutes.

Gold waited patiently, wondering what was coming next and, at the back of his mind, praying that help would come soon. He wasn't sure how long he could keep this up. 'You said you were going to untie me,' he said more boldly than he felt.

'What..? Oh yes.' The man put the knife down and undid the ropes round Gold's ankles then those round his wrists. Quickly he picked up the weapon again. 'And no funny business or…' He pointed the blade at the policeman. Gold tried hard to control the quaking he felt inside.

Chapter 19

*A **level crossing** is an intersection where a railway line* crosses a *road* or *path at the same level, as opposed to the railway line crossing over using a bridge, or under using a tunnel.*

MILLS DROVE back from Dungeness at a much more sedate pace. The open brandy bottle was wedged between his thighs so he could take a drink every now and again. As he became progressively inebriated his driving became increasingly erratic. He was starting to see double and was having trouble discerning which side of the road he was on. Mercifully there was little traffic and apart from startling a young lad on a horse-drawn cart when he veered too close, he'd managed, purely by luck, to avoid causing a nasty accident. When he neared Angus Goodyear's he slowed and considered dumping the stuff in the barn. But quickly dismissed the notion. The farmer had made it patently clear he wanted nothing more to do with him so he carried on. He took another swig from the bottle, swerved across the road, bumped up the verge and almost lost control. He wrestled with the steering wheel and managed to get the truck back in an almost straight line. His vision was becoming increasingly blurred and he was glad that he didn't have far left to travel.

~o~

'What plan do you 'ave when we find this Jack Mills, Sonny?' They were travelling along the Military Road. Russell was really pushing the Wolseley – the tyres squealing as he took the bends at speed. Bruissement was hanging on to the grab handle above the door to stop from being thrown sideways.

Russell turned the wheel hard again, correcting a slide. 'I'm not sure, Guillaume. I'm hoping we can drive him off the road. If he's as drunk as Edna suggested it shouldn't be too difficult.'

A little way behind them Weeks was struggling manfully to keep up. 'You're doing a great job, Johnny, considering how much you dislike this car,' Nettie observed.

'It's just the gears, really,' he said, as the vehicle slewed round a corner. He swung the wheel. 'It actually handles quite well. I'm unused to the boss driving like a madman – I'm only just managing to keep up. I don't know what's got into him.'

'I suppose he's keen to catch Mills red-handed. He needs to show Stout that he can at least do that.'

'True.' They were fast approaching the junction with the Appledore road. The brake lights on the Wolseley came on and both vehicles came to a halt. Weeks got out and trotted up to the other car. Russell wound down the window. 'What's the plan now, Sir?' Weeks asked.

'Same as I said in the station, lad. You position yourself by the bridge and I'll go ahead. If I miss him, make sure you stop him from getting to the pub. Right, we're off.' Russell banged the car into gear and shot off, one rear wheel lifting as it went over the bridge and round the tight bend on to the Rhee Wall.

~o~

Mills had slowed almost to a crawl. His eyelids kept closing and he struggled to focus on the road. The truck was spending more time on the wrong side and it was only when the front tyre bumped against the verge that he wrenched the wheel across to the other side. As he approached Appledore station, he made no attempt to stop at the level crossing even though the crossing keeper was starting to close the gates. At the last moment he twisted the wheel, narrowly missing the man who shouted and shook his fist. Mills was oblivious to him and carried on his way.

~O~

'Now get in the driver's seat – and remember, I've got this.' Atlas's face showed grim determination as he flashed the knife. 'I mean it. Do anything stupid and I won't hesitate to use it.'

Trying not to show his fear, the young PC put his foot on the step and hauled himself into the cab. He was just about pull the door closed when the strongman gripped the edge.

'Not so fast!' I *know* you can drive, but I doubt you've ever driven one of these before.'

'Er no. I haven't.'

'Thought not. It's a bit different from usual, see?' He pointed to the pedals. 'The accelerator is in the middle and brake is on the right. Got it?'

'I think so,' Gold said slowly.

'*Think so*? You need to know so. You've got to drive this thing for 30 miles without attracting attention.' The knife came up close to Gold's throat.

'Okay. I've got it.'

Atlas slammed the door and walked round to the passenger side. With surprising ease for one so large he swung himself into the seat. 'Right, start the engine and drive on. You've got time to get used to the controls before we hit any traffic.'

The young policeman twisted the key. The engine turned over a few times then finally coughed into life. Gingerly he depressed the clutch pedal and pushed the gear lever. There was a slight clunk as the cogs engage. Lifting his foot he let out the clutch. The truck lurched and the engine stalled.

'Fool! You didn't take the handbrake off!'

Gold sensed the tension in the other man – like an overwound spring, ready to uncoil at any moment. 'Sorry.'

'You will be. Now try again.'

This time the actions were smooth and the truck started to roll forward. Gold could feel the weight of the heavy caravan holding him back and increased the revs. He continued to drive slowly in first gear until they got off the track and on to the lane where he risked changing up into second. Already the noise in the cab from the engine in its housing between him and his passenger was growing louder and he could feel heat rising from the floor. In a few hundred yards they had reached the junction with the road and he remembered to move his foot to the right to brake. Beads of sweat were already forming on his forehead and starting to trickle down the sides of his face.

'Good boy – well done,' Atlas said sarcastically.

Gold risked a glance sideways and could see that the strongman was grinning. But it wasn't a friendly grin more like the grimace of a stone demon carved to frighten children.

They pulled out on to the Rhee Wall road and if Atlas had looked to his left he would have seen the police car stationed just beyond the bridge.

~O~

'Johnny! Look at that!' Nettie leaned forward and peered through the windscreen into the gathering gloom.

'*What the hell*? It's a truck and a caravan.'

'The DI thought we'd made a mistake with Pint-sized Charlie. Could this be the one?'

'Only one way to find out – we'd better follow it.'

'But what about Mills? The Inspector said we had to wait and head him off.'

'We'll have to take a chance. We may well see him on the way. Hopefully they'll have got him by now.'

~O~

Russell approached the bend before the level crossing at speed. As he turned the corner he had to brake hard and swerve as a pickup truck came towards him – on his side of the road. The truck swerved too late and clipped the front wing of the Wolseley before careering off. This pushed the police car up the bank, where it came to a sudden halt in a hawthorn thicket.

'*Merde*!' Bruissement cried, as he was thrown forward.

'Sorry, Guillaume. Are you okay?' Russell asked as he thrust the gear into reverse and tried to extricate the car.

'I think I might be. Was that 'im?'

'Almost certainly.' He pressed down on the accelerator. The wheels spun; the car juddered until finally the tyres gripped and they shot backwards. 'Hold on my friend. We've got to catch him.' He executed a messy three point turn, put his foot down and they thundered up the road after the pickup.

~O~

Weeks put his foot down and swung the wheel hard to the left. Nettie had to hang on for dear life or she would have ended up in his lap. 'I've got to get in front of the lorry,' he said. They were gaining on the truck and Weeks pulled out. He was just about to overtake when he saw another vehicle coming straight towards him. 'Bugger!' he yelled, and quickly pulled back in.

~o~

Russell came round the bend before the long straight and they could just see the pickup in front. Suddenly, it veered across the road – right in the path of an oncoming lorry. '*Oh my God*!' he cried.

'*Oh mon Dieu*!' Bruissement echoed.

The DI stamped on the brakes and the two men watched, appalled, as the pickup crashed into the lorry, bounced off to the left and into the field where it rolled over and came to an abrupt halt. The driver of the lorry reacted and tried to swerve out of the way. But it was too late. Through a combination of the collision and the sharp turn the caravan began to fishtail. The momentum caused the lorry to lose control and the policemen watched as if hypnotised while, almost in slow-motion, truck and van travelled diagonally across the unfenced grassy bank, through the reeds and tipped over into the canal, only just remaining upright but sinking slowly in the water. The caravan remained buoyant but the heavier truck sank until only the roof was visible.

Weeks brought the Ford Pilot to a screeching halt. Both doors flew open as he and the WPC leapt out. Nettie started unbuttoning her tunic.

'What are you *doing*?' Weeks demanded.

'We can't let them drown,' she shouted, kicking her shoes off. She began to run towards the water.

Weeks went after her. 'It's too dangerous – leave them!' he shouted. He snatched at her flailing tunic but, as Nettie gave it a final shrug from her shoulders, the garment came away in his hand and he fell to his knees in the mud.

The young policewoman tore down the bank and immediately dived into the water. The light had all but gone from the sky and the canal was so murky she couldn't see anything, but by feel alone she managed to find the handle on the driver's door. She pulled and pulled and just before she ran out of breath it opened. She reached blindly inside and her hands came into contact with a sleeve. She gripped the material, braced her feet against the sill and heaved. Miraculously the driver came free and floated out of the cab. Wrapping her arm under his chin she kicked her legs and propelled him to the surface where she gratefully gulped a great mouthful of air. It was only a few feet to the bank where Weeks and Russell were standing in the shallows. Together they grabbed the figure and pulled him to the side.

'Bloody hell! It's Andy Gold.'

'The bobby from Appledore?' Russell asked.

'Yes.'

'What on earth was he doing in the lorry?'

The PC groaned and coughed. A gout of water came out of his mouth. His eyes flickered open. 'Where am I?' he said weakly.

'You're okay. You've had a bit of an accident.' Gold coughed again and shivered. 'We'd better get you out of those wet clothes as soon as we can and wrapped up in a blanket,' Russell said. He took his coat off and laid it across the man. 'This will have to do for now.'

Gold's eyes widened. 'He's still in the truck!'

'Who is?'

'Atlas. He made me drive. He's the murderer.'

There was a sudden splash and Weeks turned in time to see Nettie heading out towards the lorry again.

'Where are you going?' he shouted anxiously.

'I've got to go and get him out of there.'

'You can't!'

'I can.' And she disappeared below the surface. It seemed like an age until her head appeared above the water again. 'It's no good. He's stuck.'

'Nettie, leave it!' Russell cried. But the girl dived again. She was gone for much longer this time. The dark water was almost still; just the odd ripple and a few bubbles rising to the surface and bursting. Long minutes passed.

'Oh God. I hope nothing's happened to her,' Weeks said. He started peeling off his jacket and was about to go in after her when she came up again, spluttering.

'It's no good. I can't shift him.' If water hadn't been streaming down her face they would have seen tears welling in her eyes. 'I tried, I really did. I think it's too late anyway.'

'Come on, lass,' Russell said gently. 'You've done your best. Let's get you and Gold wrapped up. There are blankets in the car.'

The four of them clambered back up the bank, the detectives supporting Gold who, though dripping with water, seemed remarkably unscathed. Bruissement was standing by the cars which were slewed untidily across the road. 'I don't think 'e is going anywhere.' He pointed with his good arm towards the field where they could just make out the shape of the pickup truck in the gloom. It was wedged, upside down, between two elder saplings jamming the doors shut. A column of steam rose lazily from the engine and shouts and a stream of foul language was emanating from inside the cab.

'Radio the station, lad,' Russell said. 'Get them to send an ambulance and the fire brigade. We'll need a tow truck too. This is going to cause quite a stir.'

Chapter 20

*Seeing a **red mist** can be brought on by extreme stress or anger. Losing control and raging, destroying things or people nearby, can actually cause internal blood vessels in or near the eyes to start leaking. The blood can sometimes spill into the inside of the eye, causing the one affected to see everything through a '**red mist**', hence the name. At this point, however, the person is so angry that they completely lose control and essentially go insane* for a time.

THERE WAS a buoyant, almost celebratory mood in the police station that early evening. Surprisingly, following his imprisonment by the murderous strongman and his ducking in the canal, a change of clothes and a stiff drink helped PC Andrew Gold to seem little the worse for wear. Someone had been to the off-licence for a crate of brown and light ales while a couple of bottles of duty-free brandy had somehow found their way from the wreckage of Jack Mills's pickup truck. It was rumoured that a bottle of Superintendent Stout's single malt might make an appearance but that hadn't happened so far.

Mills had been freed from the upturned truck, shaken and bruised, with maybe a couple of cracked ribs, but apart from that was astonishingly unscathed. The officers joked that the amount of booze he'd drunk had anaesthetised him. He was now sleeping if off in a cell. Charles Atlas had not fared so well.

'I'm afraid he didn't stand a chance.' John Crooks was standing in the centre of the main office with a glass of brandy in his pudgy hand, holding court. He'd been there when the CMP lorry had been pulled out of the water.

'When the truck left the road and plummeted into the canal he must have been thrown forward,' he explained. 'Unfortunately, the strongman was still holding the knife and he managed to impale himself upon it.' Crooks turned to Nettie, the heroine of the hour. She'd been lent a spare tunic and trousers. Despite them being several sizes too large she still somehow managed to look demure and attractive. 'Even if you had succeeded in freeing him,' the pathologist said. 'It would have been too late as, in my opinion, he was already done for. The knife had gone straight up into his heart.'

'So he managed to dodge the gallows by doing himself in,' Russell mused.

'It looks that way.'

'So why do you think he went on a killing spree, John?'

'You're the detective, Sonny.' Crooks took a drink from his glass. 'But as I'm feeling magnanimous I'll give the benefit of my wisdom.'

'That's good of you.'

'Yes, it is.'

'So do tell.'

'Someone find me a seat and I will.' A chair was quickly produced and the portly pathologist took time settling himself. When he was comfortable and had everyone's attention he began. 'I can't be one hundred percent certain, but I think, to use layman's terms, he flipped. He couldn't cope with rejection and something happened to his brain – the logical side was buried under the emotional part and he couldn't control his actions. He felt the whole world was against him and he just let rip.'

Crooks had been closeted with Gold before the party started. The young PC had related the conversations he'd had with Atlas and had been questioned closely as to actual words the strongman had used. Gold had been an extremely reliable witness and the pathologist was able to form a comprehensive picture of the mental state of the man.

'You really believe that he didn't know what he was doing when he killed the gypsy, Ivy Rose Lee?' Russell asked.

'I do. I think a red mist descended and he acted automatically – there was no premeditation, no planning, just a man out of control.'

'And the other fortune teller, Petulengro?'

Crooks took a sip of his drink and frowned. 'I think that was slightly different. He really did think he stood a chance with him. They were both homosexuals and Atlas couldn't understand why his feelings weren't reciprocated.'

'Killing him stills seems rather drastic.'

'Again, I can only suggest that emotions took over and he had no control over his actions.'

'Fair enough. I can't argue with that. But what about Stern, the fisherman?'

'Now that wasn't the same at all. I doubt we'll ever know what actually happened but I'm prepared to accept that it was an accident. For a start, it was nothing like the other deaths – a knife wasn't used.'

'But what about the Tarot card that was found with him?'

'Well that was different too. The two clairvoyants had cards stuffed in their mouths. His was wedged in the boat.'

'Fair enough.'

Crooks suddenly sat up. 'Oh, I forgot. I found this clenched in the strongman's hand.' He pulled an envelope from out of his inside jacket pocket. Everyone leaned in. Like a conjuror he carefully extracted a piece of crumpled card. He leaned forward, placed it on the nearby desk and gently smoothed it out.

'Is that what I think it is, John?'

'If you mean another Tarot card, Sonny, then yes. I understand that it's known as *The Tower*, but I've no idea of its significance.'

'It is a belief of mine that you know someone who could 'elp.' Bruissement had been quietly listening while he remained in the background. Heads turned towards him.

'Who do you suggest, Guillaume?' Russell asked.

'Someone you know very well, Sonny. Your friend, Isobel.'

'Of course. I never did get to hear what she had to say the other evening. Perhaps we'd better pay her a visit when we've done here.'

~O~

Stout's beloved single malt still wasn't going to make an appearance for a while. As soon as Russell had returned from Appledore he had telephoned the Super to tell him what had happened. At first Stout was extremely irritated – he was ready to go out to an old pals' reunion dinner and didn't like his plans to be disturbed. 'What the bloody hell are you doing ringing me at home?'

'We've caught the murderer, Sir.'

'*What?* You can't have done.'

'We have,' Russell said emphatically.

'Not possible. Parker has got him in custody.'

'As I've maintained all along,' Russell continued, his voice even, 'he's got the wrong man.'

'And I suppose you've got the right one?'

'Yes, Sir. Most definitely.' Before Stout could interject he quickly outlined the events of the afternoon.

'Bloody hell!' the Superintendent said when Russell had finished. 'This puts a whole different complexion on it.'

'And there's something else you should know about Parker.'

'Oh yes?'

'It was something the desk sergeant said. Something rather serious.'

'Can you tell me what it is?'

'I think I'll leave Wickstead to tell you himself.'

There was silence on the other end of the line, then a huge sigh. 'Right. I'm coming in. Make sure the sergeant is there to talk to me. Oh, and don't let DI Parker leave the office.'

~o~

The party continued, but at a slighter more subdued level when Stout arrived. They were used to seeing him in his full dress uniform on occasion. But this was a very different looking Superintendent. A crisp white wing collar pushed up against his substantial double chin and his ample girth strained against the silk cummerbund round his waist. They had little time to gawp though, as he sailed through to his office calling: 'Send Wickstead in please.'

They were closeted for no more than ten minutes before the desk sergeant came out. Russell looked questioningly at him but Wickstead's face remained noncommittal. He spoke quietly. 'Do you know where Parker is?'

Since returning from the burnt out caravans Parker had remained holed up in his office with his sidekick, Clyde Barrow. The door was firmly closed. He hadn't been invited to the party and, if he had, wouldn't have wanted to take part. He knew the rough details of what had happened and couldn't face the others. Wickstead banged on the door.

'Yes?'

The desk sergeant pushed the door open and a pall of grey smoke drifted out. He could have be jubilant – many would have revelled in the dressing down he knew the DI was going to get but instead he spoke in a measured tone. 'The Super would like to see you.' Barrow started rising. 'No just you.' He pointed at the DI. The room went quiet while Parker, hands thrust in pockets and head lowered, came out of his office and slouched down the corridor. A condemned man couldn't have looked more wretched.

Stout sat back in his chair, his hands linked across his stomach. His eyes were narrowed, his gaze steady. He stayed like this for some time while Parker twitched and fidgeted. Finally he spoke. 'Have you got anything to tell me, Inspector?'

Parker frowned, perplexity clouding his features. 'Sir?'

'Don't play the innocent with me, man. You've had a suspect banged up for more than two days for a crime he didn't commit.'

'But the evidence, Sir…'

'Don't give me that rubbish. We both know there *was* no evidence.' Stout's colour was rising at the same rate as his temper.

Parker continued playing the innocent. 'Not sure what you're suggesting, Sir.'

Just managing to keep his voice under control the Super said: 'Sergeant Wickstead has suggested that you falsified evidence to get a conviction. What do you say about that?'

'I don't know what he means, Sir.'

Stout sat up straight and hit the desk with the flat of his hand. The noise made the DI jump. 'You planted the neckerchief. *Didn't you!*'

Parker realise he'd been backed into a corner. 'Umm…'

'*Didn't you!*' Stout repeated.

The DI couldn't have looked more unhappy. 'Yes, Sir,' his voice barely a whisper.

The DI twisted the knife. '*Speak up man*! What did you say?'

'I said yes, Sir.'

'And why the hell did you do that?'

'I though the gyppo – I mean Boswell was guilty.'

'But he wasn't.'

'No, Sir.'

'Now we stand a good chance of being sued for wrongful arrest and false imprisonment.'

Alarm filled Parker's face. 'Surely not?'

'I bloody hope not! But if he does, it's your neck on the line. As it is you're suspended, pending an inquiry.'

'When, Sir?'

'As of this instant. Now get out of my sight.'

Parker turned and slunk out of the office. The Super sat for several minutes, breathing heavily. How on earth had had he allowed himself to be taken in by the man? Just because he'd had some moderate success in the past it shouldn't have lulled him into believing that Parker knew what he was doing this time – when patently he didn't. He had grudgingly to admit that Russell had been right after all. He'd have to make it up to him. He sighed. Reaching across he opened the lower drawer of the filing cabinet and retrieved a bottle of Talisker he'd been saving.

When he entered the main office a cheer went up. He smiled acknowledgement and brandished the bottle. The cheer grew louder. He handed the whisky to Russell. 'Well done, Sonny. You were right all along.'

Russell was momentarily stunned into silence – not because he'd been praised but because Stout had used his Christian name – for the first time. But also, he'd been wrong about the strongman at the outset. He stood grinning inanely for a few moments until he found his voice. 'Thank you, Sir, but it wasn't just me, it was a team effort.'

'Come, inspector, you're being too modest.'

Russell held up his hand 'No, if it hadn't been for PC Gold and his bravery I don't think we would have got the result we did. Then WPC Sharpe…' He held out his arm signifying inclusion. 'If she hadn't dived in the muddy canal and got him out of the truck, PC Gold may not have been here. Unfortunately she was unable to save Atlas but, according to the pathologist…' The arm was held out to Crooks, still sitting centre stage. 'It was too late anyway.'

A shadow of a doubt crept into Stout's mind. He was still feeling cautious after Parker's sordid folly. 'I suppose you're certain that Atlas *was* the murderer?'

'No doubt at all,' Russell said. 'I'm pretty sure his confession to PC Gold would be enough on its own. It seems he wore gloves, most of the time, but now we know it was him, I'm certain that we'll find more incriminating evidence. The caravan has been pulled out of the canal and Lewis and his assistant are currently going over it.'

'Good. That's what I wanted to hear. What about the gypsy, Boswell?'

'He's been released without charge. He wasn't happy at first but when he was reminded of the assault on Parker he went quietly.'

'And the other fairground worker?'

'Pint-sized Charlie?'

'Yes.'

He's been released with an apology. And a tow truck has been sent to free his caravan.'

'Oh, and the other man, Mills?'

'He's in the cells. He'll be charged with receiving and selling stolen goods.'

'Excellent. A satisfactory result all round.' A spare glass was found, a good measure of the single malt was poured into it, and handed to the Super. He took a sip and smacked his lips. 'What I don't understand is the significance of these Tarot cards.'

'Nor do I, Sir,' Russell said. 'But I know someone who does.'

~O~

Russell sneaked out of the party while it was in full swing. Only Bruissement saw him go but just smiled and gave him a wink. It was late when Isobel opened the door to her cottage. Her look of suspicion turned to one of delight when she saw who it was. She opened her arms wide and embraced him. 'Sonny! What a wonderful surprise.' Aggie rushed in and danced around their legs, wanting to join in. 'To what do I owe this pleasure?'

'I wanted to pick your brains,' he said, smiling happily.

'And I thought you just wanted me for my beauty.'

'That too.'

'First things first. What would you like to drink? Wine – beer?'

'I'd love a cup of coffee, if possible.'

'Certainly.' She was just turning towards the kitchen when she said: 'Oh, have you solved the case then?'

'Yes, with a little help from my friends.' He briefly outlined the events of the evening. 'I'll go into more detail later, if you're interested.'

'Of course I am. Let me organise the coffee first.'

Russell sat down to wait. The room was charming. A warm glow came from a couple of table lamps and a coal fire burned in the hearth. Music was playing softly in the background. He recognised it as Debussy's *Clair de Lune*, one his favourite piano pieces. Isobel brought the coffee in. When they were settled with their drinks and Aggie had made herself comfortable on the sofa Isobel said: 'Right, what is it you want to know?'

'What can you tell me about Tarot cards?'

'Oh yes. The conversation we didn't have when you rushed off the other evening.' She had a cheeky grin.

'Sorry about that.'

'It didn't matter. Guillaume was very good company.'

'Not too good, I hope?' Russell asked.

Isobel gave him a playful punch. 'I do believe you're jealous. Don't worry, I didn't succumb to his Gallic charm.' She snuggled up close and tucked her legs under her. 'I much prefer an *English* policeman.'

'Glad to hear it.' He kissed the top of her head. Her hair was soft and smelled of some delicate perfume.

She sat up and looked directly at him, her green eyes sparkling. 'Did you know he has a nickname?'

'No.' Russell was intrigued. 'What is it?'

'It's Morse.'

Now he looked puzzled. 'As in Morse code?'

Isobel smiled. 'No, it's French.'

'You'll have to enlighten me; my French isn't all that good.'

'It means walrus.'

Russell was still puzzled. He knew his friend was short and a bit on the round side…

The smile turned into a tinkling laugh. You don't get it, do you?'

He shook his head. 'You'll have to tell me.'

'It's because of his walrus moustache!'

Russell joined in with the laughter. 'Well I never. Yes, I can see that now.'

Isobel sipped her coffee. 'Now what is it about these cards? I'm intrigued.'

Russell reached into his pocket and produced a piece of paper. Unfolding it he placed it on the low table in front of them. 'These are the ones and who they were found with:'

Death – Gypsy Ivy Lee

The Lovers – Pilgrim Petulengro

Justice – Albert Stern

The Tower – Charles Atlas

Isobel studied the paper for some time before speaking. 'Remind me what you know about the first gypsy.'

'Apparently Atlas was on good terms with her – to begin with. Then she suggested that his friendship with the boy…'

'Which boy is this?'

'Oh, sorry. Duke Boswell. He's the son of the fairground owner.'

'The one who Bonnie Parker was convinced was guilty?'

'That's him. Anyway, she insinuated that Atlas's friendship with Duke was less than healthy. That soured the relationship and it made him angry. He said he didn't know what happened. Just found the knife in his hand and blood everywhere.'

'Mmm.' She uncurled her legs, stood up and walked over to a bookshelf. Running her fingers along the spines she stopped. She pulled out a slim volume and went back to the sofa. 'Now let me see.' She flicked through the pages. 'I thought as much.'

'What's that?'

'The meaning of *Death* varies depending on which way up the card is.'

'Difficult to tell as it was shoved in her mouth.'

'It doesn't matter, as in the circumstances the meaning is pretty clear.'

'What do you think it is?'

'Well the book says, *change, transformation and*, most telling, *endings*, which I think is pretty conclusive. Amazing that he had the forethought to choose a fitting card though.'

'I suppose he had moments of rationality between bouts of madness.'

'Perhaps.' Isobel drank from her cup. 'Now about the second death.'

'Pilgrim Petulengro. That doesn't make sense. Atlas said he loved him.'

'*The Lovers.* On the face of it looks pretty straightforward but if the card is reversed it can take on a whole new complexion.' She turned a few pages. 'Reversed, it means *disharmony, imbalance, self-love,* and fittingly, *misalignment of values.* I think that says it all.'

'The third one puzzles me. According to what Atlas told Gold, this death was an accident.'

'Was the card found in his mouth – like the others?'

'No. It was wedged between the timbers of the boat where he was found.'

'Ah. Then I agree he didn't mean to do it.'

'Is that what the cards say?'

She chuckled. 'No, that's my feminine intuition. Reversed *Justice* can mean *lack of accountability.*'

'Well, if it was an accident, that makes sense.'

'Quite. But the final one, *The Tower*, is more perplexing. Upright it can mean *sudden change* or *upheaval.*'

'He was certainly going through that.'

But… If reversed: *personal transformation.*'

'That also fits.'

'You said it was found clenched in his hand?'

'That's right.'

'Mmm. Perhaps you'll never know.'

'Probably not,' Russell mused, staring pensively into the crackling fire.

Isobel yawned and stretched. She turned towards him and lightly gripped the lapels of his jacket. She looked into his eyes. 'Well, Detective Inspector, Are you going to stay the night, or do you have to get back to your cosy little railway carriage?' Next to them Aggie stretched, yawned and went back to sleep.

The End

Blood on the Tide

A DI Sonny Russell mystery
Chris O'Donoghue

WHEN A gruesomely mutilated body trussed up in a distinctive fashion washes up on a lonely stretch of the south coast in the 1950s, DI Sonny Russell is soon struggling to unravel an intriguingly knotty puzzle. And as more bodies, similarly tortured, appear he begins to realise that, for some at least, the war is far from over.

A trail of intrigue leads him to Europe where he befriends a French detective and together they set out to track down the villains.

Blood on the Tide is a story of the sea and boats, murder and Nazis that begins in a sleepy coastal backwater and takes the reader through post-war France and Germany.

'The writing is concise but vivid and authentic – clearly carefully researched. It would make a great film with its evocation of the sights and sounds, cars, boats and trains and way of life in the 1950s.'

'The pace doesn't falter at any point and the book is hard to put down.'
'A post war murder mystery with a difference. I was swept along with the characters in this wonderfully, intelligently written book.'
'Chris O'Donoghue expertly conjures up the atmosphere of Britain in the 1950s. He has a feel for place and an eye for the telling detail.'

'I'm a big fan of Simenon and I'm sure anyone who is will enjoy this tale of the quirky DI Sonny Russell who is a vegetarian and lives in a railway carriage.'

'Like the best books in this genre you will not want to put it down until all the loose ends are tied up.'

Blood on the Shrine

The second DI Sonny Russell mystery
Chris O'Donoghue

SNOWED IN on a Buddhist retreat DI Sonny Russell isn't peaceful for long. A monk is found dead in the shrine room and two men also staying at the centre quickly arouse his suspicions.

Meanwhile his sidekick, DC Johnny Weeks meets a small time crook who, thinking he is trustworthy, asks the policeman to participate in a daring train robbery.

The action begins in Russell's sleepy corner of the South-East, travels to Eire and has its denouement in France, skilfully engineered by Russell's wily old friend, Inspecteur Bruissement.

Blood on the Shrine is a story of Meditation and friendship, deception and intrigue, which tests DI Russell to his limits.

'It grips the reader from the beginning. Not only does the author continue from his previous book, Blood on the Tide, but a new tale is intricately woven throughout with familiar characters including Sonny's dog, Aggie.'

'I really enjoyed this sequel to Blood on the Tide and especially loved the way that the new plot became interwoven with a continuation of Chris's last storyline.'

'It's a neatly-crafted work that carries on from Chris's first novel and carries the reader at a brisk pace to a climax that leaves plenty to expand on in his next book, Blood on the Strand.'

'A book that once you've started you will put off all other jobs to carry on reading. Can really picture all the characters and think it could make a really good TV series.'

'A really cracking read, so full of atmosphere, ties up the loose ends from Blood on the Tide nicely, bring on book three.'

Blood on the Strand

The third DI Sonny Russell mystery
Chris O'Donoghue

IN A RAGING GALE a heavy crate is washed up on the beach near Compass Point. DI Sonny Russell and his sidekick DC Johnny Weeks happen upon it while braving the weather near Sonny's home. Puzzled, they go to get help to recover it, but when they return it has gone. So begins a thrilling and dangerous search for stolen Nazi plunder. It leads the detectives, ably assisted by an eager young policewoman, Nettie Sharpe, on a twisting trail that encompasses Hastings fisherman, their iconic net huts, ruthless foreign criminals and the shady side of antique dealing. BLOOD ON THE STRAND is a story of intrigue and drama, set on the sleepy south coast in the post-war mid-fifties.

Chris O'Donoghue has kept up the suspense and action in this, his third Sonny Russell story. Sonny and his sidekick Johnny Weeks are joined by a WPC to solve the riddle of stolen Nazi treasure.'

'Great to return to familiar characters and see them evolve, as well as meeting new ones. Some unexpected twists and interesting plot.'

'Another good Sonny Russel mystery from Chris O'Donoghue. I recommend this series of books, proper 50s police detective work.'

Chris O'Donoghue trained in industrial ceramics at Bournemouth Art College and worked at Poole Pottery and Cranbrook Pottery in Kent before setting up on his own in Rye. He later specialised in model making and sculpture.

When much of the kind of work he did began to be made in the Far East, Chris, having always loved the outdoors, decided on a change of direction and started gardening. His design ability led him to create three medal-winning gardens at the Chelsea Flower Show.

A lifetime's passion for the sea, crime novels, the simple pleasures of the Fifties and railways – he is well known on the model railway scene – led him to combine all three in this, his fourth published book.

The first three DI Sonny Russell mysteries

BLOOD ON THE TIDE
BLOOD ON THE SHRINE
&
BLOOD ON THE STRAND